PENGUIN BOOKS

And Leave Her Lay Dying

John Lawrence Reynolds' first novel, *The Man Who Murdered God*, was published to critical acclaim and won the Arthur Ellis Award for Best First Novel. The third mystery featuring Joe McGuire, *Whisper Death*, is also published by Viking Penguin. Mr. Reynolds lives in Burlington, Ontario.

AND LEAVE HER LAY DYING

JOHN LAWRENCE REYNOLDS

Penguin Books

PENGUIN BOOKS
Published by the Penguin Group
Penguin Books Canada Ltd, 10 Alcorn Avenue, Toronto, Ontario,
Canada M4V 1E4
Penguin Books Ltd, 27 Wrights Lane, London W8 5TZ, England
Penguin Books USA Inc., 375 Hudson Street, New York, New
York 10014, U.S.A.
Penguin Books Australia Ltd, Ringwood, Victoria, Australia
Penguin Books (NZ) Ltd, 182-190 Wairau Road, Auckland 10,
New Zealand

Penguin Books Ltd, Registered Offices: Harmondsworth,
Middlesex, England

First published in Viking by Penguin Books Canada Limited, 1990

Published in Penguin Books, 1991

10 9 8 7 6 5 4 3 2 1

*Publisher's note: This book is a work of fiction. Names,
characters, places and incidents either are the product of the
author's imagination or are used fictitiously, and any resemblance
to actual persons living or dead, events, or locales is entirely
coincidental.*

Manufactured in Canada

Canadian Cataloguing in Publication Data
Reynolds, John Lawrence
    And leave her lay dying

ISBN 0-14-012298-2

I. Title.

PS8585.E96A85 1991   C813'.54   C89-095244-2
PR9199.3.R496A85 1991

American Library of Congress Cataloguing in Publication Data
Available

For Jeffrey David
&
Courtney Lee

Laughter, laughter
All their shining days.

AND
LEAVE
HER
LAY
DYING

CHAPTER ONE

He made another perfect cast.

A gold and emerald jewel suspended between two blue worlds, the fly hung at the crest of a graceful arc before descending, with an accuracy born of skill and practice, to the surface of the water where it twitched once, then twice, and waited patiently to be devoured.

Ollie Schantz grunted approval, swaying with the motion of the flat-bottomed boat beneath his feet. His quick overhand sweep of the split-bamboo rod had deposited the lure on target, just beyond a granite outcropping where the river entered the lake.

He grunted again. Should be a mess of them there. That's where all the smart guys are. The clever old ones. Hiding out at the mouth of the river, knowing I can't reach them from the shore. Takes a boat to put you in the right place for big land-locked salmon. Especially those guys, smarter'n your average truck driver. Dumb youngsters stay in the river where you can practically wade in and scoop 'em up. Gotta come at these guys where they don't expect it. Surprise them when they're lying back, feeling safe. They see a fly over their heads and it's Good morning, breakfast.

His right hand held the rod delicately between fingers and thumb, like an artist's brush. Across his other hand he draped coils of double-tapered line, ready to provide slack when the salmon struck. His right wrist quivered for an instant and the lure twitched in response, spreading orbits of ripples across the glassy surface of the water.

The fly lived. It struggled and tempted.

"Must have their mouths watering by now." Ollie spoke aloud for the first time, enjoying the sound of his voice sounding low and relaxed, free of tension and care. It felt good to hear it that way. "Gotta be prowling for food, tying on their bibs, reaching for the ketchup," he said more loudly, an overweight middle-aged man talking to himself alone in a boat, far from home. He laughed at the image and his belly shook in agreement.

He sat gently down on the seat of the boat, a contented man on a remote, peaceful lake in the endless sunshine that floods the northland in autumn, his eyes shaded by a floppy cotton hat perched lightly on a basketball head: round, bald, large, red and leathery. Two woollen lumberjack shirts protected him from the lingering morning chill; wide crimson suspenders held up a pair of oversized army surplus pants whose pockets bulged with fishing gear. On his feet he wore a shiny pair of Timberland boots purchased directly from the factory door just a week earlier.

He shot another glance at the fly on the water before transferring the loose coils of line to his right hand and reaching for a plastic cooler on the seat of the dinghy. Flipping open the lid, he withdrew a sandwich loosely wrapped in waxed paper, set it at his feet, and returned to the cooler for a bottle of beer.

He slid the fishing rod under his arm and twisted the cap off the bottle with his free hand, covering the opening quickly with his mouth to capture the foam, still chilled from the cold air of the previous night. He wiped his mouth with the back of his hand and turned to sweep the New Brunswick scenery with his eyes.

From the near shoreline of the lake, pine trees stretched away to distant hills, their thick greenery broken only where a mud road ended in a turn-around at the water's edge where Ollie's station wagon was parked beneath the low-spreading branches of a shoreline tree. Inside the car were his sleeping bag, a portable radio, a change of clothing, extra fishing equipment, a cache of ham sandwiches, beer, coffee, butter, spices and cooking equipment. He would eat pan-fried fillets of salmon and drink cold beer each night for the next three days, watching the moon rise over the lake and wondering, like a young lover greeting the morning from his bed, how anyone could possibly be happier.

He smiled up at the cobalt sky. Three days of weather like this would be —

An explosion of silver, alive and thrashing, erupted from the water near the shore. On instinct, Ollie raised the fishing rod vertically and began paying out line, giving the fish room to run. He stood and leaned forward, squinting against the sun for a view of his prey. The boat rocked beneath him, protesting the abrupt shift of weight. He stumbled, regained his balance, and began reeling in excess line.

Too much excess line.

As suddenly as it had come to life, the line went slack and dead. The fly floated back to the surface, spat out by the salmon, and the fish gave Ollie a flaunting wave of its tail as it disappeared beneath the water.

Ollie shouted a curse of anger and frustration; the words echoed back from the shore, taunting him as the salmon had, while he wound in the line. He repeated the curse, softly this time, and once again smiled at the absurdity of the scene.

"One for you," he said aloud, grinning even more broadly. "But that's all you get. That's all you get, my friend!"

He pulled the fly out of the water, inspected it for damage, and sat gently down in the boat, which continued to rock like a cradle beneath him. Gotta be more careful, he told himself. Just relax. Me and the fish, we've got all the time in the world.

In the excitement of the strike, he had dropped the bottle of beer. Now it rolled lazily amid islands of foam near his feet, back and forth with the sideways motion of the small craft. "Lots of time. Lots of beer," Ollie muttered, nudging the bottle away with the toe of his boot.

The lure had survived the salmon's attack without injury. Ollie stood up carefully, dropped the bamboo rod over his right shoulder and with a single, smooth motion launched the lure back to the little cove beyond the granite point. Responding to his deft motions, the fly pirouetted a few times on the surface of the water. Ollie sat gently in the boat again and leaned back, resting his elbow on the gunwale. The sun bathed him in soft warmth and for a few moments he lay without moving, forgetting the fly and the fish, feeling the silence of the New Brunswick interior envelop him.

Damn, he grinned to himself. I can't stop smiling. Life has finally got so good, I can't stop smiling about it.

. .

An hour later, the sun had climbed almost overhead and shrunk the shadows with its glare. Ollie removed his outer shirt and unbuttoned the one beneath it, exposing his pink stomach, round and jolly. He stood again, watching the lure play at his command on the water beyond the rocks. Empty beer bottles rolled on the bottom of the boat colliding with balls of waxed paper and bread crusts.

Two salmon, tethered through the gills, hung over the side of the boat on the end of a cotton rope. Ollie glanced down at the fish. Large enough for dinner. He would fillet them in the last light of the day. Or maybe split them along their backbones, nail them to a wooden plank, and slow-smoke them over a hardwood fire.

The beer and sun were making him drowsy. He turned to

check his car, still waiting in the shady glade. A nap later. Another beer by the lake, a short sleep, then fish some more.

Boston was far away on a distant planet, grey and grimy. There, bodies lay waiting to be discovered at the top of tenement stairs. But no more for Ollie Schantz: never again for him some dead eye focused on eternity, not another hateful face to confront.

One more cast. He wound in the line, lay the rod behind his back and snapped it over his shoulder as he had done dozens of times that morning, watching the fly soar and sink lightly in the shadow near the shore. One twitch, another . . .

The water beneath the fly boiled and the lure vanished beneath the surface. The reel began to sing as the line stretched, throbbing and taut, into the water.

"You old son of a bitch!" Ollie shouted. A burnished gleam like prized old pewter flashed in the sun as the fish broke the surface. Alternately reeling in the line and releasing tension when the salmon turned back to shore, Ollie played the fish closer to the boat and whooped aloud when his prey swam past him barely an arm's length beneath the surface.

"Got a poor memory, huh?" Ollie shouted as the salmon darted by. "Too hungry for your own good, huh? You tough old bastard you!" He laughed aloud, and in the gleeful sound he made and the wide expression on his face he was no longer an overweight retired homicide detective but a twelve-year-old boy on summer vacation.

The fish was tiring as Ollie looked around for the landing net. Big old boy must be twenty, twenty-five pounds, he told himself as he watched it swim in circles near the boat. Bending at the knees, he kept his eye on the salmon and reached blindly with one hand for the net.

Damn, where the hell was it? The boat lurched suddenly with his shift in weight and he sat down quickly to stabilize it. There's the net, near the bow. He stretched his heavy body forward, lying prone across the middle seat, to retrieve it.

Must look like a fat old fool, he grinned to himself. Then he eased himself back to a standing position.

And felt his heart sink.

There was too much slack in the line. It dropped vertically into the darkness of the water from the tip of his rod. He cursed the fish, cursed the net as he dropped it at his feet, cursed the boat that shuddered beneath him, cursed himself for his stupidity, all the while reeling in yards of line.

But the salmon had been resting in the shadow of the dinghy. As Ollie wound slack line onto the reel it darted away again with a last burst of energy before growing tired and disoriented. Ollie took back the line he had given the fish, telling himself to calm down, damn it.

With the fish within sight again, Ollie locked off the reel and stooped to seize the net, then stood up and yanked quickly on the line to summon his catch alongside the boat. Bending from the waist, he positioned the net ahead of the fish, jerked the line again and scooped the netting to ensnare the salmon.

He laughed and cursed again, hefting the fish upward with his left hand gripping the net handle. More weight than he expected. And his arms were more tired than he thought. With the salmon thrashing wildly, threatening to burst out of the netting, Ollie spread his feet apart for more stability. The boat protested with a sudden yawing motion. Instinctively, he shifted his weight in the other direction to counter the motion and lifted his left foot to retain his balance, bringing it down on something round, something rolling across the bottom of the dinghy.

His foot shot out from under him and he tried to lean forward, tried to prevent himself from falling. But the momentum of heaving the fish into the boat continued to propel him backwards. Now his other foot slipped forward too, and as he tumbled back, his arms outstretched, flinging net and rod away, he looked up at the clear New Brunswick sky and asked himself, What the hell's going to happen now?

. .

When he opened his eyes again he was sprawled on his back, his neck across the gunwale of the boat. As he fell, he had heard the sound of someone breaking a twig just behind his right ear. He had heard it snap. A dry twig under a heavy foot snaps like that. But there was no one around. And there was nothing at his right ear. Only the hard edge of the gunwale. A hard unyielding edge he could no longer feel.

Something was flopping in the water beside him. Something else was thrashing at his feet. He heard the wind; when had the wind come up? How long had he lain there? He felt the sun on his face, smelled the freshness in the air.

He gathered his will and turned his head slowly to the right. The sound of footsteps on loose gravel scratched inside his skull. Twigs and loose gravel. What had snapped? What had splintered? He knew. With welling fear, he knew.

Now he could see his arm flopping in the water, the entire limb trembling like a hysterical child. Curious, he watched his hand dance its spastic dance; panic-stricken, he tried to feel the water, feel the chill of it. And felt nothing.

Get up, he told himself. Move, he instructed his body.

But only his hand moved, shaking in uncontrollable spasms, skipping in the water to frantic unheard music.

At his feet another rhythm was being played out, softer and sporadic. Another dancer, this one performing on the end of a double-tapered line, the lure through its mouth.

Tears came to his eyes.

Ollie Schantz lay paralysed in the sunshine and listened to the salmon, tangled in the net near the bow, die in long convulsions through the rest of the perfect day.

CHAPTER TWO

Later, there were some at Berkeley Street Police Headquarters who would say the case had been practically
wrapped up, the jury would have had to be deaf, blind
and drunk not to convict the creep. Others would claim that
it was never that solid, it would have been a touch-and-go
trial that could tilt either way depending on the skills of the
attorneys, the whims of the jurors or the mood of the trial
judge.

But even the sceptics agreed that the prosecution had been
gaining ground until Joe McGuire lost his temper and assaulted the defence attorney.

McGuire had spent the third day of the trial on the witness
stand, verifying evidence presented by the prosecuting attorney in the morning and enduring an hour of intensive cross-
examination after lunch. He had begun with a spectacular
hangover and a desperate longing to be somewhere else, anywhere but Courtroom B. His lunch had consisted of a bowl
of chowder and a bottle of Kronenbourg beer, which had
helped neither his digestion nor his disposition. In fact, his
headache became so intense that during the afternoon ses-
sion, responding to questions from the defence attorney de-

livered in a rapid-fire staccato manner, McGuire frequently swept his hand through his hair, sometimes trying to ease the pain and at other times searching for a hatchet handle protruding from his skull.

It was almost three o'clock. His waistline was edging uncomfortably over the belt on his trousers; he shifted his body and crossed his legs, dangling one tassled black loafer over his knee.

McGuire dressed in defiance of fashion, favouring tailored British woollens of no particular style which he could wear for years with white Egyptian-cotton button-down shirts and plain knit ties. His trousers were dark and pleated and his jackets Scottish tweed. It was McGuire's uniform, worn in three colour variations: blue, grey and brown. Today's was brown.

The defence attorney, a ferret-faced man named Marv Rosen, had vowed to the press before the trial began that he would not only secure an acquittal for his client but expose moral rot and decay in the Homicide Division of the Boston Police Department. Now he stood at a table shuffling papers with exaggerated drama while McGuire, the jury and the rest of the courtroom attendees waited patiently.

McGuire ran his hand over his head again. His hair, still shining chestnut brown except for silver filaments woven through the short sideburns, barely hinted at its owner's middle age. Soft curls coiled around his ears and up to a widow's peak above a broad forehead, and his surprisingly dark, piercing eyes studied the world with extremes of fierce anger or deep concern.

Above his upper lip, a white scar cut at an angle through the shadow of his beard, a trophy awarded ten years earlier by a pimp on Washington Street. Women liked the scar. McGuire himself had grown fond of it. When relaxing with a book or listening to music, he would unconsciously trace its line with his forefinger.

Joseph Peter McGuire was of average height, which made

him short for a police detective. As many men do when they are smaller than those around them, he carried himself with an air of controlled aggression, a muted sense of impending explosion in his carriage, the effect either softened or made more intense by the expression in his eyes.

Now his eyes expressed only fatigue as he drew his finger over the line of the scar and let his mind wander to picture the woman he hoped to see that evening, the softness of her lying beside him and within reach . . .

". . . Isn't that correct, Lieutenant McGuire?"

Rosen, the defence attorney, was speaking from his desk near the jury box.

McGuire blinked. All day long he had replied to questions in the carefully phrased artificial jargon of formal police reports. "To the best of my knowledge." And, "We observed the victim lying in a fetal position parallel with the bed, her head towards the north-side wall of the room in question." McGuire despised using the phrases because they were devoid of emotion and caring, distant from real life. And death.

Now he spoke directly — "I'm sorry" — and stretched his neck to ease the knotted muscles at the base of his skull. "Could you repeat the question, please?"

"Repeat the question?"

Rosen lifted his head from the papers he had been studying to stare at McGuire. He stood erect, tall and lean, and echoed McGuire's words: "Repeat the question?" His close-set eyes grew wide and he stretched his arms out from his body like a man who had been challenged with a riddle to which there could be no answer. He strode around the desk, his arms still extended, his eyes moving to the jury, to the judge, to the spectators, to the bailiff, urging them to share his incredulity.

"Lieutenant McGuire wants me to repeat the question," Rosen said in a singsong manner. "And may the court note that this is at least the third time . . ." He looked back at his assistant, a smallish man with an enormous moustache, sitting at the defence desk. The assistant held up four fingers for Rosen and everyone else to see. "Correction, the fourth time during cross-examination that the attention of the witness has wandered from this vital, critical topic at hand."

"My attention hasn't wandered, counsellor —" McGuire began.

"*May I remind you, Lieutenant, that my client has been charged with a brutal murder of which he is totally innocent, and has suffered assault at the hands of you and your fellow officers?*" Rosen exploded.

"Counsellor, counsellor." The soft voice of Judge Garnett Scaife sounded from above McGuire's right ear. "No need to flirt with hysterics here, Mr Rosen." The eyes of the judge crinkled behind rimless glasses. "I think that all that's necessary is for you to repeat the question as Lieutenant McGuire requested, and I expect this time the police officer will do his utmost to listen."

Rosen approached the bench as though wanting to discuss a confidential legal matter. When he spoke, his voice carried far enough for everyone in the courtroom to hear without difficulty.

"Your honour," Rosen began, "a basis of our defence is the open hostility which has been shown towards my client —"

Judge Scaife remained smiling but raised his hands to silence the lawyer. "Counsellor," he said, in the same soft, indulgent manner, "your client has been charged with a particularly heinous murder. In my experience, police officers tend to be a touch belligerent with people they suspect of committing those kinds of crimes. Of course, if you wish to submit evidence of harm to your client's person by any of the officers, I will certainly be pleased to hear it."

Retaining his smile, Scaife scanned the courtroom, projecting an image of a strong, kindly judge determined to show no favouritism.

Rosen tightened his stomach and straightened his

shoulders. "Your honour, my client shouldn't even be in this courtroom," the lawyer declared. "But as long as he is subjected to this procedure, he deserves respect from the prosecution witnesses and most certainly from the police officers." As he spoke, he pulled the cuffs of his shirt beyond the ends of his jacket sleeves and the diamond chips on his gold cuff links danced in the courtroom lights for the entertainment of the spectators.

"So he does, Mr Rosen," Judge Scaife nodded. "So he does. Now please repeat the question. We are waiting with great anticipation." He looked up and smiled out at the courtroom once again.

While the lawyer pleaded for justice and the judge projected wisdom, McGuire shielded his eyes and tried to hear music in his mind, a jazz tune, a chorus from a favourite Brubeck recording. Somewhere else, he pleaded silently as he recalled the music in his head. Take me somewhere else, anywhere but here.

Removing his hand from his eyes he looked up to see Rosen's client, a skinny acne-faced young man named Arthur Trevor Wilmer, slouched behind the defence desk in an ill-fitting polyester suit. The shirt collar was too large for his thin neck, the sleeves too long for his short arms. As McGuire watched, Wilmer picked diligently at a hangnail on his thumb; the concentrated effort forced the tip of his tongue to emerge from behind his stained, protruding upper teeth.

McGuire knew Wilmer's history, knew of the squalor and poverty he had been born into, knew of the abuse he suffered at the hands of his mother and a series of her live-in boyfriends, knew of his drifting between jobs in car washes and short reformatory terms for petty thievery. He felt pity for Wilmer: a predestined loser, a social misfit fated to die clutching a wine bottle beneath a bridge in the Public Garden.

But he felt only loathing for what Wilmer had done to a

twenty-year-old Boston College student who endured three hours of rape and torture on a warm spring afternoon before Wilmer plunged a kitchen knife into her chest.

McGuire narrowed his eyes and watched Wilmer tug at the errant hangnail, finally lifting his thumb to his mouth and biting off the sliver of skin. Wilmer raised his head and caught McGuire's stare before dropping his hand into his lap and smiling — *smiling!* — at McGuire, the man who had formally arrested him and then, in the alley behind Wilmer's rooming house, lifted him bodily and thrown him into the rear seat of the squad car.

Wilmer hadn't complained about his treatment. He would never have mentioned the incident at all except in response to intense questioning by Rosen, his court-appointed lawyer. McGuire's action had been just another part of Wilmer's world, a world which had no room for pleasantries or careful deportment, where there were few expectations and fewer courtesies.

Rosen scanned the jury, ensuring that each member had absorbed his loud and passionate declaration of his client's innocence, before strolling back to the defence table where Wilmer now sat, self-consciously erect. The lawyer scooped a sheaf of papers from the desk and ambled towards McGuire.

"Lieutenant," he said, scanning the papers as he approached, "you stated that you visited Mr Wilmer's apartment on Tuesday, the sixteenth of May, the day prior to his arrest." He smiled coldly at the detective. "Is that correct?"

"That's correct," McGuire responded. "We had a proper warrant, documented and —"

"I'm not interested in the warrant, Lieutenant." Rosen waved the idea away with a sweeping gesture of his hand. "I am interested only in what happened at Mr Wilmer's apartment in his absence."

McGuire frowned. "I'm not sure what you mean."

"I mean to make two points, Lieutenant." The expression remained frozen on the lawyer's face, less a smile than a tightening at the corners of his mouth. "Point number one. When no one answered your knock on Mr Wilmer's door, what did you do?"

McGuire shifted in the chair. "I asked his landlady to unlock the door for me. Our warrant clearly stated —"

"Please, Lieutenant, please!" The smile broadened into something even colder and more cynical. Rosen lifted his hands to his ears as though trying to shield himself from McGuire's words. "We've heard enough about your warrant. Let's not bore everyone here with the details of your warrant, shall we?" Dropping his hands, the lawyer turned to the jury again. "Kindly tell the court exactly what Mrs Hoskins did when you made the request."

McGuire ran his hand through his hair again as the invisible hatchet blade worked its way deeper into his skull. He lifted his eyes to look at Rosen, who was studying the jury with an expression of pained patience, and replied in a flat voice, "She unlocked the door for us."

Rosen snapped his head in McGuire's direction, his eyes burning. "And you entered Mr Wilmer's room?"

"I have testified to that."

"And what did you find?"

"A mess."

"Is Mr Wilmer charged with being a poor housekeeper?" Rosen asked in an icy tone.

"No, he's not, counsellor —" McGuire began.

"Then let's not treat this matter so lightly, shall we? The point is, Mr Wilmer was not at home, was he?"

"No, he was not."

Rosen walked casually back to his desk where he dropped the papers and thrust his hands in his trouser pockets. "We have heard that Mr. Wilmer's quarters consisted of one room with one small closet," he said over his shoulder. "He shared a bathroom with other tenants. Is that right, Lieutenant?"

"That's correct."

"And how long were you in Mr Wilmer's room during that first visit?"

"Long enough to convince myself that he wasn't there."

"More specific, please."

McGuire shrugged. "Ten, fifteen minutes."

Rosen turned to face the jury and the corners of his broad mouth tightened once again. But this time the eyes crinkled. This time there was warmth in the smile McGuire could not see. "Did Mr Wilmer reside in a penthouse, Lieutenant?"

"I'm not sure what you mean."

His smile erased, Rosen looked sharply at the witness stand. "Did his residence cover several hundred square feet?"

"Hardly."

"In fact, it was one small room, wasn't it?" Rosen took a step in McGuire's direction.

"As I have testified, yes."

Another step. Rosen was bearing down on him like a . . . like a snake, McGuire thought. Body smoothly gliding, eyes unblinking, confident. A snake. "And you did conduct a thorough search, did you not?" Another step.

McGuire folded his arms across his chest. He breathed deeply and slowly, trying to prevent anger from inundating his voice, trying to avoid the unpardonable sin of losing his professional demeanour, his calculated and aloof coolness under pressure. "You know we did not, counsellor," he said, hearing the edge in his voice, feeling a tightening in his larynx. "Our warrant did not cover a search. It authorized us only to arrest Mr Wilmer or to confirm his absence in the event —"

"For the last time, Lieutenant, we *know* about the warrant you had sworn out with only the most tenuous of evidence —"

Don Higgins, the prosecuting attorney, stood and called out in a weary voice, "Objection —"

"We had a witness —" McGuire began.

"Your honour, I must object," Higgins called out.

"But not a witness to the murder!"

Thwack! — a slap from Judge Scaife's gavel. Rosen ignored it and jammed his fists against his hips.

"You had a lonely old woman sitting by her window who believed she saw —"

"Counsellor . . ." Scaife said in a voice he might use to caution a young and impetuous boy.

The hatchet cleaved deeper into McGuire's skull and he tried to shout down the pain. "She didn't *believe* it, damn it, she *testified* —"

Two strokes of Scaife's gavel failed to halt Rosen's momentum, and his words were derailed only momentarily by McGuire's interruption. "Who *believed* she saw Mr Wilmer enter the building —"

THWACK! THWACK! The gavel pounded louder, the strokes stronger and closer together. "*Mr Rosen, for God's sake, get to the point!*" the judge thundered. "It's on the record that Lieutenant McGuire and other officers entered the premises of the accused and they were authorized to do so. Now tell us why you are pursuing this line or I will direct you to discontinue cross-examination."

McGuire glanced over at Higgins. The prosecuting attorney shrugged his shoulders and sat down slowly. Let Scaife handle it, his expression said. Let the judge do our blocking for us.

"My point is this, your honour." Rosen strode back to centre stage again, where he spoke with equal attention to the judge and jury. "Lieutenant McGuire and his partner both confirmed the absence of Mr Wilmer from his apartment. Considering the modest size of the room, this should have taken only seconds. Yet they remained in the room for at least fifteen minutes. My question is simple: Why?"

The judge sighed audibly. "Answer the question, Lieutenant."

"We questioned the landlady," McGuire replied. "Her answers are on the record —"

"Wrong, Lieutenant." Rosen spoke in a weary voice as though dredging up a last reservoir of patience. "It wasn't 'we.' Mrs Hoskins has testified that your partner questioned her. My question, Lieutenant, is this: What were you doing during this time?"

"I was looking."

"At what?"

"At the room. At the posters on the wall, the pornography on the bed —"

"And you touched nothing?"

"Nothing I didn't have to touch."

Rosen turned away and studied the floor as he spoke. "Isn't it interesting, Lieutenant, that when Mr Wilmer was arrested the following morning and you finally had a search warrant in hand, you directed your colleagues to one specific shelf in Mr. Wilmer's closet?"

The prosecuting attorney rose to his feet, calm and assured. "Your honour, there has been no testimony to this effect —"

"My client will testify —" Rosen snapped, spinning to face Higgins.

"Mr Rosen —" Judge Scaife began in his pleasant voice.

Rosen's arm shot out in McGuire's direction, his finger extended. "— that when Lieutenant McGuire entered his premises and arrested him —"

Scaife banged his gavel with little enthusiasm. "Mr Rosen, I cannot permit the introduction of evidence —"

"— and directed two officers —" Rosen roared on, his finger still pointing at McGuire but his words directed to the jury.

"Counsellor, I'm warning you!" The judge's voice rose in pitch and he banged his gavel while Higgins sputtered objections from the prosecution table.

"— *to one specific shelf for the only evidence* —"

"DAMN IT, COUNSELLOR, SHUT UP!"

The court bailiffs turned in surprise to stare first at the

red-faced judge, then at each other. They raised their eye-brows and tightened their chins in unison; no question about it, Rosen had gone too far this time.

But the outburst worked. Rosen turned slowly to glare at McGuire and lower his arm to his side. The courtroom spectators remained frozen, the jury leaned forward in fascination, and prosecuting attorney Higgins stood with one hand raised.

Judge Scaife took a deep breath to regain his poise. He seemed on the brink of apologizing, then stood up quickly and looked at Rosen and Higgins in turn. "I want to see both of you in chambers," he instructed, and exited quickly through a side door, followed by a frowning Higgins and a confident Rosen.

McGuire slumped in the witness chair with his eyes closed for several minutes before opening them to watch Arthur Trevor Wilmer clean his fingernails. The ritual, he told himself. The importance of the ritual cannot be ignored. We are following a ritual here, each of us knowing Wilmer belongs out of society, each of us forgetting the innocent victim whose life he took, because the ritual demands it. It's not truth or justice that counts, it's the ritual that must be followed. . . .

The door to Judge Scaife's chambers burst open and the judge entered the courtroom, grim-faced, followed by Higgins and Rosen.

Rosen won, McGuire realized. Look at him, he's practically strutting.

The judge scanned the courtroom, scowling back at every eye caught in his gaze. "Mr Rosen has convinced me of the validity of his line of questioning and I have determined that it may continue, within limits." He looked at McGuire and added, "I shall remind the Lieutenant that he is still under oath."

Rosen smiled at Judge Scaife, then avoided McGuire's eyes as he spoke.

"Lieutenant, we were discussing your presence at the arrest of Mr Wilmer. We have heard your colleague testify that he found a brassiere, which he claimed belonged to the murder victim, on a closet shelf in Mr Wilmer's apartment."

Rosen continued to scrutinize the floor as he walked towards McGuire.

"At that time, you were in possession of a second warrant to search the apartment in question, is that correct?"

"That's correct," McGuire replied.

"And you arrived back at the apartment just as your partner was arresting Mr Wilmer, is that correct?"

"I have testified to that, yes."

"And you, along with two uniformed officers and two members of the Identification Bureau, were present, as I recall. At which time, in the presence of my client, you directed Sergeant Burns of the Identification Bureau to a specific drawer in Mr Wilmer's closet by saying 'Check the top drawer, Izzy,' did you not?"

McGuire shifted in the chair.

Jesus. He couldn't be suggesting. . . "I can't recall," McGuire said, looking up at the courtroom ceiling. "We had a blanket search warrant that time."

"Of course you did." Rosen walked casually over to the witness chair and spoke directly to McGuire for the first time since leaving the judge's chambers. "You're very thorough in your application of search warrants, aren't you? Just as you were very thorough in your search of the victim's apartment, weren't you?"

McGuire glanced over at Higgins. What the hell's going on? he asked with his eyes, but the prosecuting attorney folded his arms across his chest and looked away.

Rosen was leaning closer. McGuire could smell peppermint on the lawyer's breath. "In fact, Lieutenant, you visited the victim's apartment at least three times after the initial discovery of her body, didn't you?"

Use her name, McGuire wanted to shout back at him. She

wasn't a victim until that scum-bag, your client, mutilated her. She was young and beautiful and a good person and her name was Diane Linda Hope and she had made the Dean's List at Boston College working towards a master's degree in psychology, use her name, damn it.

Without waiting for a reply, Rosen pressed on, his eyes growing wider as he spoke. "Another fact. After your first visit to Mr Wilmer's apartment you visited the murder scene for the last time, didn't you? You met Sergeant Burns there and sent him on to Mr Wilmer's apartment alone, saying you would meet him there shortly. Is that not correct, Lieutenant?"

It was correct. After Burns left, McGuire had stood in the victim's room staring at the floor where Diane Linda Hope had screamed silently into a knotted towel through a warm spring afternoon. McGuire had listened for the echoes of her screams, tried to feel the depths of her agony, tried to make them as real as the brown and crusted stains on the carpet at his feet.

"We're waiting, Lieutenant."

McGuire blinked away the memory. "That is correct."

"And you arrived at Mr Wilmer's apartment from the scene of the murder, entered Mr Wilmer's closet, and when Mr Wilmer arrived a few moments later you instructed Sergeant Burns to examine a specific shelf, didn't you, Lieutenant?" Rosen leaned even closer as he spoke, so close McGuire could feel the other man's breath on his cheek.

"Yes, because —"

"Because you knew what he would find at the back of that shelf, didn't you? You knew he would find a brassiere belonging to the victim because you had put it there, hidden under some of Mr Wilmer's possessions."

"That's a lie!" McGuire responded.

"Because it was all you had to connect Mr Wilmer to the murder and without it, you had no evidence —"

The pain, the fatigue, the anger all coalesced into an explosion as McGuire leaped to his feet to seize Rosen by the lapel of his jacket with one hand and grip the lawyer's neck with the other, watching Rosen recoil in fear, hearing the judge thump his gavel over and over like a low drumroll, seeing the bailiffs charging at both of them, knowing he had broken the code and betrayed the ritual and not caring any more, not caring at all.

CHAPTER THREE

rom atop the fireplace mantel, the face in the photograph shone out at the world, filled with innocence and
more than a little beauty. The hair was lustrous and
black, the skin pale and smooth, the chin firm and finely
boned.

But the eyes owned the face. Large and clear, they laughed
back at the world even while their expression suggested
something deeper, something wistful, perhaps: a Gaelic sense
of tragedy.

Thirty years after the photo was taken, only the eyes, as
clear and blue as ever, remained unchanged. The coal of her
hair had changed to snow, the skin had weathered, the chin
had grown heavy. But the eyes were still focused on the
laughing side of life.

She had been christened Veronica Louise Hennessy, but
from the day of her birth she was known simply as Ronnie.
Two weeks before her twenty-first birthday and six months
after meeting an off-duty policeman on the day-ferry to Provincetown, she became Ronnie Schantz.

Along with her Gaelic eyes, she inherited a streak of fatal-
ism. When Ollie Schantz, Boston ·Police Constable First

Class, caught her as she stumbled down the ferry steps, the gears of fate had begun to mesh. They had spent the afternoon together, Ronnie so lost in Ollie's quiet strength and maturity that she forgot about the girlfriends who had accompanied her on the day's outing to Provincetown. There had never been, she knew, a day that had shone so warm and so clear on the fingertip of Cape Cod. She and Ollie sat on the pier and watched the gulls soar, nibbled on fried clams, tossed food to a solemn-looking pelican, talked incessantly on the shore and held hands in silence together on the ferry back to Boston.

Only fate could have brought them together like that.

But fate had shown her the other side of laughter as well. Fate had tugged little Jordie, their beloved Jordie, onto North Shore Road on the first warm day of his sixth spring, tiny legs churning until he froze at his mother's belated scream and the sight of the MTA bus bearing down upon him.

In the space of a heartbeat the world turned to reveal its other side, its darker side, its unfair side.

Through the years since, she refused to feel bitter about the death of her only child. It took strength to smile at young children playing among the leaves of autumn or the flowers of spring. But she did. And doing so over the span of all the years gave her something no one and no other twist of fate could ever steal from her. It gave her dignity.

· ·

It had been two months since the doctor at Mass General patiently explained the injury to her husband's fifth cervical vertebra, how the brittle bone edge had sliced through much of the upper part of his spinal column, severing nerves as cleanly, as quickly as . . . as a young boy can flee his mother's distracted attention to dash away between parked cars on a warm spring afternoon.

"One nerve is only partially damaged," the surgeon explained to her. He seemed young, far too young to be entrusted with the life of her Ollie, but she nodded and tried to smile. "We have attempted to repair it. If it works, he should have some use of his right hand, perhaps some movement in the arm as well." He paused, staring at her, waiting for her courage to dissolve into helpless tears. When it didn't, he said, "I wish I could promise more. But I can't."

She reached out and touched his hand, as though he were the one who needed strength and she was dispensing it. But she said nothing. Only her eyes spoke, smiling and thanking him for his honesty.

. .

Those same eyes smiled back at McGuire when Ronnie opened the door of her home in Revere Beach on that blustery November evening.

They reached and hugged each other without a word of greeting. Then, his hands on her shoulders, he held her at arm's length and studied her.

"How are you?" he asked gently.

"Tattered around the edges but holding together." She reached her hands to his and gripped them tightly. "It's been a bad day for Ollie. None of his days are good any more. Some are bad. The others are worse. But at least he's off the respirator, breathing on his own. Times like these, you cling to all the good news that comes your way, I guess. And that was good news."

She leaned closer and lowered her voice. "Maybe you can make him laugh, Joe. I can't. Nobody has come to see him from the department since he came home from the hospital. They were almost his family. It's like his whole family has forgotten about him."

She tried a smile, with only partial success. "You used to make him laugh. I remember, he would come home and drink his tea in the kitchen, leaning against the refrigerator and telling me about some funny thing you had said or done that day, standing there and laughing about it all over again . . ."

Her eyes blinked quickly and she brought her hands to their corners.

"I'm sorry, Joe," she said through her fingers. "No, it's all right," turning away as he reached for her. When she lowered her hands, her eyes were steady and shining. "I've started baking again. Can you tell?"

McGuire nodded. "Smells like what? Cake of some kind?"

"Lemon chiffon. Just took it out of the oven." She guided him down the hall, her hand on his elbow. "Go see him and I'll bring some in with coffee."

· ·

When they brought her husband home from the hospital, his head fixed rigidly in a stainless steel device clamped between his shoulders and his skull, Ronnie had prepared the den for his comfort. A motorized adjustable bed sat beside a window looking out on Massachusetts Bay. With a touch of the control from his good hand, Ollie could elevate the bed enough to see sunlight dancing off the water and gulls riding thermals in the sky. Another touch and the bed would glide back to a horizontal position for sleep and for Ollie to read the three words Ronnie had written with a broad felt-tip pen on the ceiling directly above his head: I Love You!

A remote control television set hung from the ceiling, angled towards the bed. Beside him on a night table was Ollie's police scanner-radio, equipped with a remote switch that responded to the same light touch as the motorized bed.

McGuire entered the room to see his former partner sitting upright, staring out the window at the black water. The scanner crackled with the chatter of police patrols located all along the shore from Lynn to Weymouth.

"They got a floater in Quincy Bay," Ollie said in a flat voice as McGuire lowered himself onto the hard-backed chair next to the bed. "Off Moon Island. White male Caucasian."

"How are you doing?" McGuire asked.

Ollie ignored the greeting. "First thing you do with a floater is, you leave it on its back," he said after a long pause. "Don't want to drain the lungs. Leave them for Mel Doitch to check. You got to watch all that stuff until Doitch arrives. Let him figure it out. What he finds in the lungs, that's important. Salt water, fresh water, no water, how much water, it all tells that fat-assed Slav something."

"Mel's okay," McGuire offered.

"Mel spends too much time around corpses is Mel's problem. He talks like 'em, he smells like 'em. He keeps stuffing his face with kielbasa and cabbage rolls, he'll look like that floater you and me checked down near Carson Beach couple of years ago."

McGuire began to speak but Ollie continued, neither his voice nor his eyes wavering.

"Remember that poor sucker? Time we found him he was so grey and bloated you wanted to paint 'Goodyear' on him and fly him over the Orange Bowl."

A smile darted across Ollie's face, then dissipated quickly somewhere behind his eyes.

"You get that floater on Moon Island assigned to you, make damn sure the whistle who answered the call didn't turn the poor bastard on his stomach. And remember to check his shoes. . ." Ollie's voice faltered and his eyes blinked quickly. They flew from the bay towards McGuire and back to the window. "You can . . . you can tell a lot . . . from a floater's shoes."

Ronnie entered with a mug of coffee and a slice of cake. Placing it carefully on the small desk beside McGuire's chair, she smiled at his whispered thanks and left as silently as she had entered.

"I won't get the case." McGuire sampled the cake, light

and tart with the clean scent of fresh lemons. He set it aside and stood up, his hands in his pockets.

"What, you too busy with old stuff?" Ollie asked from the window.

"No, it's Kavander. He's pissed at me."

"He's pissed at the world, you know that. He's always been meaner than a constipated crocodile. Me, I always thought he kind of liked you."

"Not after today."

Ollie's eyes clicked in McGuire's direction.

"I grabbed a defence attorney in court," McGuire explained. "Tried to beat the crap out of him from the witness stand. Right now, the attorney's probably sipping Chivas and scribbling out assault charges. Worse, there's a chance his client could walk from a rape and Murder One."

"The Hope murder?"

McGuire nodded. He scooped another large helping of cake.

"Who'd you beat up on?"

"Marv Rosen."

Ollie grunted. "Can't blame you. Son of a bitch is the kind of guy who'd piss on your shoes and say it's raining. Who was the judge?"

"Scaife."

"So, you gonna tell me what happened or you gonna stand there and do your imitation of a tree stump?"

McGuire smiled and sat down again. Between samplings of the cake and sips of coffee, he recited the day's events, including the pain of his hangover and his absolute belief in Wilmer's guilt.

"You plant the bra?" Ollie asked when he finished.

McGuire tilted his head. "What the hell, Ollie —"

"Just asking."

"I saw it there. On the first visit."

"When you guys were talking to the landlady."

McGuire nodded. "But I couldn't seize it. Couldn't even touch it legally. Should have had a blanket warrant, search and arrest. Did you know it takes two signatures for one of them now? I would have wasted at least an hour lining up another judge and I wanted to be there early in the morning. Thought I would catch the little bastard in bed. So I just went with simple arrest on suspicion. Figured we'd come back after laying a charge, do a total search."

"And you saw the bra but couldn't touch it so you went back for the blanket warrant."

"I stopped at the girl's apartment to check things out."

"Women tend to wear the same brand of underwear."

"Same brand, same bra size. She had three others."

"Still not a clincher."

"Blood on the one in the closet. It was her type. Semen stains on it match his blood type." McGuire shrugged and spread his arms. "Witness sees him enter the apartment on the day of the murder. Hell, it's a tight case."

"And Rosen played statistics."

"Said half the women in Boston had her blood type, half the men had his." McGuire stood up again and stared out the window at the darkened water. "I've never lost my cool like that, Ollie. I've had worse handling by lawyers on the stand before and I was able to laugh it off. Now here I am with Rosen threatening a civil suit, Judge Scaife thinking about contempt of court, and Kavander wanting me in his office tomorrow, first thing."

Ollie Schantz smiled weakly. "Joseph, you get yourself in more trouble than a hound with the shits in a swimming pool."

McGuire drained the rest of his coffee. "I keep thinking about the old days. You and me standing in drizzles on surveillance. Tossing drunks out of bars on Dorchester. Never thought I would but I miss those days. Things aren't the same."

"*Nothing's the same, God-damn it!*" It was more a hoarse

whisper than a shout, all that the older man could manage from his weakened body, but it snapped McGuire's attention back to the bed, where Ollie's face had flushed and the strain around his eyes intensified. "Nothing's ever the same. Nothing's ever going to *be* the same again!"

"Hey, I know that. I'm a big boy. But lately, I've been thinking —"

"Of checking out, right?" Ollie interrupted. "You'll tell Kavander to shove it and you take a hike. Then what'll you do? Open a book store? Go up to Vermont and tap maple trees?"

"Wait a God-damn minute."

"No, you won't do that, McGuire. You'd figure you're still a cop so you'd get a job with some piss-ass police outfit in the Berkshires. Tough Boston cop winds up directing tourists through town. Hell of a way to end a career like yours."

"You think it's fun getting my ass bitten by Kavander?"

"No, it's not." Ollie shifted his eyes back to the window. A navigation light on Bass Point across the bay winked back at the pace of a sleeping heartbeat. "No, it's not," Ollie repeated softly.

"Kavander could hang me for this."

"He won't," Ollie replied. "He would rather you hung yourself. Kavander's all shit and no flies. He doesn't want to leave himself open for making a bad decision. Guy like you, all those commendations. . . . 'Course, if you want to walk, he'll open the door for you." He swung his eyes back to McGuire. "Don't you give him a chance to say you walked away just because he's uglier than you are. You remember what I used to say about ugly guys?"

In spite of himself, McGuire grinned broadly. "Yeah. Never get into a fight with somebody uglier than you because the other guy's got nothing to lose."

"Damn right. You leave Berkeley Street, you leave because you want to, not because of Kavander."

McGuire glanced at his watch. "Speaking of leaving . . ."

"Yeah, I know. I know."

"I'll drop in tomorrow. Keep you posted on what's happening."

"Only if you've got the time." Ollie's eyes swung back to the light across the bay.

"Thank you, Joe," Ronnie said to McGuire at the door. "He really appreciated you coming. I could tell by the sound of his voice." She stood on her toes to kiss his cheek. "That's the happiest I've seen him since he came home."

CHAPTER FOUR

"Jack the Bear" they called him, for his disposition and his oversized, shaggy appearance.

Jacques Charles Kavander stood six-foot four and weighed two hundred and fifty pounds. His mother, Marie, a volatile and fiercely proud Québécoise, had been working as a cook in a Maine lumber camp when she first tangled with Charlie Kavander, a cutting crew foreman with massive arms and a constant snarl. Their marriage produced dozens of physical battles, three charges of disturbing the peace, and one son. Over the years they were separated only long enough for Marie to storm out the door and ride a bus back to her family in Rivière-du-Loup where she would call Charlie, demanding that he drive up and bring her home immediately. Which he always did without fail.

When Jacques was sixteen years old, his father sat watching him chop wood, approached him and rested a hand on the boy's shoulder. "You're going to be a big guy," he said. "Big mean guys like you and me, there are two things we can do. We can stay here, work in the lumber camps, ducking trees and axes, getting drunk every Saturday night. Or we can become cops. I think you should be a cop. It's safer."

His son shook his head. "I'm going to do both," he said. "I'm going to work with you in the bush and save my money for college. Then I'll be a cop. But not a dumb one."

He obtained his degree in criminology, graduating *cum laude* and with more than passing interest from two professional football teams, whose entreaties he ignored. In over twenty years as a Boston beat cop and detective, Jack Kavander drew his service revolver only once although he was shot at on three different occasions. On one occasion he had been hit, and with a 38-calibre bullet buried in his thigh had launched himself at his assailant with such ferocity that the man, a parole violator caught ransacking a warehouse, turned to flee just as Jack the Bear's massive hand clamped on his shoulder.

Later, Kavander and the fugitive both rode in the same ambulance to the hospital. Kavander was released several days before the other man, who was treated for several broken ribs, a broken jaw, a severely sprained arm and mild concussion suffered from falling downstairs while attempting to escape custody. Or so it was recorded in the official files.

Now nearing sixty, Kavander still carried his massive frame ironing-board erect. His hair was white and close-cropped, the limp from the bullet wound grew more noticeable every year, and his voice had acquired the rasp and growl of an idling diesel.

Kavander's appointment as Captain of Detectives ten years earlier had at first elated the Boston police force. "He's one of us," the officers nodded to each other. "A cop's cop. He knows what it's like out on the street." But the optimism soon grew jaded. Within months, Jack the Bear began his conversion from top cop to common bureaucrat, distancing himself from the everyday concerns of police officers and placing emphasis on procedures.

"You have to admit, Kavander's living proof of the theory of evolution," Ollie Schantz once observed over an after-hours beer. "Trouble is, he's evolving the wrong way. First he was a whistle, then he was a badge. Now he's a suit that's turning into a jock-strap."

. .

Sitting across from Kavander in the captain's office, McGuire remembered Ollie's joke and smiled.

"You think this is funny, McGuire?" Kavander growled.

"Not a bit, Jack."

"Damn right it isn't. Look, I don't care if Rosen says you sleep with diseased camels, you don't lose your cool in court and try to pop a defence lawyer in the mouth." He pulled a toothpick from the box in his desk and began chewing on it, the residual habit of a reformed two-pack-a-day smoker. "What if this bag of shit, this Wilmer kid, what if he walks?"

"He can't walk," McGuire protested.

"Higgins thinks he will."

"Higgins can't let him. He knows the kid is as guilty as Judas."

"Rosen's going after bail until the trial is rescheduled." Kavander examined the end of his toothpick. "He'll probably get it too. Won't be the first time."

"It's a wonderful world," McGuire muttered.

The telephone on Kavander's desk rang. He picked it up, snarled his name, and grunted single-syllable words into the receiver before crashing it down again.

"The kid walks," he said, staring out the window to Berkeley Street. "Judge Scaife declared a mistrial. Higgins is pissed. We're months from a new trial date, and the commissioner wants to see me in an hour." He swung his head to face McGuire. "What the hell am I going to do with you, Joe?"

"I could always resign."

"The very idea is giving me a hard-on."

"Want to call your wife, give her the good news?"

"You used to be funny, McGuire. Keep it up, you could be the funniest unemployed cop in town."

"Then you'll have to push me, Jack. Because I'm not jumping."

"The commissioner will want your ass."

McGuire felt the colour rise in his face. "Tell him to come and get it," he spat at Kavander. "Tell him by the time he arrives I'll let every paper in the state know this is the same commissioner who awarded me three commendations in the last five years —"

"You and Ollie," Kavander growled.

"What?"

"He gave them to you and Ollie together. And frankly, McGuire, since Ollie retired you haven't been worth a hell of a lot to me."

McGuire lowered his voice, trying to keep his emotions under control. "We had the best conviction record in the state —"

"And the more I think about it," Kavander exploded, "the more I'm convinced there was only one brain between the two of you and it's lying in bed over in Revere Beach!"

McGuire stood up, his hands in his pockets. "Jack, I'm as good a cop as you've got here."

"Then prove it to me, McGuire." Kavander's voice softened. "Find a way of proving it to me and keeping your nose clean until we put Wilmer some place where he can spend the rest of his life being gang-banged on a fixed schedule."

"You got any ideas?"

Kavander leaned back in his chair. "Yeah, I got some ideas. Sit down and I'll tell them to you."

· ·

"Grey files? He's got you doing grey files?" Bernie Lipson poked at the slice of lemon in his soda water, not believing what he heard.

McGuire nodded and sipped his Kronenbourg, savouring the slightly sweet French beer.

"That's only until the new trial, right?" Ralph Innes surveyed the interior of Hutch's, the dark Stuart Street clam bar favoured by headquarters cops. "They get that snot-nosed Wilmer back in court, you testify again, and you're back in harness, am I right?"

"If I want it," McGuire replied. He slumped against the back of the booth.

"You've got to want it, Joe." Bernie Lipson stared solemnly back at McGuire. "Guy like you, you can't throw away a career just because you tried to rearrange a lawyer's face." Lipson grinned. "By the way, apparently Judge Scaife can't talk to anybody about what happened in court yesterday without breaking up. He says the expression on Rosen's face when you grabbed him was the funniest thing he'd seen in thirty years on the bench. He wanted to do it himself, that's what I bet."

"Oh my goodness," Ralph Innes interrupted. "Here comes paradise, mounted on the two longest legs in the city."

The other men looked up to see Janet Parsons striding through the crowded bar to their table. On the way, she acknowledged greetings from police officers and ignored the stares of strangers admiring her lean figure, her long dark hair swaying in a loosely-curled ponytail. The strangers assumed she was a fashion model; only the police officers knew she was in fact Detective First Class Janet Parsons, Homicide Squad, Boston Police Department.

"Hi, sweetie," Innes said as he slid along the booth to make way for her. "What do you say we go back to my place from here? Just you and me and a whip and two midgets."

"Jesus, Ralph, don't you ever stop?" Bernie Lipson scowled at the younger man. Devoted to his family, Lipson rarely engaged in after-hours social sessions. The news of McGuire's confrontation with Kavander had drawn Lipson to the nearby bar for one glass of soda water.

Lipson had become McGuire's partner when Ollie Schantz retired, but when his relaxed style conflicted too often with McGuire's intensity, Kavander had split the team and reassigned them. They continued to take an interest in each other's concerns. Especially when it came to dealing with Jack the Bear.

Janet Parsons settled herself in the booth and waved the waiter over, ignoring Innes's comment. She ordered a Dubonnet on ice and smiled at McGuire and Lipson.

"Can't figure you out, Legs," Innes grinned. "With all my other girls I'm a regular Rudolph Vaselino."

"Ralph," she replied, looking down at her lap as she smoothed her skirt, "sometimes you are so repulsive I'm surprised your right hand still goes to bed with you." She turned quickly to catch McGuire's eye. "I don't believe what I heard. Has Kavander really got you working the files?"

"Grey files," McGuire nodded. "Review them, look for screw-ups, see what's worth running down, then send them off to the Bomb Shelter."

Grey files were dormant, unsolved homicide cases. No murder case was officially declared closed until a conviction had been secured. When a team of detectives had exhausted all leads and moved on to a new case, the information they had assembled was "grey-filed" — set aside; the case remained open but inactive. All the documentation was stored in grey envelopes identified by file number, victim's name, and date and location of the crime. Data in these four categories were entered into the department's overloaded computer for cross-indexing while the paperwork — autopsy reports, crime-scene photographs, witness statements, investigation memos — were transferred to a basement area known as the Bomb Shelter. The majority of grey file murders remained unsolved; convictions happened only as a result of blind luck, guilty conscience or death-bed confession.

"First you bury the victim, then you bury the files," Ollie Schantz once said to describe grey-filing. "Only difference is, after a year it's easier to find the victim than the files."

"All the grey files?" Janet Parsons asked, leaning across the table to McGuire.

"Last year's," McGuire answered. "My choice. I take a bunch of them, walk through the records, assess how efficient the investigating team was, maybe check out some new angles." He rotated the beer glass in his hands. "If this was the army, it would be one step above cleaning the latrines."

"That's disgusting, Joe." Janet sat back in the booth and shook her head. "A guy with your experience, all those years you put in. Kavander's acting like a bigger ass than ever."

"He wants me to resign," McGuire said, smiling warmly at her.

"Will you?" Lipson asked.

"Not yet. Not until I'm ready."

"You got any back-up?" Innes inquired.

"I've got a car, a desk and a computer terminal. That's it." McGuire drained his beer, then looked around at the others, who studied him with solemn expressions. "Come on, it's not so bad. The retrial is scheduled for six months from now. We'll get Wilmer put away and I'll be golden again. Meanwhile I get to come and go as I please. Even work at home." He grinned at Lipson. "Just might do me good. No nice Jewish boy bringing me bagels and blintzes to stuff in my fat gut."

"Hey, Joe," Innes said. "If you need something, anything, you call me, right? Bernie and me, we'll get you whatever you need. I'll bet you even put away some of those grey file cases." He turned to look at the others. "Ten bucks says Joe comes up with something, something solid so he can put the grab on a guy, get a conviction. Am I right?"

"Ralph, it's a clerk's job," McGuire said before anyone could respond. "Let's not make a big deal about it, okay?"

Innes shrugged, then slid along the booth to bump Janet Parson's hip with his own. "Hey, how's your love life, Legs?" he asked. "You getting all you need without me around to sizzle your cymbals?"

"It's none of your business, Ralph," she replied, staring at McGuire.

"Which means it ain't so hot, right?" Innes placed his arm delicately around her shoulder. "What you need is a young stud like me. If things were good in the sack, you would have said something. They're not so good, so you tell me to mind my own business." He took a long swallow from his drink. "I rest my case."

"Also your cock," Janet said, and Lipson exploded in laughter while McGuire smiled in silence.

· ·

"Anything left in your glass?"

She raised herself on one elbow and reached across him to the night table, the motion pulling the sheet from her body and exposing the gentle slope of her back, the slight hollow of her waist, the smooth swelling at her hips.

McGuire traced the lines of her body with his hand, sweeping his fingers back along her stomach, dragging his nails against her smooth skin.

"Don't," she giggled. Janet Parsons lay back and studied him, the glass of rye and water in her hand. "You know the best part about sex?" she asked.

"Damn right. It feels good."

"No, I mean philosophically."

"Parsons, you're the only woman I ever met who could get philosophical about sex."

"Listen to me. Making love forces you to live in the moment." She reached out with her free hand to touch the scar on his upper lip. "We spend so much time regretting or missing the past, or worrying about the future. Both are a waste of time. But when you're making love, you're totally wrapped in *now*. That's what makes it so special, isn't it?"

"Well, I'll agree that it's never a waste of time, anyway." He took her hand in his and brought it to his lips.

"Ralph was getting to you tonight with his wisecracks about me, wasn't he?" She withdrew her hand and drained the glass.

McGuire shook his head.

"Yes, he was." She twisted backwards to replace the empty glass on the other night table. "I could see it all over your face. I thought you were going to reach across and punch him at one point."

"You don't need any help from me handling Ralph."

She turned to face him again, a new expression of concern on her face. "Are you really going to be able to handle working alone?" she asked. "It looks to me as though Kavander is trying to humiliate you. He's trying to drive you a little nuts maybe."

"Better to be crazy and know it than be sane and have doubts."

"That's good. Where did you read that?"

"Ollie used to say it."

"God, what a tragedy." She sat on the edge of the bed, turning her back to him, and began dressing. "I'll never get over what happened to Ollie. And I don't think you will either." She stood to pull on her pantyhose. "Do you think Bernie knows?"

"About what?"

"About us. You never can tell with Bernie, can you?"

"No, you can't." McGuire sat against the headboard, his hands clasped behind his head. "What about Max?"

She was slipping her bra straps over her shoulders. "What about him?"

"Does he know?"

"Come on, Joe . . ."

"Jealous husbands have a way of ruining your whole day with a shotgun blast to the crotch when you least expect it."

"Not Max. He's too wrapped up in the restaurant. Besides, I think he may be making it with one of the waitresses. Some little honey he hired last month." She stepped into her skirt and pulled it up to her hips. "Silly old fool, going through male menopause. Damn this zipper!"

At the door she turned and kissed him lightly. "Thanks, Joe," she said.

"For what?"

"For making me feel good." She smiled and walked down the hall to the stairs, knowing McGuire was watching her but not looking back. She never looks back, McGuire mused.

It always bothered him that she never looked back. And he never knew why. Never tried to wonder why.

CHAPTER FIVE

PRELIMINARY INVESTIGATION REPORT

FILE #:   884-239A

INVESTIGATING DETECTIVES: E.D. Vance, T. Fox

DATE: 3/5/89

VICTIM'S NAME: Peter Michael Genovese

VICTIM'S ADDRESS: 2349 Chestnut Hill Drive, Brookline

VICTIM'S AGE: 42

MARITAL STATUS: Single

CRIMINAL RECORD, IF ANY: See attached sheets

INVESTIGATING POLICE OFFICERS: T. Radinsky, D. Barker

DATE/TIME OF INITIAL CALL: March 5, 12:13 A.M.

REPORT DETAILS: Call received on 911 re: hit and run, Atlantic Avenue, S. of Beach. Officers Radinsky and Barker arrived at scene approximately 12:20 A.M. Victim discovered against curbside power line pole; constables confirmed apparent instantaneous death from multiple injuries suffered a) by collision with unknown automobile; b) by secondary impact with power line pole.

Standard procedures followed re: measurement of point of impact from body, location of body, etc. (See attached H&R traffic report #3896509.)

Also automotive parts collected at scene (see above report).

Initial case conducted as standard H&R until approx. 3 P.M. 3/5/89 when unidentified witness called from telephone booth (confirmed via trace: Washington & Winter Streets). Witness reported details of collision with above victim (see attached witness report).

INTERVIEWS (LIST ON REVERSE IF NECESSARY):

_____

_____

_____

NONE: [X]

AUTOPSY REPORT: Attached [X]

Not attached [ ] Why not?

_____

_____

CURRENT STATUS: N.M./N.S.

McGuire poured another inch of brandy in his coffee mug, stretched his legs in front of him, and looked out the apartment window at the floodlight towers of Fenway Park three blocks away.

"N.M./N.S." No Motive/No Suspects. Fat Eddie Vance had written it under "Current Status" before transferring the Genovese case to the grey files.

McGuire smiled coldly. Silky Pete Genovese had been the most ruthless loan shark in the city, which provided all the motive needed for someone to run him down at midnight on a lonely street near the dockside warehouses. When news of Silky Pete's death spread through the city, drinks were hoisted and prayers of thanks were offered by hundreds of men who could now afford to miss a payment without the risk of having their kneecaps shattered.

McGuire sipped his coffee and brandy before turning to the traffic report in the Genovese grey file.

PERSONAL INJURY/DEATH TRAFFIC REPORT

REPORT #:   89-3871

DATE: 3/5/89

LOCATION: Atlantic Avenue & Beach Street

TIME OF ACCIDENT: 12:00 A.M. (approx.)

INJURIES TO (PROVIDE ALL DETAILS):

	VICTIM NAME	EXTENT OF INJURY
1.	P. M. Genovese	Death
2.		
3.		
4.		

HOSPITAL(S):   MORGUE

INVESTIGATING OFFICER REPORT: Call received on 911, approximately 12:13 A.M. re: H&R, Atlantic Avenue, reported by pizza delivery driver (name, address, statement on attached sheet). Officers arrived approx. 12:20 A.M., discovered victim against power line pole #335-A, located 14 feet south of Beach Street. Secured area, called for Medical Examiner, identified collision point as 52 feet south of Beach Street, 3 feet from east curb. Collected following debris:

    1 headlight rim
    Various headlight glass shards
    1 parking light lens

    1 chrome strip, approx. 2-½ feet long

Debris was subsequently confirmed as consistent with standard equipment on 1988 Buick Le Sabre, Embassy Blue colour.

PRELIMINARY FINDING: Victim was struck at curbside by above-described vehicle (first impact); victim struck power line pole (second impact). Driver of car unknown. Vehicular homicide suspected.

INCIDENTAL INFORMATION: Victim was identified through papers on person; victim was well-known to rackets squad with extensive record of charges and prosecutions. Victim was in possession of $2,380 cash. Victim's vehicle (1987 Mercedes-Benz sedan, plate #920AFP) was parked at curb opposite location of first impact.

Not much cash for Silky Pete to be carrying on a Saturday night, McGuire mused. But why was he out of his car, alone, on an abandoned street at midnight? He flipped ahead to the medical examiner's report.

AUTOPSY REPORT — HOMICIDE

REPORT #: 818-633-A

MEDICAL EXAMINER: M. Doitch

DATE: 3/6/89

VICTIM: Peter Michael Genovese

DETAILS & DESCRIPTION: Victim is male Caucasian between 40 and 45 years of age, 5 feet 10 inches in height, weight 190 pounds, in apparent good health prior to incident in question. Distinguishing marks include scar approximately 8 inches long on anterior of upper left arm.

    Victim has been dead approximately 34 hours (it is now 10:04 A.M. March 6). Massive contusions and fractures to left anterior of thorax, especially infrascapular and axillary areas, resulting in ruptures to major organs. Similar injuries to general skull area including severe shattering of maxilla and right temporal regions resulting in extensive fractures and substantial loss of brain tissue.

CAUSE OF DEATH: Massive trauma

PRELIMINARY FINDINGS: Victim suffered thorax injuries in collision with automobile; skull injuries were suffered through impact with heavy fixed metal object 10 to 12 inches in diameter, i.e. power line pole.

RECOMMENDATIONS: None.

McGuire tossed the report aside and reached for his coffee mug, draining the contents in one long swallow before leaning back in his chair and pondering everything he had learned.

Silky Pete Genovese had been set up and run down by a Buick. Probably ducking as he ran for his car. Gets hit on the right side. So why wasn't his arm injured? His arm would take the first impact. McGuire flipped back through the autopsy report again. No mention of an arm injury. Mel Doitch would have noted a detail like that.

He sat back in the chair again. Silky Pete's arm wasn't injured because it was raised, probably. With what? A gun? He's running, crouching, arm raised. He had to have a gun.

McGuire scanned all the investigation reports in the Genovese grey file but found no evidence of a thorough search of the area. He pictured Atlantic Avenue near Beach at midnight: desolate, with vacant lots between the warehouses. Genovese gets thrown forty feet through the air, hits a light post. A weapon in his hand could have been flung a hundred feet.

SUPPLEMENTARY WITNESS REPORT

To be completed only when supplementary information on existing matters arrives from unanticipated third party source(s). All primary information MUST be entered on PRI-MARY WITNESS REPORT, BPD Form #36-880B

CASE #:   884-239A

OTHER RELEVANT FILES: Autopsy Report 818-633-A

INVESTIGATING DETECTIVES: E. Vance, T. Fox

CIRCUMSTANCES: H&R resulting in death

WITNESS NAME: Unknown

REPORT (PLEASE BE CONCISE): Call received 2:56 P.M., March 5 on 911 line (tape #3-3-05-89) from pay phone location, Washington & Winter Streets. Male voice indicated he had witnessed incident from opposite side of Atlantic Avenue. No other information or circumstances provided. Witness reported victim had been shining flashlight in parked cars when a vehicle one block south pulled away from curb and approached victim at high speed with its lights turned off. Witness claims vehicle in question was dark in colour, no further details. No licence identification. Victim cursed loudly and began running across Atlantic Avenue but was unable to avoid speeding vehicle. Following impact, subject vehicle proceeded north on Atlantic and east on Summer Street. Witness ended report abruptly; trace and investigation of telephone booth were unproductive.

McGuire turned the form over to study the gruesome death-scene photographs for the first time. They showed several angles of a man's body crumpled against a metal pole. Silky Pete had been Boston's best-dressed loan shark, partial to alligator shoes and silk clothing. In the pictures on McGuire's lap, portions of the silk shirt and suit not stained by blood glistened in the harsh light of the photographer's flash.

So who did we check out? McGuire stroked his scar and searched for interview reports. It seemed every underworld figure in Boston had been visited by one of the detectives, although many were identified only by code words: "Herbie Two," "Violet Kid," "Little Sam." All were street finks, contacts supported and jealously guarded by detectives the way diplomats run spies in hostile countries. Each claimed to know nothing about the death of Silky Pete Genovese. And no one expressed concern that his skull had been broken in a gutter, scattering his brains as though someone had spilled porridge from a cereal bowl.

So you go to the car, McGuire told himself. Where's the trace report on 1988 Buicks, Embassy Blue?

The state vehicle registry listed eighty-six Buicks of that year, model and colour on the road as of March 5. All owners were traced and interviewed between March 7 and April 3. Owners' names and addresses were listed on a separate sheet. McGuire counted them. He counted them again. They still totalled only eighty-three.

What the hell was this? He reached for the phone, dialled Berkeley Street and asked for Timmy Fox, who answered on the first ring. Fox, a tall wiry black who wore a constant grin without seeming to find anything amusing about life, was surprised at McGuire's interest in the Genovese case.

"The hell you wasting your time on that piece of crap for?" he asked.

"Just reviewing things before they go back downstairs, that's all," McGuire replied.

"Best news of the year was Silky Pete making like a wounded duck, nesting in a streetlamp pole."

"Yeah, I know. Look, Tim, the only thing that doesn't fit is the car description you checked against all the registry files."

"I didn't check them. Whistles did."

"Okay, but we got eighty-six from the registry and I count only eighty-three checked. What happened?"

"Accidents happened. Two of them, anyway. Let me think. I remember at least a couple had been totalled before somebody tried to turn Silky into a hood ornament. And seems to me one moved out of state."

"To where?"

"Hell, I don't know. He left before it happened, I think. Look, we didn't have a plate on the car. It could have been from Florida for all we knew. We had to start and end somewhere so we made it state cars only. It wasn't exactly the governor who was used as a manhole cover, right? So how far were we supposed to go?"

McGuire grunted into the receiver. "You remember anything about the two cars that were totalled?"

"Like I said, both of them happened before Silky got hit. Whistles checked them. I think they were down state somewhere."

"Who verified the dates?"

"Investigating officers, I guess. You know the routine, Joe. Cops go in, say 'You got a car, matches this description?' Guy says 'Yeah' and the whistles look at it. Guy says 'No, I smashed it up' or 'My kid totalled it,' cops get the date."

"And verify it with what?"

"Anybody. Registry, neighbours . . ."

"Accident reports?"

Fox paused. "Yeah, I guess. That's another way."

"Thanks, Timmy. How you getting on with Fat Eddie?"

"I'd like to get on him with a ball-peen hammer."

After hanging up, McGuire tossed the Genovese file aside, counted another ten grey files to review, and went into his small kitchen for a coffee. Working alone wasn't so bad, he decided. And he thought he knew a way to make it even better.

CHAPTER SIX

"**S**loppy work, Ollie. Nothing like the way it was when you were there." McGuire shook his head in wonder. "Half the files shouldn't be grey, they should be C and C." He finished the slice of Ronnie's lemon cake and set the plate aside.

Solved cases were stamped "C&C" before the files were transferred to a warehouse. It meant "Convicted and Closed." Law and order prevail. Take a bow. Have a drink. Get some sleep. Tomorrow there'll be another corpse to view.

Ollie Schantz watched McGuire through half-lowered lids. The bed had been raised to sitting level and the limbs of his body, their corners sharpened from the weight loss he had endured, poked against the covers. Beyond the window the coast light winked through the November dusk, flashing off and on, monotonous, precise, comforting.

"Nothing new about sloppy work," Ollie said.

McGuire nodded. "But coming at the cases fresh, you see all the mistakes hanging out there like rooming house laundry." He sat back and studied the blinking light shining across the water. "You know, there could be a real need for a guy like me to do nothing but review grey files."

"Second-guessing your old buddies." Ollie moved his head in a pale imitation of a laugh. "You do that, Joseph, and you'll be as popular as a nudist at a Baptist meeting."

The door opened behind McGuire and he turned to see Ronnie standing there in a woollen winter coat, a kerchief tied over her head. "I'm leaving now," she said to Ollie. "You're sure you'll be all right?"

"Don't plan on going anywhere," he replied, staring out the window, avoiding her eyes.

"You really want me to get them?" she asked. She turned to McGuire. "Tennis balls. He wants me to buy him a can of tennis balls." She shook her head and left, closing the door gently behind her.

"What the hell do you want with tennis balls?" McGuire asked.

Ollie turned his head from the window and studied McGuire cooly. "Tell me about the files."

"Which ones?"

"The good ones."

"Maybe two are worth working on. The rest are drunks run over in alleyways, dead-end John Does, stuff that was never meant to be solved. But there's Silky Pete Genovese. Remember him? Hit and run down on Atlantic near Beach one Saturday night? Lot of people assumed it was a professional hit."

"Running down a guy in the street, that's Hollywood stunt man stuff."

McGuire nodded assent. "And if it wasn't pros, it was some poor sucker being shook down by Silky at a hundred percent interest a month. Which means it was somebody local, because Silky wouldn't deal out of state and risk a federal charge."

"We check his records?"

"Found a whole book of them back at Silky's apartment

but nobody could break the code. It's all initials and nick-names only Silky knew. Besides, he kept most of his business in his head."

"Who worked the case?"

"Fat Eddie Vance and Timmy Fox."

"That explains it. Eddie needs a road map to find his own pecker and Timmy can't see anything when that fat tooth-brush Vance keeps getting in his way."

"There's no record of body work on Buicks like the one that hit him, and the state bureau can account for all but three of them registered this year. One's in California, the other two were wrecked before Silky died."

"So what's your problem?"

McGuire began pacing as he talked. "No confirmation is my problem. Sloppy work. It all needs checking out. Maybe we should subpoena financial records, see if any owners had money trouble that might link them with Silky."

He looked down to see the other man's eyes closed, his breathing slow and shallow. McGuire spoke Ollie's name softly once, twice.

"I hear you," Ollie answered. When his eyes opened they were shiny. "Want to watch the Celtics?" His right hand flopped in short hops to pounce on the remote control. The ceiling-mounted television set flashed to life; slim bodies raced across its face, silhouetted against a golden floor. "There's beer in the fridge," Ollie said without shifting his eyes from the screen. "I'd get you one myself but . . ." His oversized mouth widened into a grin without warmth or hu-mour.

"I'm okay," McGuire answered, and he sat beside his friend for the next hour, both of them motionless, one by chance and one by choice, as they watched tall young men running, leaping, soaring across the floor of a distant arena.

With two minutes remaining and the Celtics leading by a slim three points, the front door opened and Ronnie Schantz walked lightly down the hall to Ollie's room. Before the door opened, Ollie's hand tripped the remote control and the images on the television set faded.

"Hi, guys." Ronnie Schantz entered, her kerchief wet with rain. "Terrible night out there." She reached into a plastic bag and withdrew a can of tennis balls. "Found them for you," she said to her husband, who had turned his face to the window. "Hard to get this time of year, that's what everybody told me. Unless you go downtown. But a place on Winthrop had them."

McGuire said goodbye to Ronnie, brushing her cheek with his lips, then turned and began shrugging into his topcoat. "You going to tell me what you want with tennis balls?" he asked the figure on the bed.

"Sure," Ollie said to the light across the bay. "Plan to play a set with McEnroe. What else you do with tennis balls?"

. .

By morning the rain had been swept out to sea and the drab autumn landscape lay bare beneath a brilliant sun.

Using one of the department's portable computers to gain access to law enforcement data banks in California and Massachusetts, McGuire confirmed that one 1988 Buick Le Sabre had been destroyed in a highway accident on New Year's Eve, the driver charged with D.W.I. A second Buick matching the description of the car that killed Silky Pete had been registered in La Jolla, California since February fourth. Its owner, a retired newspaper publisher, still resided there. He was seventy-three years old and had sold his weekly paper for a substantial sum before trading the Massachusetts winter for California sun.

The third Buick had been involved in a fatal accident on an interstate highway near Mansfield in the early morning of . . .

McGuire blinked. March fifth. The lone driver, killed in the accident, had been a thirty-eight-year-old resident of Taunton. He had owned a chain of three restaurants in the Taunton-Brockton area.

McGuire made two telephone calls before driving south to Taunton, cursing the sloppy police work he had exposed.

Five hours later he was sitting in Kavander's office on Berkeley Street.

"He was doing at least ninety when he hit the bridge abutment," McGuire said. Silky Pete's grey file lay between them on Kavander's desk. "State cop I talked to said they literally peeled him off the concrete."

"Go on." Kavander looked bored, restless. He removed the toothpick from his mouth, examined the tip, and replaced it between his teeth.

"Dumb whistles talk to the wife and she tells them it happened on Saturday night. The cops check their calendars, say Gee, that's March fourth. Too bad. We're looking for a car involved in an accident on March fifth. Sorry to bother you, have a nice day, la-di-da, let's go have a coffee. See, it happened within an hour of Silky being hit. All the cops are given is a date. One o'clock in the morning, the wife still considers it Saturday night. No witnesses, but a truck driver said he saw the car come up behind him maybe a mile ahead of the bridge. He said the Buick passed him at close to a hundred. Guess how he remembered the car."

Kavander shrugged.

"It had one headlight. Only the left one was working. The right headlight was out. This guy in the Buick, his name was Skerrett and he was in trouble at the beginning of the year. Bad money trouble. The bank was ready to call its loan, he's behind on payments to his suppliers, he's working with nothing but a skeleton staff at his restaurants. Then, end of January, he pays a big chunk on the bank loan. He gets the suppliers off his back, hires enough staff to get customers back, and he's golden. Nobody knows where he gets the money. And he's not talking."

Kavander studied his fingernails.

"You seeing a pattern here?" McGuire asked.

"You got more?"

"Lots more. I visit Skerrett's widow. Big house on a hill in Taunton. She's got two kids and some young guy has moved in with her. She sold the restaurants, even though she didn't have to. Skerrett's insurance company paid off on a half-million dollar accidental death policy with a lot of reluctance. I just finished talking to the investigator with the company and he's convinced Skerrett didn't fall asleep at the wheel. He figures the guy aimed the God-damned Buick at the wall because his business was going under."

"It's happened before."

"But it wasn't going under, Jack. He'd turned it around with about two hundred grand in cash. So where did he get it?"

Kavander inspected his toothpick again and began breaking it into tiny pieces. "How the hell do I know?"

"You know where he got it. He touched Silky for it and when he couldn't make the vigorish, or didn't want to, he arranged a meet. Silky figures the guy's a cream puff, he's standing around Atlantic Avenue looking for Skerrett's car and here comes the Buick. Silky's caught like a rabbit on the road. Bang, Silky's dead, and on the way home either Skerrett figures it's all over, because he knows we'll trace him and collar him, or maybe he planned to do it from the beginning. Anyway, there's a bull's-eye on a concrete wall ahead . . . ." McGuire halted his gesturing. "You listening to me?"

"Yeah, and I'm hearing nothing." Kavander tossed the toothpick splinters into his wastebasket. "Nothing we can ever take to the D.A.'s office anyway."

"What is this, Helen Keller day? All of a sudden you can't hear, you can't see —"

"Hey!" Kavander pointed his finger at McGuire like a loaded weapon. It shook as he spoke. "You don't come in here accusing fellow officers of shoddy police work just because some guy turned himself into wallpaper paste against a highway bridge."

"It *fits*, Jack."

"It fits your ass, McGuire!" Kavander shook his head and leaned back in the chair. "Damn it, don't you know when to back off?"

"You going to mark it C and C?"

"Only when you bring me facts. Not opinions. Hell, even the insurance company paid up, didn't they?"

"They wouldn't have if they'd known what we know now."

"We don't know anything, McGuire. We're doing a lot of guessing but we don't know a damn thing. What else are you working on?"

McGuire stared at Kavander in angry silence before turning away to look out the window. "There's only one other file worth anything. The Cornell murder. All the rest are whores in ditches and drunks in back alleys —"

"I hear Rosen's suing," Kavander interrupted.

McGuire swung his eyes back to the police captain. "Suing who?"

"You. For common assault. And the city. For endangerment of a bona fide court official."

"For Christ's sake."

"And he'll sue the department for harassment and false arrest of his client, Arthur Trevor Wilmer."

"Why haven't I heard about this?"

"Because he hasn't announced it." Kavander lifted his wrist and glanced at his watch. "He's holding a press conference right now to formally tell the world. Timed it just right to be the lead story on every TV channel in the state tonight." He opened his desk drawer for another toothpick. "You got a lawyer, McGuire?"

Kavander's door opened and a round face peered in, looking with uncertainty at McGuire and Kavander. "Sorry, Captain," Fat Eddie Vance said in his baritone voice. "Didn't know you were busy. Hi, Joe," he added in response to McGuire's glare.

"What do you want, Eddie?" Kavander demanded.

"I was looking for some files and they told me you had them." Vance smiled warmly at Kavander. "Thought I'd examine some old cases on the weekend, see what's worth reviewing."

"What files are you talking about?" Kavander turned to a stack of folders on the shelf behind his desk.

"Just a few of the grey ones from last year. Silky Pete was one, and that Fens murder."

"I've got them," McGuire snapped.

Vance's eyebrows shot up his forehead. "You have?" He paused, waiting for a response. When McGuire provided none, Vance continued: "Well, you need any help, Joe, you just call me, okay?" He smiled at Kavander. "Talk to you later, Chief."

Kavander stared at the door for a moment before saying: "I know what you're thinking, McGuire. But Vance is just overloaded, that's why things are a bit sloppy. Extra work comes along, Vance is the first in line to take it on. When he's got the time to do it right, Fat Eddie is the best detail man in the department."

"Maybe," McGuire muttered. "Just one thing I can't figure."

"What's that?"

"If God created the world, how come he had to make both Vance and maggots?"

. .

"Son of a bitch!" Tim Fox grabbed for his beer and drained the glass in one swallow.

"Bad clam?" Ralph Innes reached into the oversized bowl in the centre of the table and selected another steamed clam. "Gotta expect one now and then, Timmy," he said, prying open the shell. "Little guy'll get his revenge on you while you're sleeping tonight. Just make sure yo mama's not between you and the john."

Every Wednesday was Bucket Night at Hutch's, when six

dollars bought all the steamed clams you could eat, with bowls of garlic butter and cocktail sauce set among baskets of crusty bread and pitchers of cold beer.

"You married, Timmy?" Janet Parsons held a small uno-pened clam delicately between the tips of her fingers. With a deft movement she separated the two halves of the shell and transferred the meat to her mouth. The entire motion, smooth and graceful, was watched with an expression of hunger by Ralph Innes.

"Just six months," Fox answered. He frowned; the clam had left a sour, unpleasant taste.

"Still on your honeymoon," Janet smiled at him.

"I was almost married once," Ralph Innes offered, trying to decide which clam to devour next.

"What happened, Ralph?" Janet Parsons asked. "Did her father run out of shells for his shotgun?"

"Look at this fat little guy," Innes said, holding an over-sized clam for everyone to admire. "Naw, Janet. I just figured that the screwing you get isn't worth the screwing you get." He pried the shell open and looked around at the others at the table, his eyes settling on McGuire. "You've been married, right Joe? Couple of times, weren't you?"

McGuire nodded but didn't reply. He wanted out of there.

"Janet, you're married to the luckiest hash slinger in town." Ralph Innes skewered the clam meat with his fork and waved it in her direction. "Now there's a guy to envy. A bar full of booze and sweet old Janet to come home to every night."

"How are those grey files coming, Joe?" Tim Fox was waving a waiter over to the table.

"One down, a million to go," McGuire replied.

"Have you come across the Cornell file?" Ralph Innes asked.

"The one in the Fens?" McGuire shook his head at more beer. "Just to look at. I'll start working on it in the morning."

"Broad gets her head conked over in the Fens," Ralph Innes began explaining to the others as he sorted through the remainder of the clams. "Falls in the water and drowns. Me and Bernie, we worked on it, looking for her brother. Best lead was her brother . . . Archie, Allen . . . Andrew, that was it. Then we got yanked. The case died after that."

McGuire looked up from his clams. "Who yanked you?"

"Jack the Bear. Said we weren't getting anywhere so he moved Fat Eddie Vance on it. Fat Eddie went nowhere, far as I know. Thing's cold now, worn down like a hooker's heels. We had three good suspects too." Innes looked up at McGuire. "Take a look at that one, Joe. You figure it out, you're Sherlock Holmes, I swear."

Tim Fox snapped his fingers. "I remember that one now," he nodded. "Fat Eddie spent maybe two days scoffing some free drinks from a bar where the victim hung out. Did it all alone too. Kept me on the desk scratching my ass. Fat jerk."

"That's a case for you if there ever was one," Ralph Innes said, pointing his fork across the table at McGuire. "I can see you and Ollie Schantz taking that one apart. Old Ollie, he'd sit back, shake out all the garbage, and write it up over a bowl of chowder. Am I right, Timmy?" Tim Fox nodded agreement. "Hell, he was some guy, wasn't he?" Innes rambled on before launching into a story about Ollie Schantz. The tale had the smooth burnish acquired from being told many times over many bowls of clams and pitchers of beer. The others chewed and sipped in silence while Innes dotted his story with laughter and obscenities, speaking of Ollie Schantz as though he were a legend from a distant era.

. .

The telephone was ringing when McGuire arrived at his apartment near Kenmore Square. He walked briskly to his desk at the bay window facing Commonwealth Avenue and picked up the receiver while watching Janet Parsons back her Honda into a parking space.

The caller introduced herself as a reporter from the *Globe*. "Do you have any comment on the charges made by lawyer Rosen today?" she asked.

McGuire told her he hadn't seen them.

"But they were covered by all the television stations this evening," the reporter noted. "How could you miss them?"

"I was performing my duties," McGuire said. Down in the street, Janet stepped out of her car and locked the door.

"Your police duties?"

"That's right." Janet glanced up at his window and waved.

"Did you assault Arthur Wilmer?"

"I have never assaulted a prisoner in my life." He leaned forward to watch her climb the steps into his building.

"Did you plant evidence that might implicate him?"

McGuire turned to study his apartment door, visualizing Janet ascending the staircase to his second-floor apartment. "Don't be ridiculous," he said in a tired voice.

"Would you consent to an interview tomorrow?"

"Only if you clear it with Berkeley Street first," he replied. Promising to get back to him quickly, the reporter hung up.

By the time McGuire had begun to make coffee, he could hear Janet tapping at his door. When he opened it she was leaning against the frame, eying him from behind lowered lids. ·

"What kept you, sailor?" she smirked.

"Some reporter," he answered. He checked the hallway, then closed and bolted the door behind them. "Rosen's press conference has stirred up —"

The telephone rang again.

"She's back," McGuire shrugged. "You want to finish making the coffee while I get rid of her?"

He strode to the ringing telephone, seized the receiver and barked his name into the mouthpiece.

There was no voice on the other end. Instead, McGuire heard distant rock music hovering above a soft roar like running water: the background noise of a busy diner.

Finally, a hoarse whisper: "She's there, isn't she?"

"Who?" McGuire asked. "Who are you talking about?"

In reply he heard the distant wail of an amplified guitar, and then another wail, closer to the telephone, this one soft and human, before the man hung up.

McGuire replaced the receiver and turned to see Janet watching curiously from the kitchen door.

"Your husband," he said, answering her unspoken question.

She reacted with a toss of her head. "Was he upset?"

"I guess so." McGuire sat heavily on the edge of the desk, looking at his hands. "He was crying."

·   ·

Paul Desmond's saxophone floated from the stereo, soaring romantically through the melody of an old and forgotten ballad. Janet leaned against McGuire on the sofa, her legs tucked beneath her, her hands cupping a coffee mug. Such long, slender hands. McGuire had watched those hands squeeze six shots from a Police Special .38 to score the third-highest rapid-fire score in the history of the Boston Police Department.

"Anything I can do?" McGuire asked, and she shook her head sadly.

They sat in silence as Desmond wove in and out of the melody, lighting upon it and flitting away like a hummingbird. McGuire loved jazz from the late fifties. It was a time when music fit neatly into a small number of well-defined categories. Jazz was accessible, rock and roll was for hoodlums, and the classics were highbrow.

"I used to be flattered he needed me so much," Janet said when the music ended. "He was this big, good-looking guy who could handle himself in any kind of situation, and he needed me. I had never been around an independent man who needed me like that." She sipped her coffee, staring into the darkness. "Every woman wants a strong man to need her. They're the two biggest attractions for a woman, strength and need. The strong father figure and the weak child, all in one. But the more a man like that needs you, the less appealing his strength is and the less independent he becomes. And that's what attracted you in the first place." She turned to look at him. "Can men understand that? How the more someone needs you, the less you are attracted to them?"

McGuire nodded. But he didn't understand at all.

. .

Before she left they kissed at the door, long kisses empty of passion but suffused with feeling. He watched her descend the stairs before closing the door and walking to his window, where he stood until the tail-lights of her car receded into the darkness. Then he turned and opened the thick grey folder holding details of the investigation into the death of Jennifer Judith Cornell on a soft June morning in the murky waters and tangled gardens that the people of Boston have always called The Fens.

CHAPTER SEVEN

PRIMARY HOMICIDE INVESTIGATION REPORT

FILE #: 885-531

INVESTIGATING DETECTIVES: B. Lipson, R. Innes

DATE: 6/11/89

VICTIM'S NAME: Jennifer Judith Cornell

VICTIM'S ADDRESS: 2281 Park Drive, Apt. 2A

VICTIM'S AGE: 33

MARITAL STATUS: Single

CRIMINAL RECORD: None

BIRTH DATE: 1/19/56

BIRTHPLACE: Augusta, Maine

NEXT OF KIN: Unknown (see ref. re: A. Cornell)

INVESTIGATING POLICE OFFICERS: T. Whalen, L. Wade

DATE/TIME OF INITIAL CALL: 6/11/89, 7:42 A.M.

REPORT DETAILS: Call received on 911 from two joggers (see witness/report statement) who found deceased under bridge connecting Park Drive and Fenway St. Investigating officers arrived 7:47 A.M. Head was immersed in Fens water, body in prone position resting on bank. Officers observed apparent injury to victim's head. M.O. Hayes confirmed death at scene 8:15 A.M. (approx.) Fallen branch found at scene with blood and hair adhering to one end (see forensic report #T-55980 attached) (See photos A to L, film strip #89-7639)

INTERVIEWS: (LIST ON REVERSE IF NECESSARY):

Richard Fleckstone, TV Producer

Gerald Scott Milburn, underwriter,
   Upton Insurance Company

Irene Hoffman, Proprietor, "Irene's"

Frances O'Neil, Waitress,
   "Pour Richards"

Marlene Richards, Proprietor,
   "Pour Richards"

Henry Reich, Superintendent, Parkway
   Apartments

AUTOPSY REPORT

Attached   [X]

Not Attached   [ ]

If not, why?_____

CURRENT STATUS

1.   Case reassigned, E. Vance, T. Fox, 7/5/89

2.   APB Andrew Cornell, NKA, age 36 (see attached APB #88-99310) for questioning

3. Last Update: 8/2/89

4. Authorized HOLD file status: 9/1/89

Andrew Cornell, the brother Ralph Innes had mentioned. Why focus so much attention on him? McGuire flipped through the pages, pausing at the autopsy report prepared by Mel Doitch. His eyes skipped over the usual clinical descriptions to the paragraph headed "Preliminary Findings":

> Victim expired as a result of drowning while unconscious, said condition the result of a single blow to the posterior of the right squamous temporal, producing a minor fracture and moderate bruising of adjacent parietal lobe. Estimated time of death: 2:00 A.M.

The autopsy report and the statements from the two joggers who found the body gave no indication of a sexual attack, just one blow from behind which, on its own, would not have been fatal. He scanned the rest of the details. Scars on each wrist. Old and properly healed fracture of left arm, apparently during adolescence. Small strawberry birthmark on right hip. Callous on ball of right foot. No evidence of having given birth. No other distinguishing marks or features.

McGuire read on.

She carried no identification, no purse, no keys. A passing neighbour recognized her and directed the police to her apartment building where she was positively identified by the superintendent.

Colour photographs in the file showed the grassy banks of the Fens, brilliant green in the sun of an early June morning. The body of Jennifer Judith Cornell lay under a picturesque stone bridge, hidden from the street above. She had been pulled from the water and, in a close-up photo of her face, McGuire recognized the surprised expression he had seen so often on murder victims.

Other pictures accompanied the report, including three

eight-by-ten publicity photographs of Jennifer Cornell. In these professionally posed portraits, the face that looked back at McGuire was almost beautiful. The eyes and smile were a little too wide, the eyebrows too heavy, the shoulder-length hair too perfectly coiffed. Careful lighting had almost hidden the shallow crow's-feet at the corners of the eyes but failed to conceal the desperation in their studied gaze.

He stared at the face, searching for clues to the dead woman's personality, looking for something in her that could inspire someone with enough rage to commit murder on a night in June. But all he saw was the face of a sensual woman whose expression said she was frightened and whose records said she was dead.

More documentation: transcripts of interviews; a report of items recovered from dragging the immediate area of the Fens (two baby carriages, five automobile tires, one bicycle, several dozen cans and bottles, one typewriter, one drafting table. . . . A drafting table?); a description of the victim's apartment (neat, tidy, well-furnished). McGuire frowned and reached for a pad of paper. He began making notes.

Her purse was found on a dresser with wallet, credit cards and almost one hundred dollars cash inside. Two sets of fingerprints were lifted from the apartment, both relatively fresh. One set was positively identified as Jennifer Cornell's. The other, located in the bedroom, on the closet door and the exterior apartment door, belonged to someone unknown. Nothing appeared to be disturbed.

Andrew Cornell, McGuire muttered. Tell me about Andrew Cornell.

TO ALL DISTRICTS
APB # 88-99310

STATE-WIDE: [X]

F.B.I.: [X]

DATE: 6/21/89

B.P.D. CASE #: 885-531

NAME: Andrew ("Andy") Cornell

SEX: Male

RACE: White Caucasian

ALIAS: None known

AGE: 35 to 38 (approx.)

HEIGHT: 5' 8"/5' 10"

WEIGHT: 150-165 lbs.

HAIR: Brown

EYES: Brown

BIRTHPLACE: Unknown

BIRTH DATE: Unknown

SOCIAL SECURITY #: N/A

DISTINGUISHING MARKS/CHARACTERISTICS:

1. Walks with limp (right leg)

2. Speaks with slight lisp and southern accent

3. Well-proportioned physique; may frequent body-building gyms, etc.

WANTED FOR: Questioning regarding murder of sister, Jennifer Judith Cornell

LAST KNOWN ADDRESS: 2281 Park Ave., Apt. 2A

McGuire read on through the night, filling his notepad with scribbles. He wrote reminders to himself, sketched a map of the murder scene, and drew lines to connect names and locations until the sheet of paper resembled a perverse maze. When he finally stretched and looked at his watch, he was surprised to discover it was past three in the morning and he forced himself to set aside the files.

Later, waiting to fall asleep, he visualized the body of Jennifer Cornell in the last photographs ever taken of her, lying on her back, her wet hair clinging to the shape of her head, her eyes staring out in perpetual surprise.

. .

He stepped out of the shower stall to hear the telephone ringing, and left a wet trail to his desk where the details of Jennifer Cornell's murder still lay.

"You got the media on your ass yet?" Kavander snarled before McGuire finished answering.

"About what?"

"Hell, you don't watch TV?"

"Somebody from the *Globe* called last night —"

"Yeah, you're on their front page this morning. Saying 'No comment.' Very original, McGuire. You write that yourself?"

McGuire rubbed his head with the bath towel. "Jack, I just got out of the shower and I'm standing here looking like a hockey stick with hair. Get to the point, will you?"

"The point is, I need your butt here by ten o'clock. In case you don't wear your watch in the shower, that's forty minutes from now."

"What's happening?"

"You, me and Don Higgins, we're going to talk about this mess. Then we're going to face the hounds from the press and try to convince them that Boston cops don't go around kicking puppies and beating up defence lawyers. Wear something in sincere blue," Kavander ordered and hung up.

. .

Prosecuting attorney Don Higgins wore sincere blue suits exclusively, usually Brooks Brothers. In his profession, political instincts and a thrust for the jugular were deemed essential.

Higgins achieved success with minimal quantities of either, replacing them with keen intelligence and an unshakeable code of ethics in a job which frequently scoffed at both.

Tall and movie-star handsome, Higgins seemed cursed with what might have been an insurmountable handicap for a criminal law career: naivete. Democrats and Republicans alike had approached him to run for office in almost any capacity he desired, convinced that his good looks and squeaky-clean image would harvest votes in bumper-crop numbers. But after extensive conversation, the political scouts soon cooled their enthusiasm.

"Guy is as clean as an Eagle Scout," said one Democrat following an afternoon with Higgins. "But nobody's ready to vote for a forty-two-year-old guy who still says 'Golly!' and thinks being underprivileged means not going to Disneyworld every year."

Now, in a subtle blue pin-striped suit and quiet striped tie, Higgins rose from his chair in Kavander's office and extended a pink, perfectly manicured hand to McGuire. "Hiya, Joe," Higgins smiled. "Jack says he has you on special assignment."

"I'd like to have him strung up by the thumbs," Kavander growled, leaning back in his chair. "Let's get to it."

McGuire sat in the other chair, facing Kavander's desk. "Why not start by filling me in?" he said, ignoring the captain's outburst.

Kavander swung his feet on the desk and talked around the toothpick in his mouth. "The good news is, Judge Scaife isn't pressing contempt charges against you. The bad news is, Rosen has launched two million-dollar law suits against the city like we expected. One is for him, charging criminal assault and naming you and the entire B.P.D. The other is for that weasel client of his, charging false arrest and harassment, naming you and the great city of Boston."

"They are both without merit, in our opinion," Higgins said, his smile erased. "We'll propose a simple apology for the assault, since it's clear that no injury was made on his person. He'll sputter and complain, but the citizens of Boston won't want to see a million dollars of their money going to a lawyer who owns a garage full of Ferraris."

"The false arrest, it's all grandstanding, right?" McGuire asked.

"Even less chance of succeeding than the assault charge," Higgins smiled. "But it will let him keep his client off the street and delay proceedings. We'll be fortunate if we can go back to trial within a year."

"And every prospective juror from here to Cape Ann will believe we're railroading Wilmer," Kavander muttered. "Which is just what Rosen wants."

"So what's happening today?" McGuire asked.

Higgins leaned back in his chair, his hands clasped behind his head. "We'll try to neutralize the impact in the media. We can stop saying 'No comment' and begin stating that Rosen's charges are baseless and that we have total confidence in the Boston Police Department staff in general and you in particular."

"Very kind of you," McGuire said grimly.

"Hey, Joseph!" Kavander removed his toothpick and pointed it at McGuire. "You're not in any position to make smart remarks, okay? All you have to do is dance to our choreography, don't trip over the footlights, stay away from here, keep your lip —"

"Stay away from here?" McGuire echoed, rising out of his chair.

"— keep your lip buttoned and we wait —"

"Back it up, Jack!" McGuire shouted. "What the hell does 'Stay away from here' mean?"

Higgins was smiling and waving his hands at the other men. "Hey, fellows, come on."

Now Kavander was standing too, his hands on his hips. He swivelled to stare at an empty corner of his office, breathed deeply once, and turned back to face McGuire.

"That's the deal, Joe," he said in a soft, almost conciliatory voice. "The official word is, you're on special assignment. You keep your pay, your pension and your badge. Most of all, you keep your nose out of here."

"Just until Rosen milks whatever he wants out of the charges and drops them," Higgins added quickly.

"You want me to disappear?" McGuire asked, looking from one to the other. "Go away, sit home, watch soap operas?"

"I don't give a fuck if you fly to the moon on a broom," Kavander snapped. "Just don't show your face around here for a couple of weeks at least."

"What if I stay out of here permanently?" McGuire asked. He reached inside his jacket to retrieve his badge.

Kavander sat down. "Suit yourself," he began, but Higgins interrupted, reaching to touch McGuire lightly on the arm.

"Not a good idea, Joe," the prosecuting attorney said gently. "If you resign it will be construed as an admission of culpability. Rosen's case would immediately become strong enough for litigation. And that would be just the beginning."

"Of what?"

"According to our legal advice, resigning now would leave you open to full indemnity on both million-dollar suits filed by Rosen. The city would be relieved of the financial risk and of any obligation to provide you with legal support."

McGuire stared at Higgins to be sure he was serious — a wasted effort. Higgins was always serious. "You mean I would be out on my own, facing two million dollars in law suits, and the city would be off the hook?"

Higgins nodded, a look of concern on his face.

Kavander was less comforting. "Not everybody would be sorry to see it happen, McGuire."

"Does that include you, Jack?" McGuire demanded.

"Hey, what difference does it make?" The captain leaned back in his chair. "What are you, too proud to take a paid vacation?"

"We're looking at a month, two months at the most,"

Higgins said. "When Rosen drops his suits, everything is back to normal."

Kavander rustled in his drawer for a fresh toothpick. "For once in your life, McGuire, be reasonable. If I was you, I'd be out booking a cruise, getting away from this lousy weather, maybe hustling rich old broads all over the Caribbean."

"What about the grey files?" McGuire asked.

"Leave them. I'll pass them on to Eddie Vance, see how he does with them."

"Fat Eddie's the reason most of them are grey in the first place, Jack. I solved one of them in a day."

"You came up with a half-assed theory is what you did." Kavander looked across at Higgins. "Silky Pete Genovese, remember him? Buick used him for a bowling ball and a telephone pole for the head pin. McGuire thinks it was a murder and suicide. Some guy's way of handling a customer complaint with his friendly neighbourhood loan shark. Trouble is, nobody cares."

"I care, Jack," McGuire said. "The real trouble is that nobody else cares that Fat Eddie is blowing half the cases assigned to him. I'm looking at one now, a woman who drowned in the Fens last summer. There are leads everywhere, including an APB for her brother that was never followed up, and Fat Eddie writes 'NETGO' on it, leaves it in the drawer —"

"Writes what on it?" asked Higgins.

"NETGO," Kavander said, staring down at his lap. "Nothing else to go on." He was a different Kavander now, sullen and quiet. "Joe, you want to work on that one, you go ahead. I'm just telling you you're on your own. You don't show up here until I give you the word, and you work with whatever you already have." His eyes snapped up and met McGuire's. "That's the deal. You either make the most of it or you book passage out of town, I don't care. I just don't want people around here tripping over you until Rosen's off our back."

"Why?" McGuire asked quietly.

The word detonated another explosion in the police captain. "There's no 'Why?' There's only 'Do it.'" Kavander slapped his hand on the desk. "You're a fucking loose cannon, McGuire. You've been that way since Ollie Schantz retired, flying around, bouncing off things." He shook his head as though to erase his mood and force himself to grow calm again. "You ever play football in college, McGuire?" he asked in a quiet voice.

"Never went. After I graduated from high school, my old man told me I already had twice as much education as he did and I'd better get a job and start paying board."

"What did you play in high school?"

"Usually dead."

Kavander smirked. McGuire knew the captain had been an all-star guard at Boston College, a bruising blocker who remembered every opposition player he had ever knocked down. "I could tell you didn't play team sports. Because you've never been a team player around here, McGuire. You're a solo artist, you never learned how to put the team's interests ahead of your own."

Higgins glanced at his watch. "They're waiting for us downstairs," he interrupted, straightening the crease in his trousers. "The TV crews were setting up when I came in. We should get going."

Kavander placed his elbows on the desk. Holding his head in his hands, he stared at a typed sheet of paper in front of him. "Joe, listen to me," he said without looking up. His voice was low, his tone avuncular. "Trust me. I'm doing you a favour. Just lay low for a few weeks. It'll do us both good. That's all I'm asking. Just a few weeks, all right?"

When McGuire didn't reply immediately, Kavander swept the sheet of paper from his desk and rose from his chair. "Let's go," he said, walking briskly to the door. "And for Christ's sake, McGuire, try to keep your cool."

CHAPTER EIGHT

No weather is as unwelcome in New England as November rain. After scouring the North Atlantic, the cold air sweeps ashore and chills the land with its dampness. Too late in the year to nurture life and too early to soften the landscape as snow, the rain is suitable only for a grey world where Indian summer and all of its colours have faded and fled.

When the rains begin falling after sunset, they drive New Englanders deeper within the caverns of their minds where their thoughts focus on the pleasures of dry warmth and their souls weigh the dubious prospect of another sunrise.

That evening, a grey November rain deluged New England and the frame houses lining the streets of Revere Beach. Inside the white house on the hill with its view of the Sound, McGuire basked in the warmth of a fire, the aroma of fresh-baked pastry and the comfort of quiet conversation.

He sat back in his chair, a glass of Scotch in his hand, describing the morning's press conference and Kavander's insistence on McGuire's absence from the Berkeley Street headquarters building.

Ollie Schantz lay propped in a sitting position. The fingers of his right hand tightened and relaxed around a tennis ball as he spoke. "Kavander doesn't want you away from Berkeley Street," Ollie said as McGuire sipped his Ballantyne's on ice.

"He says it's his choice."

Ollie grunted. "Jack's not the wind, he's the weathervane. Somebody else doesn't want you there. Somebody higher. Commissioner's office, maybe."

"Whoever it is, I'm not going."

"Not going where?"

"Out of town." McGuire turned and stared out the window where the raindrops gathered on the glass and migrated downwards, seeking the sea. He felt old and defeated, more useless than his former partner lying paralysed beside him. He grimaced in a bitter imitation of a smile. "It's your classic decline and fall of civilization as we know it, Ollie. You're here, I'm on the street, Fat Eddie Vance is golden, and the guys in the pinstripes are calling the shots."

"Fat Eddie's the only guy I ever met, can't get out of his own way." Ollie turned his head to follow McGuire's gaze through the window. The light across the water was obscured by the cold rain. "You say you've got one of his cases?"

"You want to hear about it?"

"I keep telling you I'm not going anywhere."

McGuire drained his glass and set it aside. For the next half-hour he recited the details of Jennifer Cornell's murder. Ollie, his eyes turned away from McGuire and searching for the offshore light, interrupted several times to ask questions. Only when McGuire finished did Ollie roll his head on the pillow to study him.

"So you've got this Cornell woman, she's working on Newbury Street."

"In a pricey dress shop."

"In a dress shop by day and at night, when she's not trying to hustle parts as an actress, she's hanging out in this bar."

"Pour Richards."

"Whatever, on Mass Avenue."

"She's a regular there."

"No husband, no boyfriend, nothing steady."

"Picks up a guy every now and then."

"She's got a history of dropping a few beans out of her basket," Ollie recalled from McGuire's briefing. "Spends some time in a shrink haven upstate. Report says she was a borderline psychotic, manic depressive tendencies. Gets straightened out, comes back to Boston, when?"

"Five years ago."

"Gets settled in and one day her brother shows up."

"Andrew."

"Andrew, her brother. He starts hanging out in this bar too. He's smooth, good dresser, good conversation, everybody likes him, everybody thinks she's a bitch."

"Yeah, she could be a real ball-breaker. That's what comes out of the interviews."

"And after she croaks they find this TV producer's name in her book and some guy, a regular in the bar, who's got the hots for her."

"Something about her employer too. Woman who owned the dress shop where she worked was really pissed at her."

"And she and her brother are living together."

"That's what the neighbours say."

"Two weeks after her brother shows up, she's found dead in the Fens and there's no sign of her brother, what's his name?"

"Andrew." McGuire consulted his notes. "Not a trace. Nothing in her apartment, no clothes, no ID. A second set of fresh prints, probably his. They were checked out and zilch came back. And there's nothing on the guy. They checked with Maine records for information and came up empty. Birth records, neighbours, none of them say Jennifer Cornell ever had a brother. Of any age."

"Any next of kin at all?"

"Not that we can find. Jennifer was born out of wedlock. Father unknown. Mother married a guy from San Antonio fifteen years ago. Died in a traffic accident there, nineteen eighty-three."

"Bernie Lipson starts the case, goes nowhere, and Fat Eddie takes it over."

"Yeah," McGuire snorted. "Sits on it for a month, loses a bunch of reports and writes it NETGO. A real Sam Spade."

Ollie breathed noisily for a moment, his eyes on McGuire. "What's out of sync, Joe?" he asked finally.

McGuire grinned. How many times over their years of working together had Ollie looked at him while sitting in an unmarked car, or walking down Boylston Street on their way to a lunch of clams and beer, or gnawing on pizza in South Boston, tossing details of a case back and forth like a couple of Celtics working a two-man press? Ollie would ask "What's out of sync?" and McGuire would review the case for him, Ollie nodding and saying "There's a hiccup" or "Gotta stare that one down" or "That's hotter than a two-dollar pistol." Schantz and McGuire: together they had more closed files, more tight-assed homicide convictions than any two people who ever walked the floors at Berkeley Street. God-*damn*, McGuire thought in silence, there were damn few grey files when they worked together, and there was none of that NETGO crap written on *their* cases.

"Have we got us a job, partner?" McGuire asked.

Ollie Schantz managed a smile in return. "Looks like we might. Go over all that stuff again. Let's see who's dragging his dick around the parade ground." McGuire watched Ollie's weak right hand making dimples in the tennis ball. The rain was still falling cold and steady on the roof, the offshore light still flashing somewhere in the mist.

They had one. They had a murder for Ollie.

CHAPTER NINE

In the early days of Boston's history, the area called The Fens was nothing more than ill-smelling marshes extending along the banks of the Muddy River on the settlement's western border. But in the mid-nineteenth century, as the city's social leaders began fleeing the squalor of the waterfront neighbourhoods and moving west, they found the mosquito-breeding Fens intolerable and converted them from putrid marshlands to formal gardens, draining the wide swamp to create picturesque waterways.

Arbours and bridges were constructed at vast expense, and by the end of the century flowers bloomed in the glades below the level of the avenues. Warm Sunday afternoons would find all of social Boston promenading along the Commonwealth Mall and down the sandy paths which wound through the Fens.

Over the years, the inner city continued to spread; after World War Two it grew to engulf the Back Bay area, and Boston's wealthy families resumed their westward flight. Their abandoned brownstone mansions were transformed into apartments and rooming houses, and soon the nearby Fens became a weedy haven for addicts and muggers.

In recent years, the pattern began to come full circle. Many Back Bay mansions were restored to their original elegance as condominiums for young well-to-do urban couples. But the Fens were unchanged. The gardens remained overgrown and the formal plantings were as wild as a Maine meadow.

On a warm day in June, a visitor to the Fens would still find rustic charm in the greenery bordering the river, and in the small flocks of ducks and geese feeding in the sluggish water. But on a chilly November afternoon, when the overnight rain had turned first to sleet and later to the season's first snow, the Fens were uninviting, cold and sad.

McGuire stood on the stone bridge crossing the Fens at Agassiz Street and stared down at the water's edge, where Jennifer Cornell had been murdered five months earlier. A dirt pathway led from an old tangled rose garden through dead grass, tracing the shoreline of the river.

He felt the flurries settle on his neck and the dampness seep through the soles of his shoes, and decided there was nothing to be gained by walking that pathway in November. He looked up and beyond the bridge to the apartment building at 2281 Park Drive.

· ·

"He's dead," the old woman told him, looking through the crack of her apartment door, open only as far as the chain-lock would allow. "Died last July. I told him, I said 'You start drinking again, you'll kill yourself,' but he never listened. Never listened to me in forty-three years."

Her face was a road map of creases. She wore a shapeless print dress and her long wispy hair was tied loosely behind her head, hanging down her back like the hide stripped from some long-dead animal.

McGuire showed his badge. "Mrs Reich, I wonder if I can speak with you about Jennifer Cornell," he began.

"Who?" The woman's voice erupted, loud and piercing.

"Jennifer Cornell. She lived here. She was murdered over in the Fens last summer."

"Oh, that bitch!" The woman looked away in disgust but made no gesture to remove the restraining chain from her door. "She was another one."

"May I come in and talk to you about her?" McGuire asked, trying to keep his voice steady. "We have reopened the investigation."

"He already told you people everything."

"Who did?"

"That dummy. My husband. He did all the talking. Even identified the body."

"Yes, I know. But there may be a few other facts —"

"He ran the damn building, I didn't. Do now. Didn't then."

"But you knew her? Jennifer Cornell?"

"Yeah, I knew her. The bitch."

McGuire's mouth broadened in a smile that failed to warm his face. "Then why don't we talk about her, Mrs Reich," he said, the words snapping like dry twigs, "before I charge you with obstructing justice? Or maybe just call some friends at the fire department and ask them to do a thorough evaluation of your fire prevention procedures, room by room?"

She stared at McGuire, then muttered something under her breath before sliding the chain aside.

McGuire entered to see her walking away to a worn armchair set beside a window. The room smelled of staleness but was surprisingly clean.

Mrs Reich — the police records listed her first name as Amanda — collapsed in the armchair and sat staring out the window at the dull sky. McGuire remained standing. Amanda. Such a romantic name, he thought.

"Do you remember any details about the morning Jennifer Cornell was found dead?" McGuire asked.

"Hell, yes," the woman growled. "Cops all over the place, coming and going. Came here asking if we knew anybody looked like her. I knew it was her but I wasn't going over there. So I had to find him. He was off getting the garbage ready for pickup the next day. He never liked cops. Hardly told them anything. Then the cops had to get a key to her apartment. The cops, they must have talked to everybody twice. Tramping in and out of here. Screwed up everything that day."

"Did you hear anything unusual the night she was murdered?"

"No. Just heard her brother going upstairs, maybe two in the morning."

"How did you know it was him?"

"He had a limp. Stairs go right over our bedroom. Can hear everybody. I think I heard her go out later but I'm not sure."

McGuire scanned the room, cluttered with cheap souvenirs and old photographs. Amanda Reich continued to stare blankly out the window at the sky. He walked around the room, touching the worn furniture, glancing at the sad stains on the wallpaper. "Tell me about Jennifer Cornell," he said finally. "What kind of person was she?"

"I told you. A bitch."

"What else? Was she punctual? Tidy? Did she have lots of friends?"

The woman's body shook in a small spasm of laughter. "She took a man upstairs every now and then. Nobody could stand her for more than one night, way I see it. One time we nearly had to call the cops. Three in the morning and she's throwing stuff — glasses, books, I don't know what all — at this guy going down the stairs. And screaming at him. Woman had a mouth like a backed-up toilet."

"Do you know who this man was?"

"Some guy. Drove one of them expensive German cars."

"Mercedes?"

"The other one."

"BMW?"

"I guess."

"Do you remember the colour?"

"White. I remember it was white. Had one of them funny things on the back. Whattaya call it?"

"A spoiler?"

"Something like that. Looked like a race car. Parked it right in front of here. Didn't give a damn if he got a ticket. Some people have money to throw away."

McGuire settled himself on an arm of the sofa and smiled. She knows everything, he realized. She listens and she watches and she knows everything that goes on around here. "How many days before the murder did this happen?" he asked.

She kept her eyes on the window but her aggressive mood had mellowed to something more passive. Acceptance, perhaps. Or sadness. "Two, maybe three weeks," she replied.

"And what was this man saying to her when she was screaming at him. Do you remember?"

"Something about her being lousy. And that she was through. 'You're through! You're through!' he kept yelling at her."

"Any idea what that meant?"

She shook her head. "That dummy, he went —"

"Who?" McGuire interrupted.

"My husband," she snapped. "He went out in the hall and told them to shut up or he'd call the cops. She went back in her room and slammed the door. Guy with the car, he just went out and drove away. Last I seen of him."

"How about her brother?" McGuire asked. "Wasn't he staying here for the last two weeks before she died?"

For the first time since McGuire entered the room, she turned to face him. "Him, he was a weird one," she said. "Scared me. Passed him on the stairs once and damn near jumped out of my skin."

"Why?"

She studied her hands. "Don't know. Something about him wasn't right."

"Can you describe him for me?"

She looked out the window again. "About your height. Maybe thirty-seven, thirty-eight years old. Good build. Had a moustache."

"You said something about him wasn't right. What did you mean by that?"

At first, McGuire thought she hadn't heard him, or was ignoring him. Then she said, "He looked familiar. Like I'd seen him somewhere before in the newspapers or on the TV or something. Reminded me of somebody famous. And he always avoided me. Once I was on the stairs and he came out of her room and saw me and went right back in again, and I heard them arguing through the door." Her chest heaved and she lowered her head. "Besides. Maybe it's because of what happened after."

"After what?"

"After the bitch died. That's when he started his drinking again."

McGuire was confused. "Who?"

"That dummy. My husband. Hadn't touched a drop in ten years. Dried himself out. Then, after the bitch was killed, he started drinking again. He'd come home, he could hardly stand up, and I'd say 'You'll kill yourself, you keep this up.' He'd laugh and tell me I didn't know nothing. He said 'I got everything figured out about that Cornell woman and her brother.' I asked him what, and he just laughed at me. Then I found out he wasn't drinking alone. He was running around with somebody."

"Who?"

She paused, swallowed once, and blinked at the sky. "I don't know. He said it was Andy."

"Jennifer's brother?"

She nodded.

"He disappeared when Jennifer Cornell died."

"I guess so," she said. "I never saw him again anyway."

"And your husband would go drinking with him."

"Bullshit." She blinked again, several times, and McGuire realized she was crying. "He was drinking with some woman. I figured it out. I could smell her on him. What the hell do you do with a man, after forty-three years, he sneaks away and goes drinking with some woman? I tell you what you do. You say 'Piss on him!' So one night I'm in bed alone and he's late, he's out with her I know, and I hear a crash, hell of a noise. I get up and get dressed and there he is at the bottom of the cellar steps. Broke his fool neck trying to carry a case of whisky down the stairs."

McGuire stood up. "A whole case?"

"Twelve bottles of rye. All of them broken and him lying there with his neck . . ." She lowered her head and hid her face in her hands.

McGuire waited, listening to traffic noises from the street and muffled footsteps from the apartment above them. "Do you remember what happened the morning Miss Cornell was found dead?" he asked gently. "I mean, before the police arrived?"

Lifting her head, she frowned at her fingernails. "Nothing."

"Where was your husband that night?"

"He was here. In bed with me. Then he got up, maybe about four o'clock. I asked him what the hell's wrong and he said he heard somebody on the fire escape. Thought maybe there were kids back there or them drug addicts from the Fens, they like to sit out there on the fire escape steps. They're crazies. Should lock them all up. So he got up and looked and came back in about ten minutes. I asked him what it was and he said nothing. Told me to go back to sleep. So I did, and then I got up in the morning and told him to move his ass out of bed, he had chores to do."

"What time would that be?"

"I get up six-thirty every morning. Always have. Him, he'd

have his fat ass in bed until seven. Sleep all day if I'd let him."

"Did he ever explain who was on the fire escape?"

"Not to me he didn't. Told the cops he thought it was her brother, sneaking out the back way."

"Where did your husband get the money for the whisky?"

She shrugged. "I don't know. Never had enough money to buy me anything. I never saw none of it. Whatever he had, he spent on the woman."

"Who was the woman?"

She exploded in fury, turning on him. "How the hell should I know? I never cared. He could do whatever the hell he wanted, far as I was concerned. He could have ten women, the dummy, I wouldn't care."

McGuire waited until she had calmed down. "And you never saw Andrew Cornell or the man in the BMW again?"

She had returned her gaze to the window, her chin on her hand, fingertips in her mouth. She shook her head.

McGuire pulled a card from his wallet and left it on a side table. "Please call me at one of the numbers on my card if you think of anything else," he said. Then he added, "I'm sorry about your husband."

"Why the hell should you feel sorry about a dummy like him?" she mumbled from the window. "Good riddance to the son of a bitch. That's what I say. Same thing to you. Good riddance. Just get the hell out and mind your own business."

He closed the door behind him, leaving her by the window, blinking up at the sky.

. .

The snow had turned to sleet again as McGuire walked to the rear of the building.

Each apartment opened to a wooden landing and fire escape leading to an alleyway running parallel with the street. He stared up at the second-floor rear apartment for several minutes. It told him nothing, so he walked back to the Agassiz Street bridge with his shoulders hunched against the wind, glancing briefly down at the site of Jennifer Cornell's murder as he crossed the Fens. The light had faded, turning the world to a still deeper shade of grey. At the end of Westland Street he walked north to Massachusetts, losing himself in the crowds of office workers rushing to the subway.

Another block and he was across the street from the rustic barnboard façade of Pour Richards. He dodged a bus, cursed at a cab that sprayed him with slush, and ducked into the warmth of the bar.

Inside, McGuire stood in the doorway while his eyes accustomed themselves to the dim light. To his left were tables with mismatched chairs. The bar itself ran along the right wall, extending into blackness at the rear of the room where a rock singer screamed from a hidden jukebox.

He chose a corner table and ordered chili and a Kronenbourg from a middle-aged waitress, then sat and watched the crowd of after-hours office workers who were enjoying a quick relaxer before heading for home. Men and women stood three-deep at the bar, laughing, shouting, ignoring the snowy image on the wall-mounted television set.

When the chili arrived it was fiery hot and thick, with chunks of stringy beef. By the time McGuire finished, most of the after-work crowd had departed. The waitress brought his check.

"Anything else?" she asked in a lazy drawl. Her hair, bleached and dyed to the colour of pineapple, was swept up on her head; a few strands had escaped and dangled over her eyes.

"Who owns this place?" McGuire asked.

"You a cop?" the waitress replied.

McGuire said as a matter of fact he was.

"We breaking any laws here?"

"Not as far as I can tell," McGuire said, smiling. "Just curious to know who the owner might be."

"Marlene," she replied. "Over there," and she jerked her head in the direction of the bar where a woman leaned against the cash register, her arms folded across her ample chest. McGuire dropped some money on the table and crossed the room to the bar, sliding onto an empty stool in front of the owner. "You Marlene Richards?" he asked.

The woman turned and studied him carefully. She apparently liked what she saw because a broad smile began to spread across her face and continued to grow wider while she spoke, in a voice whose edges were frayed by smoke and whisky. "That's me, sweetie. Somebody send you looking for me?"

"Kind of." McGuire returned the smile.

"Hope they gave me a good recommendation." She stepped forward, rested her elbows on the bar and looked coyly into McGuire's eyes. " 'Course, all my recommendations are good." He could smell her perfume, heavy and sweet. "Who did the favour, sent you looking for me?"

"Guy called Andrew Cornell," McGuire replied.

The smile froze and she straightened up, tilted her head at him and asked "Who the fuck are you?"

"He's a cop." The waitress had followed McGuire to the bar after clearing his table. Now she looked at him with distaste, stuck out her bottom lip and blew a few tendrils of hair away from her face.

"Nothing wrong with entertaining a cop," Marlene Richards said. "Sometimes get a few of them in here for a beer after work."

"Any of them ask about Andrew Cornell?" McGuire asked.

"Who?" The waitress frowned.

"Finish clearing your tables, Shirl." When she left, Marlene Richards pulled a stool out from under her side of the bar and sat across from McGuire. "Look, I went through all this crap with you guys last summer when Jennifer was murdered." She looked away, then quickly back at him. "That's what this is all about, isn't it?"

She was perhaps forty-five, her face too fleshy to be pretty and her make-up too heavy to be flattering. Her thick, dark hair fell in curls to her shoulders. Her eyes were large and lively, her lips full and almost pouting, and her hands were small and pudgy; she wore cheap silver rings on each finger.

"Did you know him well?" McGuire asked, ignoring her question.

"Not as well as some people." Reaching under the bar she retrieved a container of fruit juice and poured some in a small glass. "You drinking anything or are you going to tell me you're hard at work?"

McGuire said he was both and he wouldn't mind another Kronenbourg.

Her smile returned. "A man of taste." She turned and shouted down the bar: "Shirl! Bring a frog beer with you!"

"Should I insist on some ID?" she asked after the waitress slid a bottle of the French beer and an empty glass in front of McGuire. "You look better than your picture," she said when he showed his badge and identification. "Me, I look better *in* my pictures. Hides the sags and bags."

McGuire smiled back at her. "Tell me about Andrew Cornell," he said.

"Thought I told everybody already. First I told a couple of cops, then a team of detectives, and about a month later some fat-assed slob started coming in here and asking the same questions over again. Sat right there and drank whisky sours. What the hell happened to tough cops who drink nothing but boilermakers? Anyway, he stiffed me for two drinks, as I recall."

"Do you remember his name?"

"Naw. Had a moustache like a toothbrush and talked like he was standing in a well." McGuire nodded. Fat Eddie Vance rides again.

"Did Andrew Cornell come in here often?"

"Look, I only saw the guy over a couple of weeks. He was in here four, maybe five times before Jennifer was killed. Never saw him again."

"Do you think he killed her?" McGuire took a long sip of beer and watched Marlene Richards arch her eyebrows and shrug her shoulders in reply. "Tell me what he was like," he asked.

She stared off towards the dark end of the bar where the jukebox had grown mercifully silent. "Andy, he was everything Jennifer wasn't. She was loud, he was quiet. She was rough, he was smooth. She dressed like a ten-dollar hooker, he dressed like a window at Brooks Brothers. I remember he came in once wearing one of those French watches, the really expensive ones."

"Cartier?"

"Yeah, one of those. Jennifer wanted everybody to know about it. Andy, he wouldn't flash it, he'd just sit quietly sipping his beer. But Jennifer told me once, 'Next time you see him, check out his watch.' She was that kind of broad."

"Sounds like they were opposites."

"Yeah. Except in one way. You looked in their eyes and you could see they were both hornier than three-headed goats." She tilted her head back and laughed, her voice shattering the near silence of the almost-empty bar.

"You learned quite a bit about him in just two weeks," McGuire said when she calmed down.

"What are you saying, I took him in the back for a quick boink one night?"

McGuire smiled silently in return.

"Well, I might have. Got to know him a little better, I just might have. Guy had a good build. Looked solid in the shoulders, nice flat stomach. And there was something about him." She searched for a word in her mind. "I don't know, he was kind of . . . mysterious, I guess."

"You haven't said much about Jennifer," McGuire commented.

Marlene reached under the bar and poured herself another glass of juice. "Jennifer, she was okay. She was a little . . . intense, I guess. I heard she'd spent some time in one of those rubber-room hotels up the coast, but we all go a little nuts now and then, don't we? Some of us in public, some of us in private. Anyway, one thing I'll say for Jennifer, she stood up for her rights. Other than that, I had no quarrel with her."

"But other people did."

Taking a long swallow of juice, she rolled her eyes to the ceiling.

"You want to tell me who?" McGuire asked.

"Hey, I told you. I gave all this stuff to the other bozos last summer. What are you trying to do, catch me in a lie?"

McGuire explained he had reopened Jennifer's file and wanted a fresh perspective on things.

She drained the glass and set it under the counter, then leaned towards him with her elbow on the bar. "Well, there was that guy from the insurance company, Milburn his name was. Used to come in here. Jennifer took him back to her place for a quickie one night and he thought he was in love. Spent the last couple of weeks before she died hanging around here, him playing Bogart and her playing Bergman. All I needed was a record of "As Time Goes By" on the juke-box. . . . Anyway, one night he tried to pick a fight with Andy Cornell. Said there's no way Andy could be her brother."

"Why not?"

"Because Jennifer spread the word that Andy moved in with her. See, this guy — Gerry was his first name, I haven't seen him in here since — he knew she had a bachelor apartment. One of those sofas that convert into a bed, a kitchenette, bathroom, and that was it. I mean, this is a pretty liberal town, but brothers and sisters sleeping together, that's where you draw the line. Milburn, he was in here drunk one night. Told me Jennifer wouldn't see him because she was spending so much time with her brother. So he tried to pick a fight with Andy. Who bolted out the door like a shot."

"Was Jennifer here that night?"

"No, but she came roaring in about ten minutes later. Looked terrible, too. Wearing a jogging suit, no make-up. Jennifer, she was a woman who needed make-up. I mean, she wasn't a bad-looking broad, but she had to work at it some, you know?"

McGuire said he knew.

"Anyway, she came in loaded for bear, grabbed a bar stool and tore after Gerry before a couple of regulars could grab her. Said he had no right meddling in her life, trying to beat up on her brother, all that stuff."

"How did she find out?"

"Hell, Andy was out the door as soon as the other guy came at him. Guess he met Jennifer jogging and told her about it, she came running right in. She was all out of breath but ready to kick some ass. Thing is, this Gerry guy was a bit of a pussy himself. I mean, he's in *insurance*, for Christ's sake, and Andy, he doesn't want any part of him. Want another beer?"

McGuire turned down the offer and withdrew his notebook from a jacket pocket. "I've got two names here," he began, opening the book in front of her.

Marlene leaned closer and tilted the notebook to catch the light, almost brushing her cheek against his. "What are you wearing?" she asked, smiling at him. "Smells good."

He told her his brand of aftershave.

"That's a new one on me. I just bought a used Jag and now I'm looking for a man who sweats English Leather and pisses gasoline. Let's see who you've got here. Fleckstone. Oh yeah, big shot Fleckstone, the TV producer. Jennifer had the hots for him. Thought he was going to make her a star. Brought him in here a couple of times to show him off. I thought he was a jerk, personally. She did some TV commercials for him, pushing pizzas on channel three. Big deal. She had to put out for him to get those. Talk to Fleckstone, he'll tell you all about Jennifer, star of stage, screen and motel beds. Who else you got?"

Her face fell at the sight of the next name on McGuire's list.

"Frannie. Yeah, poor Frannie."

"Frances O'Neil. Does she work here?"

Marlene turned to take a check from a waitress. "Used to," she said over her shoulder as she rang it through the cash register, "until Jennifer was killed and Andy took off." She handed change to the waitress, returned greetings to a crowd of regulars entering the bar, and leaned towards McGuire again. "Poor thing. She left here one night with Andy. Stars in her eyes. When he disappeared after Jennifer's murder, she was crushed. Never got over it. Walked around here crying until I sent her home. I kept her on for a few weeks, but she just got worse. Turned into a bag of nerves and finally called me to say she quit. Which did me a favour, because I was all set to fire her anyway."

"Where is she now?"

"Last I heard, she was living with her sister out in Cottage Hill."

"Do you have an address?"

"Somewhere." She leaned to retrieve a stack of notepaper from under the counter. "She asked me to mail some money I owed her and I did. Here it is."

McGuire copied the address in his notebook, then paid for his beer and slid off the bar stool. "Nice to meet you," he said, nodding to her. "I might be back."

"Hope so." Marlene scooped the money and watched him head for the door. "Just remember, McGuire."

"Remember what?" he asked, shrugging into his winter topcoat.

"Love is nice, but tender lust ain't bad." She threw her head back and laughed, her voice following him through the door and out into the dark and empty street.

CHAPTER TEN

"It's just another neighbourhood bar. They get the office crowd at noon and after work, and then the regulars show up at night to watch the Sox or the Bruins, pinch a little ass, try for a pickup. The owner just might be the raunchiest female bartender you've ever met."

Ollie lay back listening, his right hand squeezing and releasing the tennis ball with the mindless rhythm of a metronome. "This Cornell woman," he wheezed. "She a regular there?"

McGuire sipped his coffee before speaking. "Worked just around the corner on Newbury. I'll stop by tomorrow, talk to the owner of the dress shop."

"The guy she had the fight with at her apartment. Who was he?"

"Don't know. It might be Fleckstone, the television producer. This other guy, the insurance man with the hots for her, he sounds promising too." He set his coffee cup aside and turned to see Ollie watching him through narrowed eyes.

"The building superintendent bothers me. After she's dead he starts drinking again, hanging around with women. Buys his booze by the case."

McGuire shrugged. "His wife says he was in bed until almost seven in the morning the day of the murder, except when he got up to check the noise on the fire escape. Either way, he was with her at the time the Cornell woman died. Tough alibi to break, him being dead too."

"So maybe he helped the brother check out when he got up at four in the morning."

McGuire nodded. "I thought about that."

"Doesn't explain the woman," Ollie began. His eyes shifted quickly to the window.

"What woman?" McGuire could hear Ronnie approaching them, coming down the hall towards the bedroom. "You mean the one Reich was seeing? His wife could be wrong. I'll bet he was out drinking with the brother. He's hiding Andy somewhere and Andy is paying him off, maybe keeping him in booze until he gets out of town."

"You think the brother did it?" Ollie asked, facing the darkness through the window.

"I'm not thinking anything until I talk to Fleckstone and the others." McGuire stood up as Ronnie entered quietly behind him. It was time for her to feed Ollie and change his bedclothes. He's like a baby, McGuire realized. He has to be bathed, fed and cleaned up after. "I'm seeing him, the waitress and the insurance man tomorrow," he said. "And the woman who owned the dress shop. I'll come back tomorrow night and fill you in." He kissed Ronnie lightly on the cheek. "Gotta go, sweetheart. Thanks for the coffee."

She gave him a thin smile, and the gesture revealed to McGuire the burden she bore and would bear for the rest of her life, caring for her husand as she would a helpless child.

. .

Half an hour later, McGuire found a parking space within a block of his apartment, congratulated himself on his good luck and began walking back along Gloucester, his head down and his shoulders hunched against the cold.

High heels clicked towards him from the opposite direction, and he looked up to see Janet Parsons. They met at his apartment house stairs and she touched his arm gently and reached to kiss his cheek, her face silent and solemn.

"How have you been?" he asked, and her eyes gave the answer.

. .

She perched on the edge of a chair like a bird poised for flight. Her coffee had grown cold in the earthenware mug on the table beside her.

"I guess I wasn't thinking when all this . . . when all this began," she said in a dull, flat voice. "I still care for you, Joe, but . . ."

McGuire poured his second cup of coffee. "You don't owe me anything," he replied. "You never did." He looked at her over the edge of his coffee mug. "What did you tell him?"

"As little as possible. Why hurt him more?"

"How does he feel about me?"

"You mean does he want revenge?" She shook her head. "No, that's not Max. He just wants me back. He wants everything the way it used to be. Like it was a year ago."

"Nothing can ever be the way it used to be. Things can't be the same ever again." He was echoing Ollie Schantz — sooner or later he always did.

"He wants it better than it was." She raised her chin and her eyes glistened in the light from McGuire's reading lamp. "How about you? How are you doing, staying away from headquarters? Bernie, Ralph . . . they're all going to miss you."

"Kavander won't."

"I hear rumours that you're not coming back. Some people are even saying the commissioner wants you gone."

"Maybe he'll get his wish." McGuire stood up and walked across the room to his elaborate stereo, the only luxury he afforded himself. "I don't miss Berkeley Street as much as I thought I would." He selected a CD and slipped it into the player. "Ronnie Schantz is trying to get me fat with her cooking and Ollie and I are working together on a case."

"Ollie? I thought . . ."

"He's only paralysed from the neck down, you know." Soft piano music filled the room, rich, slightly dissonant sounds, introspective and slow. "Know who's playing?" he asked, turning to her.

She tilted her head, listening. "Bill Evans," she said with a slight smile. "Am I right?"

"Six months ago, you didn't know him from Liberace."

"Six months ago, I didn't know a lot of things." She glanced at her watch and stood up. "I shouldn't have come here," she stammered. "Except that I felt I owed you —"

"You don't owe me a thing!" he snapped. Then, shaking his head, he said it again softly: "You don't owe me a thing. Go home, Janet. Quit feeling sorry for me and your husband. And don't ever start feeling sorry for yourself. That's one thing I liked about you. You were the only woman I ever met who I couldn't imagine feeling sorry for herself. If that was an illusion, don't spoil it now."

Later, standing at the window, he watched her leave the building and walk down Commonwealth to her car. He turned away, not seeing the man who had been standing across the street looking up at his window, and who began to follow Janet, walking several paces behind her.

. .

The morning arrived too soon and too cold. Clouds skimmed low across the sky and dampness seeped through McGuire's heavy winter topcoat, scarf and gloves.

McGuire located Fleckstone Productions above an antique store in a three-storey brick building on Charles Street. At the top of the stairs an attractive young woman looked up from behind her colonial desk and smiled as he approached. She was speaking on the telephone, and while McGuire waited he scanned the office decor, which looked like an extension of the antique shop below them. Nova Scotia pine cupboards were mixed with Pennsylvania Shaker and English Chippendale furniture for an eclectic effect, as though each piece had been selected at random. McGuire knew that there was nothing random about this collection; the style was the result of a calculated effort that bespoke money. Large sums of money.

The prints on the wall were Courier and Ives, the carpet a rich and very old Persian, the light fixtures all burnished brass. But above, thrusting itself incongruously into the period mood of the room, was a gleaming wall-mounted television monitor.

"May I help you?"

The woman at the reception desk looked up and radiated an orthodontically perfect smile.

McGuire showed her his badge, gave his name and asked to see Richard Fleckstone.

Her eyes widened slightly but the smile never wavered. She punched a button on her telephone, announced McGuire, and with the same smile directed him to the end of the hall leading off the reception area.

Walking down the hall he passed several small cubicles. From behind their closed doors came the sound of rock music or amplified, professionally modulated voices. McGuire recognized the spiel of a popular used car pitchman as he passed one closed door; the musical theme of a local public affairs television show escaped from another.

At one open cubicle, McGuire paused to watch a cluster of young people dressed in jeans and sweatshirts or outrageous punk fashions, all of them bent over electronic equipment and intently studying images on banks of small television screens, speaking among themselves in a shorthand language as alien to McGuire as Mandarin Chinese.

The elaborately carved oak doors at the end of the hall

swung open and McGuire approached a large overweight man standing in the doorway.

"I'm Richard Fleckstone," said the man slowly. His voice was deep and resonant and he breathed noisily, as though speech were an effort.

McGuire once again showed his badge and identified himself. Fleckstone nodded and McGuire followed him through the door into a large high-ceilinged room cluttered with papers, stacks of video tapes, boxes and books. One wall was devoted to electronic equipment: a computer system, an expensive rack-mounted stereo, two VCR units and a bank of television monitors. An antique barber's chair sat alone by a corner window, facing out towards Beacon Hill.

Richard Fleckstone shuffled papers on his desk, the top of which was hidden beneath layers of photographs of attractive young women. "Excuse the mess," he said, in the same bored yet almost out-of-breath manner. "I'm in the middle of casting a major shoot and I wasn't expecting company. Can I get you a coffee?" He looked up to see McGuire watching him carefully.

Fleckstone had a boxer's physique: a fighter past his prime and out of shape. His rounded shoulders flowed into a massive chest which ended abruptly at a soft, protruding stomach. His face was round, the grey hair thinning. But it was Fleckstone's stance which suggested he belonged in a ring: he stood with his stocky legs apart and balanced, the head bent slightly, the lids half-lowered, the eyes watching McGuire warily from an off-centre position — a boxer's stance.

"I'll pass on the coffee," McGuire said. "Just tell me about Jennifer Cornell."

"Thought so." Fleckstone, wearing a blue blazer over a worn sweatshirt and cotton slacks, sat down and rested his feet, clad in white tennis shoes, on the corner of the desk. "Couldn't think of any other reason for you to come."

"What the hell do you do here?" McGuire asked, sweeping his arm to take in the wall of electronic equipment.

"I used to do nothing but TV commercials," Fleckstone replied. "Still do some. But now we're into other things. Industrial movies. Corporate presentations, training films. 'Six Steps to Sales Success'. Stuff like that. Even some rock videos." He swivelled in his chair and pointed to the television monitors. "See that top screen, second from the left? Watch."

McGuire followed the producer's gesture. The monitor flashed a frozen black-and-white image of a silhouetted man in a harshly lit street. As McGuire watched, the scene shifted almost imperceptibly and the street lights acquired a blue tone. The man's hat, a forties-style fedora, faded from black to chocolate brown and in the background a white neon sign was transformed to orange.

"Colorizing," Fleckstone explained. "We take old black-and-white movies, put them through a computer one frame at a time and add colour. Gives a whole new dimension. This one's *The Communion Murders*. Old Sydney Greenstreet flick."

"Isn't there a lot of controversy about that?" McGuire asked.

"Yeah. Some. These movies, they were never made for colour. They were exposed, framed, edited, all for black-and-white."

"So why do it?"

Fleckstone smiled. "Hey, you want art, you go to an art gallery. I'm a businessman. I've got over three million tied up here in video and computer equipment and I pay sixteen people to run it. First thing I ask anybody applying for a job here, the artsy-fartsy types with their degree in video arts or cinematography, kids who grew up expecting to become Eisenstein or Spielberg, I say, 'You concerned about prostituting yourself?' If they answer yes, I say, 'So how come you're looking for work in a whorehouse?'"

"Did Jennifer Cornell work here?"

"Jennifer? You kidding?" Fleckstone looked away, shaking his head and smiling. "Hell, no."

"How did you know her?"

Fleckstone looked back at McGuire from under half-lowered eyelids. "Should I have a lawyer here?"

"You can if you want one. My suggestion is, save yourself the fee until I read you your Miranda rights."

Fleckstone considered McGuire's advice before leaning back with his hands clasped behind his head. "I met Jennifer about a year ago at a party over on Newbury Street. A photographic exhibit or something. She latched on to me as soon as she heard I was in video work. Said she'd done some amateur theatre productions and wanted a chance in commercials."

"And you gave her work?"

"A couple of local things. Carpet store commercial, some spots for a Chevy dealership in Quincy. I think she played a mother in a training video we did on dental hygiene." He grinned at McGuire. "Not as much glamour in this business as some people think, but you can make a few bucks."

"Were you ever in Pour Richards?"

Fleckstone nodded. "It's a dump. I met Jennifer there a couple of times. She liked to impress the regulars, have people meet her at her special table in the corner. She'd introduce me, saying 'This is Richard Fleckstone, I bet you've heard of him.' Most of them hadn't and I told her to knock it off, don't try to come on like a star."

"Were you sleeping with her?"

Fleckstone froze his gaze on McGuire, then allowed a smile to crease his face. "Boy, you get right to the point, don't you?"

"Beats wasting time."

The other man nodded. "Yeah, I spent a few nights at her place, she spent a few nights at mine. No big secret. I've got two ex-wives and three kids too, in case you're curious."

"You drive a white BMW, spoiler on the back?" McGuire asked.

"Sure. Parked in the lot. You want to check it out?"

McGuire shook his head. "You had a fight with Jennifer at her apartment about two weeks before she was murdered, right?"

"Something like that."

"Mind telling me what it was about?"

"The usual stuff. Greed. Lust. Lies." Fleckstone's grin widened. "Her greed. My lust. And both of us lied."

"You were using her."

"Routine as old as show business. And hey, she earned a few bucks in the process." Fleckstone jabbed a finger at McGuire. "Look, she wouldn't have gotten any work without me. I mean, she could act, but like I kept telling her, she was no Meryl Streep. So who was using who?"

"What was she like?"

"Jennifer? A little desperate. She could be calm, pleasant. And funny in a raunchy sort of way. Other times . . . hell, I guess it depended on what prescription bottle she grabbed when she got up in the morning. I see a lot of women like that her age. They dabble in acting or modelling or something, doing amateur theatre work, telling themselves their break is just around the next corner. Then one day they wake up and realize they've turned too many corners. They have no family, no career hopes, nothing. But they can't let go of that dream. So they get a little desperate. Do weird things." Fleckstone swung his feet off his desk and studied his fingernails as he spoke. "I heard, after that fight we had at her apartment, she tried to change her looks. Tried to look younger, take some years off by changing her hairstyle, buying a new wardrobe. Kind of sad, I guess."

"Was she difficult to get along with?"

"You mean bitchy? Jennifer was born bitchy. But like I said, she could be funny too. And she was bright. And I'll admit it, she had some talent." He grinned up at McGuire. "Even did a great impersonation of Richard Nixon."

"Did you ever meet her brother? Andrew?"

Fleckstone snorted. "No, he phoned here a couple of times. She even called me, pleading with me to audition him. Said she knew we were finished but that Andrew had just come to Boston and was looking for a break." He shrugged. "Whole damn family was nuts. Couple of days later I get another phone call and it's this Andrew Cornell. Before I can say anything he starts tearing into me about the way I treated his sister. Said he was coming over to have it out with me. I hung up on the yo-yo. Then, maybe a couple of days later, he calls again and apologizes. Says he has a comp sheet, a sample reel —"

"What are those?"

Fleckstone sighed. "Comp sheet, that's what models use to show how they can look in different scenes. Bunch of pictures they get taken by professional photographers. Sample reels have actors' roles on them, from commercials or films. When you call on a producer, you'd better take your comp sheets and sample reels with you or you don't even get considered. Anyway, I thought, 'What the hell is this? First the guy wants to pick a fight with me, then he wants an audition?' Well, you never know. I told him, you want to fight, you want to act, come on over. Do either one, I don't care. But he never showed."

"Think you frightened him away?"

"No idea. Anything else?" Fleckstone's eyes scanned the monitors on the wall.

"You ever hear about Frances O'Neil? Or Gerry Milburn?" Fleckstone closed his eyes and shook his head slowly. McGuire stood up, scribbled his telephone number on a sheet of paper from his notebook and handed it to Fleckstone. "You think of anything else, you let me know. Okay?"

Fleckstone rose and nodded silently.

"I'll bet you remember where you were the night Jennifer was killed," McGuire said. He was looking down at Fleck-stone's desk.

"Sure do," the other man replied. "I was in New York for the weekend. Left Friday night, came back Sunday afternoon. Still have the receipts, if you want to see them."

"Business?"

Fleckstone smiled. "Pleasure. Lots of pleasure."

"Who are all these women?" McGuire asked, waving his hand over the stack of photographs.

"Actresses. Models. Women who want to be actresses and models."

"These are comp sheets?"

"That's what they are. I use them when I'm casting a shoot. If I like what I see, I might find something for them."

"Like TV commercials for rugs and cars?"

Fleckstone's face crinkled in laughter. "You got it. I might even take one down to New York for a weekend, introduce her to a few friends, you know? Hell of a job. Doubt if I can keep doing it for more than another thirty, forty years."

He escorted McGuire to the door and watched the detective walk down the long hall and through the reception room before crumpling the paper with McGuire's telephone number into a ball and tossing it in his wastebasket.

CHAPTER ELEVEN

Driving beyond the exit to Logan Airport, McGuire turned south on Bennington and into the town of Winthrop. Tall wooden houses lined the narrow streets, forming corridors which revealed tantalizing glimpses of the sea in one direction and dramatic views of Boston Harbour in the other.

It seemed like an idyllic place to live, a residential area on a finger of land offering vistas of both the city and the ocean. But its location also meant much of Winthrop lay directly beneath the landing approach to the airport. Throughout the day and much of the night, aircraft skimmed the tops of trees, the deep roar and angry whine of their engines disturbing the tranquil neighbourhood.

At the tip of the peninsula, like a brooding menace, sat the fortress-like structure and stone guard towers of Deer Island jail.

Outside of Winthrop and before Deer Island, McGuire entered Cottage Hill and quickly found the address of Frances O'Neil, a three-storey house on the harbour side of the peninsula.

With the exception of its size and location, the building

was undistinguished, even dull in appearance, constructed in a perfect cube shape as deep and high as it was wide. White shutters gleamed against the chocolate-brown siding; brass light fixtures added in an attempt to create character only drew attention to the practical, unimaginative lines of the house.

McGuire stepped out of his car, ducking instinctively at the roar of a jumbo jet passing low overhead, and walked up the concrete steps to the front door.

At the sound of the bell, a large dog barked inside and the door opened just wide enough to reveal a weary-eyed woman in her mid-thirties clutching a robe around her body.

"Yes?" she asked McGuire. Her eyes flew from him to his car, then up and down the street before alighting on McGuire again. A black Labrador retriever stood behind her, watching McGuire carefully.

He asked to see Frances O'Neil.

"She's not here. She's out." The woman's eyes darted past him again, confirming that he was alone.

"When do you expect her home?" McGuire asked.

"Can you tell me what this is about?"

He showed her his badge and identification. "I just have a few questions for her, that's all," he said soothingly.

Her eyes widened and searched the street once more. "Is Frannie in trouble?" She bit her lower lip.

"No, ma'am. Not at all, " McGuire replied. "I'm just cleaning up some routine work before closing a case. Thought she might be able to remember something that could help me."

"She's . . . Frannie looks after my little girl, Kelly. She's gone down to meet Kelly at the school bus and bring her home. It's not due for another ten minutes but Frannie's always afraid it might arrive early and she won't be there to meet her. Frannie's like that."

"Where is she meeting the bus?"

The woman opened the door wider and leaned out, pointing down the road. "It stops around the corner, where this street curves at the sea wall. She'll be waiting there. She's wearing a blue quilted jacket."

McGuire thanked her and turned away.

"Just a minute," the woman said from the door. "Can you wait just a minute, please?" Closing the door, she disappeared inside, returning a few seconds later and thrusting a woollen scarf towards him. "Would you give this to her, please? Frannie never dresses warmly enough and there's a terrible wind off the harbour today." She smiled for the first time, a smile that brought warmth to her face but did not disguise the concern in her eyes. "You're sure Frannie's not in any trouble?"

McGuire assured her she wasn't and turned again to walk down the steps. From the corner of his eye he saw the woman watching him from a window.

The street curved left, making a switchback that led back towards Boston via Winthrop Shore Drive. On the outer edge of the curve a low stone wall separated the road from the waters of the harbour.

Another aircraft passed overhead, its engines screaming and its landing gear extended. McGuire grew convinced that views of the city skyline and the sea, no matter how spectacular, could never compensate for the noise from the busy airport flight path.

The woman was sitting on the low wall, her back to him, wearing loose woollen slacks, a tattered ski jacket and a thin kerchief on her head. She was staring not at the city skyline but at the grim black towers of Deer Island jail down the peninsula. The wind tugged at her clothing and danced with a wisp of hair dangling from under her kerchief.

At the sound of McGuire's footsteps she turned to look at him, then quickly away.

"Miss O'Neil?" he asked, stopping beside her. "Frances O'Neil?"

She looked up at him again and forced a smile across her

face. Her soft attractive features seemed to be heavily weighed by life and her eyes were dark and melancholy, the eyes of a saddened child.

"Lieutenant Joe McGuire," he said, showing his identification.

She looked at the badge without interest before turning to face the harbour.

"Are you Frances O'Neil?" he asked.

Leaning forward, she held her head on her hand and said something McGuire was unable to hear.

"I'm sorry. Would you repeat that, please?" McGuire sat on the wall with his back to the harbour and leaned to look at her.

"Yes," she said in a small voice. "Yes, I am."

"I was asked to bring you this." He handed her the scarf. "I think it's from your sister. Back at the house."

She smiled, avoiding McGuire's eyes, and accepted the scarf. "Thank you," she said, wrapping the scarf around her neck and tucking it into the ski jacket with her thin, delicate hands. "Yes, that's my sister. My older sister. Older sisters think they're mothers to the rest of the world."

He showed her his badge and introduced himself. "Did you know Jennifer Cornell?"

Frances O'Neil continued to smile sadly and nodded. "I knew it would be about Jennifer."

"Why did you know that?"

"Because she was murdered. And because you haven't found the killer yet."

"How did you meet her? When you worked at Pour Richards?"

She moved her head up and down in short, jerky motions. "I worked there as a waitress for over a year. But I guess you know all that. I told some police officers all about it after Jennifer . . . after the murder."

"What kind of person was she?"

Frances looked directly into McGuire's eyes. "She was

mean. Terribly mean. And ambitious. And sexy to men in her own way, I guess."

"Did you ever meet Richard Fleckstone?"

"Who?"

McGuire repeated the name and Frances shook her head.

"How about Gerry Milburn?"

The smile returned and she turned away to stare out at the harbour, her chin on her hand. "Gerry thought Jennifer was wonderful. And she could be wonderful, too, when she wanted something from somebody. She took him home with her once and I guess he thought it was love or something. But not Jennifer. For Jennifer it was just recreation."

"Would you say Milburn was in love with her?"

"Smitten."

"Pardon?"

She looked back at him, one hand toying with a wisp of hair that had fallen out from under her kerchief. "He was smitten with her. Nice word, isn't it? Comes from the word smite. 'She smote him a heavy blow.'" She tucked the errant hair back under the kerchief. "Sorry, I used to be a teacher. Sometimes I miss it."

"You went from being a teacher to a barmaid?"

"With a few stops in between. Now I'm just a baby-sitter. So in a way I've come full circle."

A 727 roared overhead, drowning out her last few words. McGuire glared up at it, but Frances O'Neil didn't seem to notice.

"This Milburn," McGuire began, watching the aircraft drift lower towards the runway across the water. "Do you think he was jealous enough to kill Jennifer?"

"He wasn't jealous," she replied. "He was shattered."

"But could he have killed her out of anger or revenge?"

She shrugged her shoulders. "Who knows what people can do?" she asked. "You must know that better than me. In your line of work." She stiffened, looking over McGuire's shoulder towards Winthrop. "Here comes my baby," she said, her face brightening. "Here comes my angel."

McGuire turned to see a yellow school bus winding its way around the curve. "How about Jennifer's brother, Andy?" McGuire asked. "I understand you knew him."

"Yes." She stood as the bus approached. "Oh yes, I knew Andy."

"What was he like?"

"Beautiful. Sensitive." She waved at the bus and walked to the curb. "Everything Jennifer wasn't."

The bus stopped at the curb and an overweight woman in a heavy woollen coat stepped out to help three young children down the steps. The last child to emerge was a girl about five years old. Her round face, framed in tight blond curls, shone as she reached her arms out to Frances O'Neil. "Fanny! Fanny!" she cried. Frances swept her up, and the child's tiny arms wrapped tightly around her neck.

"This is Kelly," Frances said, turning to face McGuire. "Kelly, say hello to . . . I'm sorry."

"Joe," McGuire smiled. "Just call me Joe," and he offered his hand to the little girl.

"Hi, Joe!" Kelly smiled, and Frances lowered her to the sidewalk.

The bus pulled away as the three, Kelly clinging tightly to Frances's hand, began walking around the curve of the sea wall back to the house.

"Tell me about Jennifer and her brother," McGuire said.

"What do you want to know?" They were moving slowly, matching their pace to the child's short methodical steps.

"How did they get along?"

"Wonderfully," Frances replied. "They loved each other. Everyone could see that. They absolutely loved each other."

"Did that include physically?"

"I beg your pardon?" She looked at him, shocked. "Do you mean . . . the two of them . . . ?" Looking away towards the harbour, her shoulders began shaking.

McGuire reached to touch her, but when she turned he saw that she was laughing, not sobbing as he expected. "Sorry," she said. "It just struck me funny, what you said."

"I don't understand. You think incest between a brother and sister is funny?"

Her demeanour changed abruptly. "No," she said quietly. "No, that's not what I meant at all."

"What did you mean?"

Kelly asked to be carried and Frances lifted her again and kissed the child gently on the cheek. "You had to see them together," she said, quickening her pace. "You couldn't understand unless you saw them side by side. Jennifer so independent and tough, yet so talented. And Andy the opposite: kind, gentle, sensitive." She blinked back tears. "And ethics. Andy had very high ethics."

"Were you attracted to Andy?" McGuire asked. They had reached the house and he could see the sister standing behind the aluminum storm door watching them, her arms folded across her chest.

"Yes, I was." Frances lowered Kelly to the ground. "Go to Mommy," she instructed. "Tell her I'm coming." They watched the little girl scamper up the steps.

"Where is he?" McGuire asked.

"Gone."

"Gone where?"

She looked at him, her expression saying nothing. "Gone. Disappeared. Just gone, that's all."

"Do you have any idea where?"

She shook her head. Tears flooded her eyes.

"Do you think Andy was responsible for his sister's death?" McGuire asked.

"Oh yes." Frances dabbed at her nose with a torn tissue. "Oh, I'm sure of that."

"And he's never tried to contact you?"

"No, and he never will," she said, biting her lip.

"Sometimes I dream he will, but he won't. I'm sure of it." She wiped the tears from her face. "Is there anything else?"

"You'll call us if he ever does, won't you?" She nodded silently. "Here's my card. If he tries to reach you or you think of anything else, call me right away."

She took his card and turned without a word to walk up the steps. Kelly, her jacket removed and a cookie in her hand, waved merrily at him from behind the picture window.

McGuire smiled and raised his hand to return the greeting before getting into his car.

. .

"You here for chili or to arrest me for serving you the last bowl?" Marlene Richards threw her head back and laughed, a sailor's laugh, coarse and vulgar. "What can I get you, McGuire?" she asked, after leaning towards him, her arms on the counter. "We've got clam chowder today. Shucked the clams myself last night."

"Just bring me the kettle and a long spoon," McGuire replied. He sat on the same bar stool as before. The noon-hour crowd had dispersed, leaving most of the tables empty.

"And a frog beer to go with it?"

McGuire smiled. "And a frog beer."

She brought him a cold Kronenbourg and a thick china bowl spilling over with chowder, a pat of butter floating in its own golden puddle on top.

"Well?" she asked after he sampled his first spoonful.

"Good," he said. "Damn good," and he meant it.

"Jesus, I used to look forward to hearing that in bed. Now I only hear it in my bar."

"I just talked to Frances O'Neil," McGuire said after another spoonful of chowder.

Marlene's smile faded and a look of concern flooded her face. "How is poor Frannie?"

"All right, I guess. Is she always so tense?"

"Frannie? Yeah, she's always been wound up like an eight-day clock on Sunday morning. She tell you she used to teach school?"

McGuire took a long pull on his Kronenbourg and wiped his mouth with the back of his hand. "Yeah, she told me that. Told me a few things about Andrew Cornell too."

"You think he killed Jennifer?"

"He had something to do with it. Shows up suddenly, then drops out of sight as soon as she's killed. All his belongings were gone. Not a thing in her apartment except his fingerprints." McGuire looked up at her, his spoon poised over the bowl of chowder. "Tell me more about him. How often was he in here?"

"Not that often." She looked around and lowered her voice. "Look, that rumour about the two of them sleeping together, sister and brother. I don't buy it, you know?"

"Why not?"

"Come on, McGuire. That kind of stuff happens in Kentucky maybe, up in the hills. But not in Boston. Besides, when he first came in here he said he was living in Cambridge. It was that jerk Milburn who started the story about them sleeping together. And Andy, there was something about him."

"Like what?"

"I don't know. I just had the feeling he was too cultured for anything like that."

"How did he act when he was here?"

"What do you mean?"

"Did he try to pick up women? Did he get drunk? Was he loud?"

"None of the above." She waved her hand in the direction of the dining area. "He sat over there and drank soda water and lemon by himself. The only woman I ever saw him talking to was poor Frannie." She looked quickly to the rear of the bar, then back to McGuire. "You know, that was the night Jennifer was murdered. He stayed until closing. Frannie was always stopping at his table and talking to him that night. Stars in her eyes. She came and asked if she could leave early because Andy was going and they wanted to walk home together. I said sure, what the hell, she might get lucky. Poor kid deserved it."

"Was Jennifer here that night?"

"No. I remember Andy saying he was waiting for her but she never showed. So he left with Frannie."

McGuire finished his chowder. "You say he was only in here a few times?"

"Yeah. The first week or so, they used this place to leave messages. Jennifer would come in, ask if Andy was here. Then she'd leave a message. 'Tell him to meet me back at the shop,' she'd say."

"The shop?"

"Where she worked. Irene's over on Newbury Street. It's closed now. I hear it went bankrupt. Anyway, she'd leave this message for him to meet her somewhere. You know . . ." She looked away and frowned before turning back to McGuire and whispering: "It's easy to think they had something going. Frannie was the first woman Andy really talked to here. And after Andy came on the scene, Jennifer would have nothing to do with any of the guys here. Not a thing. She'd sit here at the bar raving about him to me or one of my girls maybe, saying what a wonderful guy he was, sweet, sensitive, a hell of a catch for some woman. Like she was in love or something. So maybe . . ." She shuddered. "Hell, who knows?"

A waitress brought a check and money to the bar and Marlene turned to use the cash register. "You've got to understand, McGuire. Jennifer would have used anybody to get what she wanted. Even her own brother."

McGuire drank his beer, lost in thought, until Marlene returned to her post in front of him.

"You know what I think, McGuire?" she whispered.

"What do you think?"

"I think somebody killed both of them. And made it look

as though Andy did it. I mean, first Jennifer's killed, then her mysterious brother disappears. Hell, I'm no J. Edgar Hoover but let's face it, even I would have the bloodhounds out looking for her brother if that's all I had to go on."

McGuire dropped a five-dollar bill on the counter. "Why not just assume the brother did it himself? Isn't that more logical?"

"Not a chance," she said, scooping the money from the counter and turning back to the cash register. "Because I'll tell you, honey. Andy, he was too sweet a guy to do anything like murder. He'd run from his own shadow."

CHAPTER TWELVE

McGuire cursed the cold rain that lashed his face as he left Pour Richards and crossed Massachusetts Avenue. Two blocks east, he entered a glass-and-steel office building and rode the elevator alone up eighteen floors while he tried to identify the name of the popular song seeping through the elevator speakers. When he couldn't, he convinced himself that the failure was due to the graceless style of modern song writers and not early symptoms of Alzheimer's disease.

Upton Insurance occupied three storeys of the building. On the eighteenth floor, McGuire stepped into the firm's dark-panelled reception area and asked the receptionist for Gerry Milburn.

Within a few seconds, a door facing McGuire across the wide vestibule area opened and a slightly-built man in tweed jacket, striped tie and slacks entered, his eyes darting here and there as he walked, avoiding McGuire's. McGuire guessed he was thirty-five, perhaps thirty-seven years old. "Your name McGuire?" he asked in a hoarse whisper when he reached the detective.

McGuire reached for his identification. "Joe McGuire, Homicide —"

"I know, I know," the other man hissed impatiently. "What the hell do you want with me? Nobody told me you were coming!"

McGuire studied the man before answering. Milburn's hair was prematurely grey and his eyes were magnified by tortoise-shell glasses. One hand never left his trouser pocket, where it jingled loose change nervously.

"Well, I'll tell you, Milburn," said McGuire quietly. He tilted his head and smiled at the other man. "I need to ask you a few questions, you see. But I understand that you're a busy guy and all that, so I'll make a deal with you."

For the first time, Milburn's eyes found McGuire's. "What's that?"

"We do it here or we do it down on Berkeley Street."

Milburn swallowed, and his eyes began their dance again. "All right," he said without whispering. His voice was surprisingly high and thin. "Maybe five minutes. But not here. Jesus, not here." He led McGuire to an elevator, still jingling coins in his pocket.

The elevator doors opened and three men, talking among themselves, began to exit. Milburn changed personalities almost instantly; his thin lips broke into a smile and both hands reached out to seize the shoulder of the tallest man leaving the elevator.

"Roger, you bandit!" Milburn said. "I didn't think you'd be back until later. How did things go in Hartford?"

"Good, Gerry. Real good," the man replied, not breaking his stride. "I'll fill you in later."

"How about lunch tomorrow? I owe you," Milburn called after the man, who nodded without turning around.

In the elevator alone with McGuire, Milburn said, "That guy is the next senior vice-president of operations. And what I don't need right now is to be seen with a cop!" He punched the button for the seventeenth floor.

McGuire began to speak, but thought better of it. He watched Milburn carefully during the short ride, noting his nervous mannerisms and the tension that seemed coiled within his body.

The elevator doors opened to a small grey lobby with several doorways lining the walls. Milburn turned quickly to the right, away from a vast open area where men and women sat at identical desks punching the keyboards of identical computer terminals, and entered a washroom. McGuire followed to see him checking toilet stalls, confirming that they were unoccupied.

"Okay," Milburn said sharply, turning back to McGuire and leaning against a sink, his arms folded in front of him. "Five minutes. Nobody worth anything will see us talking on this floor. What the hell do you need from me?"

"You knew Jennifer Cornell?" McGuire began pleasantly.

Milburn slipped his hand back into his trouser pocket, where the loose change began its jangly rhythm again. "Come on, I told you guys everything last summer. Cripes! How often do I have to repeat it?"

"What's troubling you, Milburn?" McGuire asked in the same friendly tone. "You got something to hide?"

"I've got nothing to hide!" Milburn spat at him. "The night she was murdered, I was home with my wife."

"Then you've got lots to hide, haven't you?" McGuire interrupted.

Milburn glared back, then looked away.

"You're an ambitious man, Milburn," McGuire said calmly. "Probably have, what? One, two kids? Nice house, maybe out in Norwood? Commute to work every day with the same gang of guys? Got a good job with a solid conservative outfit that wouldn't exactly make you employee-of-the-month for screwing around with a woman you picked up in a bar, especially a woman who was found murdered one Sunday morning."

He leaned closer to Milburn until he was just inches from the other man's face.

"Now you talk to me, Milburn. Or I'll have my next interview in the office of your buddy upstairs, good old Roger the Bandit."

The jangling stopped. Beads of sweat flooded Milburn's upper lip, and one hand shot up to push his glasses higher up the bridge of his nose. "All right," he said, still defiant. "But make it snappy. Somebody might come in here, and get the wrong impression."

McGuire arched his eyebrows, smiled, and jutted out his bottom lip as though he found the idea amusing. "How often did you see Jennifer Cornell?"

"What do you mean?"

"Meet her. Go back to her place and sleep with her."

"Hey, give me a break here." Milburn's eyes glanced at the washroom door. "I only met her three times. I was only at her place twice."

"And the third time?"

"She said she was waiting for her brother."

"So she didn't want anything to do with you."

"That's how she acted. She said Andy was her whole life since he came back from California."

"And you were jealous of him."

Milburn gathered himself up and turned to speak directly at McGuire. "I saw something in Jennifer nobody else saw," he said, his voice losing its edge as he talked. "There was a warm, attractive woman there. And she saw something in me. That's what she told me." He studied his fingernails. "But then came her brother, and before that some TV producer."

"Fleckstone?"

Milburn nodded. "He was using her. Anybody could see that. There was no way he was going to make her a star."

"Why were you so angry with her brother?"

Milburn walked away, past the row of sinks. "I saw his

stuff in her apartment the second time I was there. His luggage. His clothes. She even showed me a watch she bought for him. Big gold Cartier. The only bed was a pullout sofa. There was no place else to sleep. And she told me to leave because Andy was coming home any minute. She didn't want Andy to find me there. I mean, what would *you* think?"

"I'd think it was none of my business. By the way," McGuire added, "did your wife know about you and Jennifer?"

Milburn pivoted and pointed at McGuire. "I'd say that was none of *your* business!" he barked.

McGuire nodded. "Could be. But you have to admit, it'll be easy to check."

His face white, Milburn looked around in mild panic, as though searching for an escape route. "Hey, you can't do that," he muttered. "Come on, you can't just go into a man's home and spill stuff like that." Grasping the sides of a sink, Milburn dropped his head and stared into the drain.

"Just tell me what I want to know, Milburn," McGuire said, walking slowly towards him. "And I'm gone."

Milburn exhaled noisily. "Her brother was a faggot," he said bitterly.

"Really?"

"You could tell by the way he walked. Kept to himself. Hardly talked to guys in the bar. Never paid attention to women."

"Doesn't make him gay."

"He was a pussy. When I challenged him he ducked away from me. Wouldn't let me near him."

"Tell me what happened," McGuire said. He leaned against the wall and watched Milburn's face as he talked.

"I called Jennifer one night. I wanted to see her, just talk to her, and she told me to . . . She didn't want to see me. So later that night I went to Pour Richards alone. I'm sitting at the bar and all I'm hearing about is Jennifer's brother Andy, what a sweet guy he is. And then Marlene, the owner, said he'd moved in with Jennifer and I thought, 'That's not right, sleeping together like that,' and I went after him." Milburn began washing his hands, still avoiding McGuire's eyes. "I'd had too much to drink. Normally I wouldn't do something like that. I walked over to him and I said, 'You can't be Jennifer's brother, you son of a bitch.' I don't know, I forget what else I said." He ripped a paper towel from the dispenser and began drying his hands.

"And Andy took off."

"Yeah. Right out the door."

"And when Jennifer came in she was ready to hit you with a bar stool."

Milburn nodded. He tossed the paper towel at a waste container and missed. "Anything else?"

"Two things. Where were you the night Jennifer Cornell was murdered?"

Milburn leaned on the sink again and stared at his reflection in the mirror. His mouth had grown slack and his grey hair no longer looked premature. "I told you guys last summer."

"Not me you didn't. Where were you?"

"I went to a movie."

"With whom?"

"By myself."

"On a Saturday night? A married man with . . . how many kids?"

"Two. Two boys."

"Name the movie."

Milburn closed his eyes, took a deep breath, and exhaled slowly. "I wasn't at a movie."

"Damn right you weren't." McGuire walked away a few paces, then returned to Milburn in three quick strides. "So where were you?"

"I went looking for Jennifer. I stopped at the bar and saw her brother, sitting in the corner by himself. I went outside and waited to see if Jennifer would show up. She didn't, so I went back to her apartment building and rang the bell. There was nobody home, or maybe she just didn't want to answer the door. But I could hear music playing in there. So I sat on a bench across the street by the Fens and watched the building for a while." He shrugged and half-smiled in embarrassment. "Then I bought a bottle of booze and took it back to the bench and drank it. I woke up about two o'clock and there were still lights on in her apartment. I went to a pay phone and called her and Jennifer answered. She sounded happy; she was laughing. She told me to call her back early in the week, she couldn't see me just then. I had the feeling there was somebody else with her. So I went home."

He looked up at McGuire with tears on his face. "That's the truth, McGuire. I swear it. That night . . . That night almost cost me my marriage. The next day I heard she was found murdered."

Laughter erupted from the washroom entrance as two men entered, one holding a sheet of paper for the other to read over his shoulder. Milburn turned away quickly, tore off another paper towel and brought it to his face. The two newcomers glanced at him, then at McGuire, and walked in silence to the urinals.

Distancing himself from the men, Milburn approached McGuire. "What was the other thing?" he asked in a low voice. "You said you had two things. What else was there?"

McGuire bent to retrieve the ball of paper towelling Milburn had tossed at the waste container. "Pick up your trash," he said, tossing it in the man's face.

. .

The wind had dropped, taking the temperature with it. Outside on Massachusetts Avenue McGuire walked through a swirl of snowflakes. At Newbury Street he trudged east to Dartmouth. The flakes were now no longer melting on contact with the pavement but were beginning to transform the city into a soft white sculpture, clinging to bare tree branches, settling on parked cars and on the heads and shoulders of pedestrians.

Just beyond Dartmouth, McGuire found Irene's Dress Shop on the elevated first floor of a restored brownstone. He slipped once on the snow before grasping the cast-iron railing and pulling himself up to the darkened door.

The letter taped on the inside of the glass was headed "Raymond D. Robinson, Attorney" in flowing script, with an address in the Hancock Tower. All enquiries regarding Irene's, according to the short typed message on the letter, were to be directed to the office shown on the letterhead.

McGuire shielded his eyes and peered through the glass into an empty store littered with cardboard boxes, empty display cases and several hundred plastic hangers on metal racks.

He entered a bar next to Irene's and used a pay phone to call the lawyer. A woman with a heavy British accent answered, took his name and put him on hold long enough for him to finish sipping his double Scotch, neat. She returned to announce that Raymond Robinson would be pleased to see him in his office at ten the following morning to answer any questions on behalf of his client Irene Hoffman.

McGuire leaned against the wall and tried to assemble all he had learned about the woman found dead in the Fens two seasons earlier. She had been a frightened woman, unstable perhaps. And yet Jennifer Cornell could also attract the attention of a television producer who used women like he used his video equipment, and infatuate a minor insurance executive to the point where he would risk his family and his career.

McGuire had known women like her in his life. During a short and stormy second marriage, he had been wedded to one. She hadn't been unstable, though, only too young and too beautiful, too in love with the thrill of turning men's heads to be satisfied with the attention McGuire paid to her. It had been his total attention, total devotion. No, he had to admit, not total. And not enough. Not enough to keep her from walking out five years ago, leaving him to work in a Florida nightclub where the patrons weren't sullen and middle-aged but young and challenging and loved to dance.

He looked around the bar, searching for the kind of companionship that began with eye contact, and estimated the average age of the patrons at twenty years less than his own. Wasn't anybody in the world born before nineteen-sixty?

Leaving the bar, McGuire paused in the doorway to turn up the collar of his overcoat and watched calmly as a small car with its wheels locked glided out of control on the snowy road surface before slamming into the rear of a car ahead of it. The small car's bumper crumpled; an enormous tail-light on the other car shattered with a delicate musical sound, muted by the snow. The two drivers stepped out of their vehicles to examine first the damage, then each other, with sad resignation.

"Florida," McGuire muttered to himself as he turned his back on the scene and walked away. "Florida," he repeated. "Hell of an idea."

· ·

He retrieved his car from a parking lot near Pour Richards and drove back to his apartment. The heavy snow and rush-hour traffic would tie up the route to Revere Beach for two hours at least. He'd wait till it let up. That would give him enough time to think about what he had learned, make some notes, microwave a dinner and read the paper before visiting Ollie.

Fifteen minutes later he was in the warmth of his apartment with a Paul Desmond CD playing on the stereo, two fingers of Scotch and some ice in a glass, and a frozen "Chicken Stir-Fry" dinner in the microwave.

He sat back in a heavy armchair, sipped the cold smoky whisky and listened to Desmond's alto saxophone dance through a Cole Porter song. God, nobody plays like that any more, he thought. Nobody ever played like that. Except maybe Lee Konitz. But Konitz was more experimental, he kept changing his sound, while Desmond polished his like an opera diva who begins singing *Aida* first as a young girl — the God-damn telephone's ringing — and then later as a mature woman — why does the fucking phone ring when I don't want to hear it? — and when she's older — son of a bitch!

"Hello!" The bark of an angry and disturbed dog.

"Joe?" The voice was dusky and warm — and hesitant.

"Yeah." He softened his tone and leaned back in the chair. "What's up?"

"You okay?"

"Sure, Janet. Sure. I'm fine."

"Joe, I'm at a pay phone." Before he could reply she added, "I'm being followed, Joe."

"Your husband?"

"I don't know. Whoever they are, they're professionals."

"Take it easy," he began.

"If they're following me, they're probably following you, too."

"Okay. But there's nothing to find with me."

"I know," she said. "I just thought I should let you know. Besides . . . I miss you."

Desmond's music was flooding the room. The scotch warmed him to his toes as he watched snow sifting down through the night to settle on his windowsill. "Yeah. Me too." He felt he should add something. "Take care of yourself," he said finally.

He could hear traffic noises behind her: the blast of a car horn, the roar of a diesel truck engine. "I will," she said. She sounded disappointed. "Sounds like you're listening to Paul Desmond," she added. "Am I right?"

"You're right," he smiled. "You've always been right," he added before saying goodbye and gently lowering the telephone.

CHAPTER THIRTEEN

Ollie's room was a warm haven in the midst of the early winter snowfall. He lay propped upright while Ronnie fed him servings of warm strudel, the air throughout the small house rich with the aroma of fresh-baked pastry, apples, cinnamon and nutmeg.

McGuire sat in his usual bedside chair. On the table next to him was an empty plate scattered with small flakes of strudel pastry, which he picked up and nibbled at as he spoke.

He recounted the day's interviews while Ollie nodded or scowled at significant information and his right hand squeezed the tennis ball, tightening and relaxing in a steady, unbroken rhythm.

When McGuire finished, Ronnie offered the last morsel of strudel to her husband, who opened his mouth dutifully and chewed silently.

"Sounds like a complicated case," she said, standing and brushing crumbs from her lap and from Ollie's blanket. "I'll leave you two experts to work it out."

McGuire turned down Ronnie's offer of more coffee and waited until she left the room before asking Ollie's assessment.

"I want to know who the brother is," the older man said, staring straight ahead as he spoke.

"You don't think they're related? The birth records could be wrong. He could have been born out of wedlock."

"Whoever he was, I'm betting he'll turn up dead."

"And whoever killed Jennifer Cornell killed the brother too."

"Something like that."

"Doesn't make sense," McGuire said, flipping through his notes. "The woman's murder has impulse written all over it. She's struck from behind by a piece of wood that's apparently just lying around. No premeditation there. And the blow doesn't kill her. Falling into the water and drowning does the job. Whoever hit her just left her there dying. But the brother, he's gone without a trace. No clothes, nothing but fingerprints. That takes planning."

"But it might explain why she didn't have any keys or identification with her," Ollie said, turning his head to look out the window. The light spilling from the room shone on snowflakes in the darkness, tracing their paths as they swirled in the air. "Work it out. Killer takes the keys, goes back to the apartment, gets rid of the brother."

McGuire nodded in agreement. "Norm Cooper says there were only two sets of fresh prints in the place. He confirmed one set is hers, the other is a John Doe's."

Ollie Schantz rolled his massive head away from the window and gazed up at the ceiling. His wife's words were still there. They were unavoidable. They spoke to him when he closed his eyes in the evening and they reassured him when he opened them the next morning.

"Reich, the apartment superintendent, he still bothers me," Ollie said after a long, thoughtful pause. "Falling off the wagon like that. Hanging around with women. Buying good booze by the case. All just after the murder. Can't get past that one."

"You think he did it?" McGuire asked.

The other man ignored the question. "By the sound of things, his wife is a tough old bird."

McGuire agreed.

"Probably knew her husband better than he knew himself. Some wives are like that. Especially ones who . . ."

"Who what?"

"Who either love you or hate you so God-damn much." He looked over at McGuire. "You believe the widow?"

"Yeah," McGuire nodded. "I believe her."

"So do I."

"But that means Reich didn't kill Jennifer Cornell. She died around two in the morning. His wife is sure he got up to check a noise out back around four. Came back to bed a few minutes later. He couldn't have made it across the street, down into the Fens, do the job and get back into bed. Even if he had a motive. The guy was over sixty years old." McGuire leaned back in the chair. "You got any ideas?"

"That's all I've got, is time and ideas," Ollie said in a flat, toneless voice.

McGuire reached for his notebook, his pencil poised over the page.

"Who saw her last?" Ollie snapped. "And who was supposed to see her next? Same with her brother. Who was the last to see him?"

"Frances, the waitress," McGuire replied, scribbling as he talked. "She left the bar with Andy the night of the murder. And I'll talk to Fleckstone again. The brother was supposed to visit him and never showed."

"How about the watch?"

McGuire looked up. "What watch?"

"The one she bought for her brother. What was it? A Cartier? What are they worth?"

"Out of my league."

"The brother had no job?"

"Far as I know."

"He wants to skip, he'll need money. Check the pawnshop

listings for a Cartier in June. See if any names match up." He frowned again. "What's this lawyer want with you tomorrow?"

McGuire shrugged. "Guess he's handling the bankruptcy of Irene's."

"The store where the victim worked?"

"Yeah. I don't expect anything much to come out of it, but the owner was interviewed by Fat Eddie. Who knows what he dropped through the cracks?"

The furrows between Ollie Schantz's eyes deepened. "Seen her bank records?"

"Whose?"

"The victim's, damn it!" Ollie barked. "Are her bank records in the file?"

"I don't remember seeing them —"

"What the hell are those idiots doing down on Berkeley Street?" Ollie demanded. "Bank records are like a diary. Better than a diary sometimes. Mark a case NETGO and don't check bank records? It's crazy!"

"They're short on staff —"

"And long on assholes! Try to get her bank records."

McGuire made his notes in silence, broken only by Ollie's laborious breathing; the right hand squeezed and released, squeezed and released the tennis ball at a faster tempo than before.

"You got inside her bones yet?"

It was Ollie's manner of asking if McGuire understood the victim totally. "Let's get inside their bones," he would say to his partner when they worked together. "Best way to know the killer is to know the victim."

"Not yet," McGuire answered, closing his notebook. "She was complex. A few people thought she was wonderful, others thought she was a bitch. She had something that attracted men, that's for sure. And she had the mental thing — three months in a loony bin. She liked her fun, she had a healthy sex drive, she took a few men home with her. She wanted more — more glamour, more money maybe, something to help get her past forty."

Ollie looked down at his hand and watched the fingers tighten and relax around the tennis ball. "Where are you going with it from here?"

"Thought I'd start with the victim's mother," McGuire replied, slipping his notebook into his jacket and standing up. "She's been dead for years, but maybe something happened while she was living in San Antonio, something we can use."

"Nice place, San Antonio." Ollie turned his head back to the window. "Went there once to bring back a crazy dude about twenty years ago. Middle of March. Colder than a witch's tit when we left here. Snow and sleet everywhere. Arrive in San Antonio and it's hot and dry, people walking around in shorts eating ice cream."

At the door, Ronnie helped McGuire into his winter coat. "He's thinking about that case of yours all the time," she whispered. "He calls me during the day and talks about it. He has me make notes and read them back to him, over and over." She touched the lapel of his coat absently.

McGuire nodded and brought his lips to her forehead.

At the end of the walk, he turned to wave to her as she watched from behind the storm door, the snow falling silently between them.

. .

Driving home, McGuire remembered Janet's warning about being followed. He exited at Charlestown, turned into a side street, accelerated quickly to the next block, turned right when he was almost through the next intersection, switched off the headlights and pulled quickly to the curb.

For five minutes he sat watching the empty street behind him in the rear-view mirror before shifting into gear again and making a fishtailing U-turn in the gathering snow to head home.

. .

The next morning dawned clear and dazzling white. McGuire stood at his window, finishing his third cup of coffee and watching Boston University students toss snowballs at each other. He set the cup aside, reached for the telephone and dialled the direct line to Ralph Innes at Berkeley Street Police Headquarters.

"Hey, big guy!" Innes almost shouted over the line when he heard McGuire's voice. "Jeez, if you don't make it to Hutch's soon they'll lose their Kronenbourg franchise, I swear to God!"

"What's going on?" McGuire asked.

"Business or personal?"

"Start with the personal, what the hell."

"Joe, I admit it. I took a date home last night for dinner. Broad was so ugly I made her sit in a corner and fed her with a slingshot. I'm telling you, it's getting tough to find a good-looking woman in this town who isn't married, knocked up, or just changed her name from George to Georgette."

"Anything else?"

"Bad news and good news."

"Give me the bad news."

"Sweet-ass Janet and her husband are talking separation." He paused, waiting for a reply from McGuire before adding, "Now do you want to hear the good news?"

"Sure."

"Sweet-ass and her husband are talking separation." Innes roared with laughter.

"Ralph, I need a favour," McGuire interrupted.

"Sure, Joe." Innes became calm and serious. "I told you, you need anything, you call me."

"It's on the Cornell case."

"Wait till I get a pencil here."

McGuire explained what he needed: A survey of routine

pawnshop reports on all items valued at five hundred dollars or more, specifically any Cartier watches pawned or sold since June, with the name of the seller. An accidental death report for one Henry Reich of Park Drive, died sometime in July. A general records report from the San Antonio Police Department regarding one Suzanne Alice Cornell, died May thirty-one, nineteen-eighty-three.

"Is Cornell her married name?"

"Maiden. Jesus, Ralph, I'm looking at the file right now. Says she married somebody and they don't even get his name. Anyway, I need the victim's bank records too."

"How far back?"

"Whatever you've got. A year will do." He gave Innes the bank and branch from the cheques found in Jennifer Cornell's purse. "And I need it all tonight," he added when he had finished.

"I'll see what I can do," Innes replied. "But listen, you didn't get it from me, right?"

"Why not? This is legitimate business."

"I know, I know."

"Kavander?"

Innes exhaled slowly. "Yeah."

"What about him?"

"He thinks you're trying to shaft the department, Joe. He's telling us to notify him about any contacts we have with you. Any at all. And he's asking everybody if they've heard you bad-mouthing him or the commissioner or the commissioner's dog, anybody. Know what I think? I think he never expected you to work the grey files. Way I see it, he figured you'd tell him to shove it and he could suspend you. Now he thinks you're just doing it for revenge and planning to talk to the papers about it, I don't know . . ."

"Ralph, I'm working on an assigned case. I don't take files home for doorstops."

Innes sighed into the telephone again, his breath making a noise over the line like distant thunder. "Joe, what can I say?

Look, I'll pass this through the channels, put a rush on it, give it a phoney file number. Nobody will ever know."

McGuire said he would call later in the day. He lowered the telephone and stared down into the street again as three young men in the grey and maroon colours of B.U. leaped from behind a parked car to pelt two laughing co-eds with snowballs, the sound of their play echoing off the buildings along the street and penetrating the dusty glass of McGuire's window.

I'm working the case until they take me off it, he said to himself. Me and Ollie. Nobody else turned up a thing in six months. Now it's me and Ollie and we'll work on it until we solve it — or they find a way to stop us.

. .

Half an hour later, McGuire walked past the mound of snow concealing his car and headed for the Hancock Tower. He found no enjoyment in the fresh whiteness of the season's first snowfall. Winters were the price of living in New England, and the price seemed to be rising with every passing year.

Arriving at the Hancock Tower shortly after ten, he rode the elevator to the offices of Raymond D. Robinson, entered and announced himself to the receptionist. He declined her offer of coffee and watched her disappear through a doorway in the elaborately panelled wall facing him. McGuire sat in a leather-and-chrome chair and wondered if law firms could function without walnut panelling. The decor seemed as important to the launching of law careers as textbooks and diplomas.

"Mr Robinson will see you now," the receptionist announced, standing in the doorway. She was young, slim and attractive; as McGuire passed her he breathed deeply, trying to inhale her perfume, and was disappointed when he detected none.

"Lieutenant McGuire."

The voice boomed from a barrel-chested man in his fifties who looked up from where he had been bent over his desk shuffling papers.

It took several paces for McGuire to cross the thick carpeting and reach the lawyer. Ceiling-high windows on the wall to McGuire's right revealed a spectacular view stretching northward from the Common to the coast, several miles distant. McGuire shook Robinson's hand and proffered his identification, which the lawyer glanced at without interest before sitting down.

"As you probably noticed," Robinson began, his eyes fixed on the papers in front of him, "I have been retained by the proprietor of Irene's to handle legal concerns regarding dissolution of the firm."

"I'm here on a criminal matter," McGuire interrupted. "The murder of Jennifer Cornell, who used to work at the store."

"Yes, yes, so I understand," Robinson added. He seemed preoccupied and unaccountably nervous.

Raymond Robinson was sketched in shades of grey. His silver hair and moustache were immaculately trimmed and he wore a subtly-patterned grey suit over a white shirt and grey paisley tie. Even his glasses were silver-grey, poised on a patrician nose set between two grey eyes that seemed to be evading McGuire's.

To McGuire, Robinson was a man who avoided spotlights, preferring to remain in the background of events.

"As it happens we're both investigating the same person," Robinson was saying. He swung the chair to his left, brought a hand to his chin, and stared out the window.

"Would you mind explaining that in detail?" McGuire asked, opening his notebook.

"My area is not criminal law, Lieutenant," Robinson replied, his focus on the scene beyond the window. He scratched his ear, smoothed his eyebrow and adjusted his tie. "But I have clear evidence that Miss Cornell was systematically defrauding my client, Irene Hoffman, over a two-year period prior to her death. These losses had a direct impact on the store's financial condition and led to its bankruptcy."

McGuire nodded as he made notes. "Any idea how much money was involved?"

"As much as fifty thousand dollars. Not an astounding amount, perhaps, but Irene's was a small exclusive shop with the usual retail cash-flow problems. Further, my client had recently completed extensive renovations which stretched her financial capacity. When she was unable to pay her suppliers' invoices, they ceased shipping new merchandise. The store, I might add, had built its reputation on offering the very latest in ladies' wear. Not being able to offer new merchandise had a negative impact on sales. Soon she was unable to meet her bank loan and things quickly tumbled from there."

"When did you discover the frauds?"

"Officially, when an audit was conducted on . . ." The lawyer swivelled in his chair to examine his notes. "August twenty-eighth of this year. Unofficially, there were deep suspicions dating back to June."

"When in June?"

Robinson's eyes fastened on McGuire for the first time. "I beg your pardon?"

"When did your client, Irene Hoffman, discover that Jennifer Cornell was robbing her blind? And where is your client now?"

"I'm not sure that's relevant —" the lawyer began, his eyes skipping from McGuire to his window.

"I'll decide what's relevant." McGuire bit off each word. For years he had harboured a casual distaste for lawyers. Now it was developing into a finely-focused hatred. "Was it early in June? Late? Middle of the month?"

Robinson's eyes dropped to his desk and he began shuffling his papers again, moving them delicately with the tips of his well-manicured fingers. "I would say it was early in June, but I can't be more specific than that."

"Which would make your client a suspect in this homicide investigation," McGuire said. "Discovering a major theft by the victim, especially one which resulted in the failure of your client's business, would constitute a motive for murder in the eyes of a grand jury. So where is she?"

"I must respect my client's confidentiality," Robinson replied. He began sliding the sheets of paper on his desk into a file folder.

"Until I obtain a subpoena," McGuire said. "You try to hide her after getting one of those and you'll be facing a charge —"

"Lieutenant McGuire," the lawyer began.

"— of obstructing justice." McGuire stood up, his hands in his pockets. "You got anything else to add?"

"Yes, as a matter of fact I have," Robinson said, rising from his chair. "Please understand, Lieutenant, that what I am about to do has no bearing whatsoever on my legal obligations either to my client or to the community at large. Nor does it constitute any obstruction of justice in the opinion of my colleagues."

McGuire remained standing, puzzled. When lawyers begin talking like textbooks, he reminded himself, it's time to duck, because they'll probably be throwing one at you.

Robinson walked to a doorway concealed in the panelled wall opposite the floor-to-ceiling windows. He opened the door slightly and stepped aside as McGuire approached. "It has been a distinct pleasure to make your acquaintance, Lieutenant," he said with excess formality. "I expect we may have occasion to meet again."

McGuire refused the lawyer's outstretched hand, returning Robinson's bland expression with a glare as he pushed through the open door into what he thought would be an outer hall. Instead, he saw three men sitting at a conference table, watching him with interest. He cursed and began to turn back but the door closed behind him, the lock sliding into place with a precise metallic click.

CHAPTER FOURTEEN

Marv Rosen leaned back in his chair, his hands behind his head. Two men sat flanking him. All three watched McGuire from across a long rosewood table inlaid with an ornate geometric pattern.

"Hello, McGuire," Rosen said with his singsong delivery. "Sorry about the surprise, but there was no time to have invitations printed."

McGuire glanced from the lawyer to the other two men. One was Rosen's young assistant, who stared at McGuire with a bored expression while pulling at errant hairs in his enormous moustache.

"You already know Ivor here," Rosen said. "He was a witness to our courtroom drama." The assistant allowed himself a small smile, his fingers still worrying his moustache. "This other gentleman is Mr Lorne Marshall, who has been retained by me." Marshall, on Rosen's left, looked blankly at McGuire through thick horn-rimmed glasses. "Mr Marshall is a private surveillance officer," Rosen added.

"I've got nothing to say to you, Rosen," McGuire spat. He turned to grasp the knob of the door behind him. It resisted his attempt to twist it open.

"My friend Raymond likes his privacy," Rosen smiled. "Actually, he's a little embarrassed at all of this, but he owed me a favour. Professional courtesy. One of my contacts told me you were working on a case involving a client of Raymond's. Knowing your complete thoroughness and utter dedication to detail, I suspected you would contact him eventually and when you did —" He shrugged. "There's a door behind us here which exits directly to the outside corridor, so you can leave any time you wish. See? No coercion at all."

"I don't talk to scum," McGuire said quietly, "unless I'm arresting them."

Rosen waved away the insult, still smiling. "Please, McGuire, pay attention, will you? I'm not asking you to talk to me at all. I'm just asking you to listen for a few moments. That's what you're good at, isn't it? Listening? Don't forget, you can leave any time at all." He angled his head in the direction of the door behind him. "Just walk out and be on your way. Or you can invest maybe two minutes in hearing what I and my colleagues have to say." He held out a hand, indicating a chair across the table from him. "Won't you sit down? There's coffee in the carafe on the side table over there."

McGuire folded his arms and leaned against the wall. "Go ahead and talk, Rosen," he said.

Rosen shrugged, widened his eyes and rolled them at his assistant. "Whatever you say, Lieutenant." He turned to the balding, dark-skinned man on his left. "Lorne? You want to read your report?"

Marshall cleared his throat, passed one hand across his mouth and lifted a sheet of paper from the desk. He began speaking in a scratchy, nasal voice with a distinctive cockney accent. Not a voice McGuire would want to hear on a regular basis. Not a voice he wanted to hear now.

"On November twenty-second, the subject departed Hutch's Bar and Grill, having consumed two bottles of beer in the presence of what appeared to be a contingent of fellow law enforcement officers. He drove directly to his residence, arriving at approximately eight thirty-five P.M., where he was joined by a woman subsequently identified as Homicide Detective Janet Parsons at eight forty-three P.M."

McGuire closed his eyes briefly before fixing them on Marshall again.

"Mrs Parsons, who at the time was residing with her husband on Bartlett Crescent in Brookline, was observed leaving the premises at ten-fifteen P.M. On the following evening, Wednesday, November twenty-third —"

"Shove it, Marshall." McGuire had heard enough.

Marshall turned to Rosen, who nodded. The lawyer placed his elbows on the table and his hands under his chin. He studied McGuire in silence before speaking. "You know the procedure, McGuire. Incidentally, we have photographs. Taken from the apartment of one of your neighbours. Or, I should say, several of your neighbours. A group of students sharing some rooms directly across Commonwealth Avenue from you. Infrared prints through your bedroom window. Very revealing. We didn't show them to Max Parsons — who, by the way, is a very broken man. But we did pass along your telephone number and suggested he call it the next time his wife said she'd be late arriving home from work. Sloppy stuff, McGuire. Should be more aware of surveillance techniques these days. Oh, and we also have some transcripts of telephone conversations. Which," Rosen added quickly as McGuire began to speak, "are not admissible in a court of law, but that's beside the point."

"You tapped my telephone?" McGuire said in a low, threatening voice.

"Not physically, McGuire," Rosen smiled. "You know very well that's not necessary any more. Just the usual radio pickup from a van on the street. Besides, I can have the transcripts destroyed and both of my colleagues here will swear I made no reference to the matter. In fact, as Raymond Robinson will attest if necessary, you stumbled into our meeting here in this room while exiting his office after a routine interrogation." He smiled and blinked several times. "Like I said, McGuire, the door is open any time you want to leave."

McGuire breathed deeply, forcing himself to stay calm. "What do you want?" he asked, speaking each word distinctly.

"Obviously, your resignation," Rosen replied. "There are a few local scandal-sheet reporters who would be very excited about your activities over the past few days. They could spin it into a series: 'Affairs between members of Boston's elite detective unit breaking up marriages.' 'Award-winning cop has love nest on fringe of Back Bay area.' So it's very simple and very persuasive, McGuire. You simply throw in the towel and I drop all charges against you, the department and the city of Boston. And don't kid yourself, McGuire. There's more than one heavyweight cop downtown who would be pleased to hear that you're leaving and taking my lawsuits with you. Jack Kavander and some others will be happy. I'll be happy. And even you'll be happy, McGuire. Because I'll destroy all my material. I won't send it to Max Parsons. And I won't send it to the media either." He extended his hands, palms up. "It's what you call a win-win situation, right?"

"It's what I call extortion." McGuire took a step towards the table. In reflex, the other three men simultaneously leaned away from him. "If I resign from the force —"

"Nobody has to know why," Rosen interrupted, his infuriating smile growing wider. "Just a quiet walk away from duty, that's all it is."

"And Arthur Wilmer? What the hell does his retrial turn into? The jury will know that you and I are already responsible for one mistrial. And you'd be sure to ask me on the stand about my resigning from the force. No jury in the world would buy my testimony completely. You know it, I know it, Don Higgins knows it. In fact, Higgins probably wouldn't even waste the taxpayers' money on another trial. And you would have another acquittal on your slimy record."

"My client is innocent —" Rosen protested.

"*Your client is an animal that should be shot and pissed on!*" McGuire shouted. He lowered his voice and rested his hands on the table, leaning even closer to the three men who sat frozen by the glare in his eyes. "And I'll risk everything I have," McGuire hissed, "to see that he is caged for the rest of his miserable life!" He straightened up and began walking quickly towards the far end of the table.

Rosen pursed his lips and shook his head sadly. "McGuire, you are the agent of your own misfortune."

Rounding the end of the table, McGuire seized the metal coffee carafe from the sideboard and, in the same motion he would have used to toss a sidearm curveball, flung it through the air in the direction of the three men, who ducked to avoid its path. The carafe struck the polished surface of the table in front of them and careened away to collide with an elaborately framed Victorian-era print on the wall at the other end of the room. The impact knocked the picture and its heavy, ornate frame to the floor with a clatter of splintered wood and shattered glass.

The three men leaped to their feet, dripping coffee. "Jesus Christ!" Rosen's assistant muttered while Rosen quietly withdrew a handkerchief from his pocket and brushed at the coffee on his suit jacket.

McGuire smiled and nodded politely before leaving the room, closing the door gently behind him. He paused, took a deep breath, and realized that, for the first time in several days, he felt good about himself.

. .

"We ain't open."

The frowzy waitress looked up as McGuire entered Pour Richards. She stood behind one of the small tables in the dining area, a cigarette dangling from her lips, filling a salt shaker from a large container.

"Don't try to seduce me, Shirley," McGuire joked. "Today I'm a man of steel."

"Any rusty parts?" The whisky voice came from somewhere behind the bar. McGuire stepped between two stools and leaned across to see Marlene Richards kneeling on the floor, stacking glasses on a lower shelf. She looked up and grinned. "How about that, McGuire? I didn't even know who I was talking to. You suppose that's how I got my reputation as a tart?"

McGuire smiled back and swung his legs astride a stool. "How's chances of getting a coffee?" he asked.

"Not as good as they are of getting a frog beer. Shirl and I finished the first pot and the lunch coffee isn't ready yet." Marlene stood up and reached for McGuire's hands, clasping them in her own. "Hey, sweetie. Your hands are freezing. What's the matter, don't you have anybody to tie a string on your mittens and hang them through your sleeves? And what've you been up to? You look too smug for your own good."

"I just threw a pot of coffee at a lawyer," McGuire grinned.

"My hero!" Marlene cried. Dropping his hands, she squeezed his cheeks and pulled him towards her, planting a wet kiss on his lips. "Did you hit him, or just fire it across his bow?" Before McGuire could respond, she turned away and went back to preparing the bar for the lunch crowd. "Did I give you my lawyer test?" she asked.

"Not yet."

"Okay, here goes." She turned back to face him and thrust one hip against the counter behind the bar. "You're lost in the desert and you come walking over a sand dune. In front of you are an honest lawyer, a dishonest lawyer and a unicorn. Which one do you ask directions from?"

McGuire shrugged. "Beats me."

"The dishonest lawyer. You want to know why?"

"Desperately."

"Because the other two are figments of your imagination." She erupted in laughter so loud that the waitress dropped the shaker she had been filling, spilling the salt across the table.

"I need to use a phone," McGuire said. "Couple of local calls."

"No problem." Marlene reached under the counter and retrieved an extension phone. "I'll go back and check on the coffee. Give you some privacy."

McGuire flipped through his notebook and dialled Fleckstone's number. The producer barked his name at the other end, the voice hard-edged and impatient.

"It's McGuire. Homicide."

"Yeah, what's up?" In the background, McGuire could hear several voices in urgent conversation until Fleckstone said "Just a minute" and then, dropping the receiver, "Hey, shut the fuck up!" The background noise disappeared and Fleckstone returned to ask what McGuire wanted.

"You said Andrew Cornell made an appointment to see you," McGuire said.

"Yeah. Wanted a screen test, drop off his comp sheet. I already told you that."

"Do you remember the date?"

"What, when he called me? Or when he was coming over to see me?"

"When he was coming over."

There was a long pause. Then: "Okay, I'm in a mixing studio right now," Fleckstone said finally, "and I'll have to check my book to be a hundred percent sure. But I'm pretty certain he was coming in on the Monday after Jennifer died."

"And he never showed."

"I told you that too."

"But when did he call, all excited about his sister? How many days before that?"

Another pause. "I don't know. Probably the Thursday before. Yeah, because I remember saying 'Hell, come on over today. Or tomorrow.' And I can hear that funny voice of his saying he'd rather make it Monday."

"What was so funny about his voice?"

"He had this kind of lisp. And a southern accent. But I know accents. Used to be married to a dialogue coach and I've got a good ear anyway. If I hear a cracker order a beer, I can tell you what part of any state he's from and give you a town within three counties, too. But I had trouble with that guy's."

McGuire scribbled "Accent?" in his notebook and thanked Fleckstone, who hung up without replying.

"Tell me more about Andy Cornell," McGuire said when Marlene returned and slid a cup of coffee in front of him.

"Like what?" she asked, resuming her position against the back counter.

"Did he have an accent?"

"Accent?" She studied the ceiling. "I don't remember any accent. You mean like New England?"

"Southern."

"Southern?" she snorted. "Hell, no. He was no peckerwood. I would have remembered that."

McGuire frowned. His eyes ran down the notes he had made during their first meeting. "You told me you could see something in their eyes, his and Jennifer's."

"I said I could tell they were brother and sister and they were both horny. Had the same *look* in their eyes. Funny thing, though. Hers were blue and his were brown. Deep sexy brown." She shrugged. "I guess that could happen in the same family." She pushed away from the counter and leaned against the bar, smiling at McGuire. "You staying for lunch? We've got shepherd's pie with mushroom gravy. Warm the old bod on a day like this."

McGuire pocketed his notebook and slid off the stool.

"Better not," he said, returning her smile. "I've got a car to dig out."

"So go back and see your lawyer friend," Marlene shouted as he headed for the door. "Those guys really know how to use a shovel!"

. .

The DC-10 dropped out of the clouds directly overhead as McGuire stepped from his car. Its engines, on low throttle, idled with a shrill whistle that pierced his ears, and he glared up at the craft's steel belly to watch it descend into Logan Airport.

He stepped carefully through the fresh snow in the gutter and stamped his feet on the shovelled walkway leading to the house. At the door he rang the bell and heard the Labrador bellow inside. A woman's voice spoke soothingly to the animal before the inner door swung open.

Frances O'Neil stood behind the outer storm door, an expectant smile frozen on her face. The smile began to dissolve, then reappeared, weaker and without conviction.

"May I come in for a few moments?" McGuire asked pleasantly.

She nodded, unfastened the inner lock and opened the door for him.

He stepped into a warm corridor which ended at a closed door. Behind the door the dog cried and snuffled.

To McGuire's right, at the far end of a large living-room, logs burned silently in a plain brick fireplace. The room was filled with undistinguished furniture, much of it covered in vinyl, arranged haphazardly on thick broadloom carpeting. Below one of the two picture windows facing the street sat a large antique steamer trunk overflowing with colourful plush and plastic toys.

"Would you like to sit down here?" Frances O'Neil asked, leading the way into the room. The next sentences emerged in a torrent of words, falling over each other as she walked ahead of him. "I can make a pot of tea. I'm not a coffee drinker. Marlene was always trying to get me to drink coffee, but. . . Mona, that's my sister, she and Kelly have gone to see Robert, that's her husband, for lunch in the city. So I made a fire, because I love fires on days like this, just sitting here with a book and with Jabs for company. Jabs, that's the dog . . ."

She turned to see McGuire watching her carefully, standing beside the sofa.

Her hands flew across her face and fluttered frantically like birds tethered on a string. Squeezing her eyes shut, she stammered, "What am I doing? I didn't even take your coat. I'm sorry. I don't know what's gotten into me."

McGuire shrugged out of his topcoat and handed it to her as she brushed by, returning to the corridor. "Hush!" she called to the dog behind the door.

He entered the room and sat on the sofa, facing the fire. The mantel was crowded with photographs of Kelly. In most of them, the little girl and Frances smiled back at the camera together. McGuire counted only three in which the girl was pictured with her stern-faced parents, the mother with her hair always freshly set, the father, balding, with his eyes challenging the camera from behind steel-rimmed glasses.

"Are you sure you don't want tea?" Frances asked when she returned. McGuire assured her he didn't.

She crossed the room and sat on a low bench near the fire, her knees drawn up and her arms wrapped tightly around her calves. Her blouse complimented her long, loosely-fitted skirt; she had applied just enough mascara to flatter her eyes and just enough lipstick to define her thin mouth. A gold chain lay around her neck and gold hoop earrings swung with each move of her head.

Not beautiful, McGuire thought as he studied her, but not unattractive, either. The kind of woman who could sit alone in a bar and not get a second look from men until after midnight.

She stared into the fire and said, in a small sad voice, "Why did you return?"

"To ask a few questions. About Jennifer Cornell. And about Andy, her brother."

"Andrew? Andrew's gone, isn't he? Can't you people believe that he's never coming back?"

"Miss O'Neil," McGuire began.

"Frances," she said, turning to look at him abruptly. "Please call me Frances."

"Frances," McGuire smiled. "It appears you were the last person to see Andy Cornell. Did he walk you home the evening his sister was murdered?"

"Actually, I walked Andrew home. He invited me back to his. . . back to Jennifer's apartment. He said he wanted company. Just company to walk home. It was such a lovely night, I remember. Warm and soft. You only get nights like that in June, don't you? Later on, in August, the nights can get, I don't know, heavy. But in June they're soft and romantic."

"What did you talk about?"

She looked back at the fire and smiled. "So many things. Andrew was interested in so many things. Books and music. And movies and plays. I told him I thought the most beautiful movie ever made was *A Place In The Sun* because it had the two most beautiful people in it, Elizabeth Taylor and Montgomery Clift. I had a mad, passionate crush on Montgomery Clift when I was a kid. I thought he was the most gorgeous man in the world. I told Andrew he reminded me of Montgomery Clift. Not in looks so much. Andrew wasn't as dark and swarthy as Montgomery Clift. But in his sensitivity. His eyes, his voice, the way he carried himself."

Briefly, she bowed her head, and then raised it again, her eyes flooded with tears.

"And he stopped and took my head in his hands and looked at me and said, 'I love you for saying that.' I thought he was going to kiss me. I was sure he would, but we just kept walking, up Westland Street and across the bridge, the stone bridge over the Fens."

She bent to rest her forehead on her knees.

"What happened then?" McGuire asked gently.

"When?"

"After you crossed the bridge."

She looked up and studied McGuire before replying in a stronger voice. "He saw the light on in his. . . in Jennifer's apartment. He said he would love to invite me up for coffee and talk about movies and books and things. But he said Jennifer was home, and Jennifer wouldn't like it. He said she was a very jealous, possessive woman. And she was. I knew that. So I asked him. . ." She swallowed, looked away, regained her strength and began again. "I asked him to come home with me. I had never done that before. Asked a man home, I mean. I just had this small apartment in Cambridge, it was nothing much. But he said no, he couldn't do that, he had to go to Jennifer."

"And that's the last time you saw him?"

She nodded silently.

"He went into Jennifer's apartment house?"

Another nod.

"Did you actually see him enter?"

"Mr McGuire, I stood on Park Drive and I watched him go in the door and I stayed there for the longest time waiting for him to come out. But he never came."

"So you went home."

"I walked. Across the Harvard Bridge all the way to Prospect Street."

"What did Andy do for a living? Did he tell you?"

She rubbed the fingertips of her hands together as she spoke. "He never said. He just told me he had travelled a lot, here and there, and that he was ready to settle down. He said he liked Boston, he had never been here before."

"Did he tell you about his limp? Did he explain it?"

"He joked about it. Said it was from a car accident. I didn't ask for details."

"There's no record of Jennifer ever having a brother. Nothing at all."

"Yes she did. It was Andrew."

"But there's no proof."

"You never saw them together like I did." She looked away and wiped her eyes. "She was so proud. So proud."

He waited until she turned to face him again, an embarrassed smile on her lips.

"I'm sorry," she said. "What else would you like to know?"

"I understand he had an accent."

"He had several." Her smile grew broader. "He liked to practise them. When we walked home that night he talked in a Georgia accent and a Texas accent, just joking, making fun of them. And he did a Boston accent, a broad one, like the Kennedys."

McGuire frowned. The picture of Andrew Cornell was becoming more clouded with every revelation about him. "Where were you the morning Jennifer was found dead?" he asked, trying another tack.

She shrugged. "In bed. Exhausted."

"What did you think about when you heard the news?"

Frances brought her hands to her face and her shoulders heaved. Standing up, she walked to the window and gazed out at the snowy landscape. "I knew Andrew was gone. I knew I would never see him again."

"Do you think he was responsible for Jennifer's death?"

She replied without hesitating. "Oh, yes. Andrew was responsible. That I'm sure of."

"Why would he kill his sister?"

Turning from the window, her face was calm again. "I don't know," she replied. "You'll have to ask somebody else. I can't answer that."

"Where is Andrew now?"

Sparks flew as a log shifted and dropped into the embers. Frances looked towards the fire. "Probably dead."

"What makes you say that?"

"I don't know. A feeling." She smoothed her skirt. "That's the logical explanation, isn't it?"

"It's one," McGuire replied. "He could be anywhere. In fact, when I was here last time you just said he had gone away. Now you suggest he's dead. Why?"

"Because I want to believe it." She lifted her head — a teacher's pose of strength and authority. "Maybe it's wrong to hope that someone is dead. I'm sorry if it is, but that's the way I feel." She walked quickly towards the kitchen door. "I'm making some tea, Mr McGuire. Are you sure you won't have some before heading out in the snow?"

. .

Her legs crossed, she dangled one shoe from her toes, swinging it back and forth as she spoke.

"There was just Mona and me," she said in a voice that was relaxed and reedy. "Mona is two years older. When you come from a family like ours, you either get hard and aggressive or you get. . . like me, I guess. I withdrew into my own little dream world where everything was sweet and romantic and everybody was nice to everybody else. Nobody was cruel. Mona, she became tough. No one ever dominated *her*. No one ever will."

She drained the tea from her cup and set it aside. McGuire had long since finished his and he sat back on the sofa, listening to her tale of two young girls being terrorized by a tyrant father as they grew up in South Boston.

He liked the delicacy of her, the slenderness of her arms and body. McGuire had known women with an inner beauty whose appeal defied physical measure alone, and women whose outer beauty was so obvious it made cosmetics superfluous. Frances O'Neil's beauty was neither inner nor obvious. It was frail, like a green bud in early spring, ready to burst into full flower or wither in the next killing frost.

"So Mona became an executive secretary. And I became a teacher. Then I worked as a librarian for a few years." She smiled at the memory. "I loved being surrounded by books. Loved having all those characters and ideas lingering between the covers. I could visit them whenever I wanted. It was a wonderful time for me."

"And then?"

She smiled and stood up, kicking off both shoes before walking to set her empty cup on a side table. He realized for the first time she wore no brassiere. Her feet were tiny and bare; nail polish flashed like costume jewellery from her toes.

In McGuire's eyes she suddenly seemed attractive, sexy, enticing, as she stretched languidly, her arms above her head, in the soft light of the picture window, in a warm room with a dying fire on a cold day.

She walked back to the fireplace and knelt to add a log.

"I only had one boyfriend in high school. And there was a nice man I dated when I was teaching," she said after seating herself once again on the low bench by the fire. "They were both quiet, gentle men. Perhaps I should have married one of them. But I didn't."

Her hands fluttered in front of her face. "I've always been a nervous, withdrawn person. But I'm getting better. I was always so afraid of becoming too involved. Too deeply involved. Being a librarian helped. I was distanced from people. I could take refuge in books."

She stood and walked back to the window. Again, McGuire was struck by her grace and delicacy.

"One day a businessman came in and asked me to help him find some reference books he needed," she said, without turning from the window. "He was in advertising. He was going to make a speech and I helped him find what he needed. We spent an hour together. He came back a week later to say his speech had been a big success and he wanted to take me to lunch, just to thank me for all the work I had done."

She turned to face McGuire, raising one hand to brush away a lock of hair from her forehead.

"Do you want to guess the rest?" she asked.

"I don't have to," McGuire replied. "How long did it last?"

"Almost three years. During the last year, his daughter started coming into the branch every Saturday. She was perhaps nine, ten years old. I recognized her from the photographs he had shown me. And I saw her name and address on her library card. He would talk about her all the time. He worshipped her. One day, when he hadn't called me for over a week, I did a terrible thing. I went to this sweet little girl and said I knew her name and to please tell her daddy to call me at the library." She returned from the window and sat on the bench again, staring at the fire.

"When he called, he was furious. He said terrible things about me. Things I couldn't believe a man would say to a woman who did nothing wrong except love him too much. He told me his family was the most precious thing in the world to him and I had almost destroyed it for him. I cried for days. Finally the chief librarian said I would have to leave. Due to my emotional state. And because someone had complained about me."

"The man's wife," McGuire added.

She nodded. "So," she said, smiling and opening her arms, "that ended one career and began another. At Pour Richards. That was my sister's idea. She told me I had to get out among people. She said one bad affair shouldn't make me a hermit. And working there was fun for a while."

"Until Andy Cornell?"

"He was part of it. I just. . . When I left, my sister told me I could be her live-in baby-sitter. I earn my room and board and forty dollars a week. And I get so much love from Kelly. She seems everything to me. Sometimes it frightens me because I know she won't always be a child. She won't always need me."

McGuire stood up. "I have to go, Miss O'Neil." He thanked her for the tea.

She walked him to the door, held his coat for him, and touched his elbow absent-mindedly. "I've never told anyone about the man at the library," she said. "Except my sister. I'm sorry if I bored you."

"You know what I think?" he said, turning to look at her. "I think you're too good a person to spend your life regretting a guy like that."

The tears began again and she bit her bottom lip. "Thank you," she said. "Thank you for saying that." Then, with a whisper of desperation in her voice: "Will you be back?"

"I might." He handed her his card. "If you think of anything else, call me."

"You already gave me one," she said accepting it. "But I'd love another." She reached to touch his upper lip with her finger. "How did you get that scar?"

"Shaving."

She smiled broadly enough to wrinkle her nose, making her look several years younger. "Impossible."

"I use a very large blade."

"You're an interesting man."

"Only on the outside."

The dog began scratching at the kitchen door, crying for attention. McGuire stepped into the chill of the day and the inhuman roar of another 727 on its way to the airport, its landing-gear extended and the sound of its engines piercing the afternoon calm.

Driving back to the city, he tried to assemble pieces of the puzzle of Jennifer Cornell's murder in his head. No matter how he arranged them, the gaping hole that always remained in the picture was named Andrew Cornell.

He hesitated at Bennington, began to turn left into the city, then jerked the wheel right towards the ocean and Revere Beach Parkway.

· ·

"Would you mind waiting in the living-room?" Ronnie said at the door, avoiding McGuire's eyes. "It's dinner time. He's not comfortable having you watch me feed him."

McGuire sat quietly in the small, tidy living-room. A game show played itself out on the television set, the contestants locked together in frenzied greed. Atop the television console, from within a sterling silver frame, the face of a small boy shone into the room. His hair was carefully combed into a shiny pompadour and he wore a printed cotton top with matching short pants. He was laughing at something above and behind the camera, his rosebud mouth spread in an expression of glee. He would always be laughing. He would always be five years old and alive.

"Coffee?"

McGuire twisted in the chair to see Ronnie beaming at him.

"He's happy you're here," she said. "He won't show it — you know Ollie — but he wants to talk to you."

She poured coffee for him in the kitchen and he entered Ollie's room, sipping from an earthenware mug.

"How you doing?" Ollie lay propped up in his bed, his right hand squeezing the tennis ball at the same steady tempo.

"First we kill all the lawyers," McGuire said as he lowered himself into his usual chair. "You?"

"You have to ask?" The large head studied McGuire, the eyes narrowed to slits. "So tell me what happened today."

For the next half hour McGuire traced the events of the day, beginning with his request for information from Ralph Innes.

"You'd better talk to Jack," Ollie offered when McGuire

mentioned Ralph's warning. "Get him calmed down. Otherwise you'll get your ass pulled into the wringer."

His eyes widened as McGuire described Rosen's ambush in Robinson's meeting room and the demand for McGuire's resignation.

"Rosen's about as smooth as stucco toilet paper, but he's not dumb," Ollie said quietly. "Bet the farm on this, Joseph. Somebody over at Berkeley Street knows what he's up to and gave him the nod. Maybe not Kavander, but somebody above him. They know about it. Otherwise, Rosen wouldn't pull a number like that on you."

"God-damn it, Ollie!" McGuire exploded. "I resign now and they'll put this Cornell case back in the grey files. Not only that, but Wilmer will walk for good. You know how testimony is useless from a cop who just resigned from the force. It's worth nothing. Less than nothing. Rosen would cut me to pieces in front of the jury. We'd have two killers still walking around out there and nobody would give a damn."

"Except the city gets rid of a trouble-making cop and out from under a lawsuit." Ollie turned his head to face McGuire. "Joe, I remember when Kavander talked to me the day I left. He said he'd bet my pension that you wouldn't last six months without me to keep you reined in."

"And what did you tell him, Ollie?"

"I told him he might be right." Ollie lowered his voice. "I also told him that if it was true, he would lose the best damn investigating cop on the force. Now, what else have you got?"

McGuire reviewed Andrew Cornell's appointment to meet Fleckstone on the day after his sister was found murdered, and his apparent familiarity with southern accents. He talked about visiting Frances O'Neil and her description of the missing brother.

"It all comes back to the brother, whoever he is," McGuire said when he had finished.

Instead of answering, Ollie studied him, then rolled his head to look out the window at the darkened sea.

McGuire looked at his watch. "I'll call Ralph Innes, see what he came up with."

Ronnie was seated in the kitchen, the evening newspaper spread in front of her. "I need to use the phone," McGuire said, adding quickly, "No, it's okay, stay there" when she rose to leave.

"We're having an extension installed in Ollie's room to-morrow," she said. "A speaker phone. That way, he doesn't have to use the receiver." Her face clouded. "After that, all he'll need is somebody to call him."

McGuire dialled Berkeley Street, asked for Ralph Innes and opened his notebook while waiting to be connected.

"Innes here," the detective answered.

"Ralph, it's Joe. You got anything for me?"

"Yeah, yeah." The other man sounded distracted. "Let me get to a different phone, okay?"

McGuire nodded when Ronnie lifted the coffee pot in his direction. She poured a cup and set it in front of him.

"Joe?" Innes came back on the line. His voice was softer, almost a whisper. "Had to get to another phone. Listen, where you calling from? Kavander's been riding everybody's ass looking for you."

"I'm at a friend's," McGuire replied. "Just tell me what you got and I'll get back to Kavander later."

"Okay. And listen, Joe, Jesus, I'm really sorry for all those things I said."

"About what?"

"Not what. Who. Sweet. . . Janet. I didn't know about you two. Why didn't you say something instead of letting me talk about her like that in front of you?"

"How the hell did you find out?" McGuire asked.

"A guy in ID heard Kavander bitching about it to some-body in the commissioner's office. Her husband called the commissioner himself and spent ten minutes blubbering about how you ruined his life. Kavander said that was all he needed, a citizen complaining about a cop screwing his wife behind his back. Hell, you know how word spreads around here. Anyway, Joe, I'm sorry for all those cracks. Just making jokes, you know?"

McGuire felt more tired than he could remember. All day long he had managed to keep memories of Janet from his mind. With difficulty. And with sorrow. He didn't want them intruding now. "Forget it, Ralph. It's over anyway. I was never comfortable being involved with a married woman. Never could be. So what did you discover?"

Innes spoke to someone at his end of the line, then returned to the receiver. "I have to make this fast," he said. "Just got a call in from Washington Avenue. Sounds like a double and suicide. Anyway, here's what I've got. Found a Cartier pawned on Dorchester, June nineteenth. Guy got sixteen hundred cash for it."

"Name?"

"One Henry Reich, Park Drive."

"Son of a bitch!" McGuire began scribbling in his notebook.

"That's the bozo you wanted to know about, right? Apartment superintendent? Fell downstairs carrying a case of booze? I interviewed him, second time around on the case, with Fat Eddie."

"What was he like?"

"Kind of arrogant, as I recall. Wouldn't offer us a thing. Acted like it was his big chance to be a pain in the ass to the cops."

"What's on his death report?"

"Accidental. Yeah, this is the guy. Age sixty-four. Weight one-eighty. Blood alcohol level was point-one-six. Old bugger was pickled like a kosher dill."

"When did it happen?"

McGuire could hear pages being turned. "July fifth. About eleven at night. No witnesses, body discovered by the wife."

"Okay, I know that part. How about Jennifer Cornell's bank records?"

More pages being turned. Then: "She made cash deposits of over three thousand dollars each on May twenty-third, twenty-fifth, twenty-ninth and thirtieth, and June second. These were in addition to regular salary deposits made by her employer. Then she withdrew almost five grand in cash on June third."

"Which, I'll bet, is what the Cartier was worth."

"Something like that."

"Anything else in the bank records?"

"Nothing special."

"How about her mother?"

"Ah, yes. Suzanne Alice Cornell." Innes read from his notes. "Died end of May, nineteen eighty-three, San Antonio, Texas, aged fifty, cause of death massive internal injuries suffered when the car in which she was a passenger collided with another vehicle on Culebra Road."

"She the driver?"

"No, her husband was. One Ernest Edward Snyder. Charged with D.W.I. Spent thirty days in the slammer and another year with his licence lifted."

"Who else was in the car?"

"Can't tell. All I got was a reading from the woman's death certificate and some info over the phone on her husband. Circumstances, that's all I asked for."

"Where is her husband? He still alive?"

"Guy on the desk down there, his name is Maydelle by the way, said he thought so. Old Ernie Snyder was no stranger to the boys in San Anton', apparently."

"They have any children?"

"Who? Ernie and Suzanne? No, nothing here."

"All right, thanks Ralph. You gave me plenty to work on."

"Ernie had a kid. Got something on him."

McGuire continued scribbling in his notebook, the

telephone receiver wedged between his ear and shoulder. "Can't be worth much."

"Maybe, maybe not. But it's interesting. See, this was his second marriage. Ernest Edward Snyder had a son from a previous marriage, born nineteen fifty-three. Guy would be in his mid-thirties now. Anyway, want to guess what his name was?"

CHAPTER FIFTEEN

"**A**ndrew Ernest Snyder!" McGuire slapped his notebook on Ollie's bed and began pacing the length of the room, almost strutting with pride. "She had a foster brother named Andrew, damn it. From San Antonio."

Ollie Schantz watched him silently.

"I'll call Kavander for an arrest warrant and take off for Texas," McGuire continued.

"How about a description?" Ollie asked in a flat voice. "You got a description to match this guy?"

"I've got a name, I've got a connection, he's the right age. Come on, Ollie. How much more do I need?"

"It would help if Kavander didn't want you waltzing away from the case."

"But if I do, who finds the killer?" McGuire almost shouted. "Fat Eddie Vance and his gang of merry men? Look, Ollie. If Kavander gets in my way on this one, I'll call every greaseball reporter in the state and tell them that our Captain of Detectives wants to suppress a murder investigation."

Ollie stared at him, blinking once, then twice. "Call him," he said finally.

Back in the kitchen, McGuire waited for a desk officer to make the connection to Kavander's office. It was five-thirty; the odds were good that Jack the Bear was still at his desk, writing sarcastic comments on investigation reports.

"He ain't here," said the desk officer when he returned to the phone.

"Who's this?"

"Sergeant Cauley. So who the hell's this?"

"Joe McGuire, Stew. How are you?"

"Hey, Joe-Joe! I'm okay, but you're three storeys below the shit-house. With the Bear, anyway."

"That's one reason I have to talk to him. So where is he?"

"Down at the Copley. Probably on his third martini. Getting ready to pinch a waitress's ass. Testimonial dinner there for the commissioner. Listen, you call him there, I didn't tell you where to find him, okay?"

"Stew, I haven't talked to you all year. Thanks."

It took three people to connect McGuire with Jack Kavander in the Waltham Room of the hotel. Against a deep layer of conversation and a thin veneer of instrumental music, he heard Jack Kavander's voice bark its owner's name.

"Jack, it's McGuire."

He waited for a response. Instead, all he heard were peals of distant laughter and two bars of "It Was Just One of Those Things."

"Jack, I know you're pissed with me, but I've got something on one of the cases —"

"McGuire?" Kavander spat into the telephone. "How did you know where I was?"

"It's scribbled in washrooms all over town. Listen, Jack —"

"God-damn it, McGuire. In ten minutes I'm making a law-and-order speech to half the politicians in the state."

"Good. Tell them what a great fucking job your Homicide squad is doing," McGuire shouted into the receiver. He glanced up to see Ronnie peering at him over the top of her newspaper, and shrugged apologetically.

McGuire counted another bar of the old song from the hotel's music system before Kavander replied in a tight, even voice. "McGuire, if you have something we should know about, you bring it to my office tomorrow at noon and you lay it out for me and Lieutenant Vance and his people. And if you have sufficient cause, we will certainly follow routine procedures to launch an appropriate investigation."

"Fat Eddie? Jack, that horse's foot blew this case in the first place."

"Preliminaries, McGuire. That's what we'll do first."

"The guy we want is down in Texas, for Christ's sake!"

Another pause. "All the more reason to do the preliminaries." Kavander lowered his voice even further. "I'm telling you, McGuire. If you have something, you turn it over to the staff. Because right now your career is hanging by a thread —"

"Which is wrapped around your balls!" McGuire replaced the receiver and stared at the telephone before looking around to see Ronnie studying him. A slight smile played across her face.

"Next time, give him Ollie's love too," she said.

He grinned back and leaned to kiss her on the forehead. "I need to make another call or two," he said. "One of them is long-distance. To Texas."

"Not a place I ever wanted to visit," she said.

McGuire grunted, flipped through the telephone book for airline listings, and within five minutes had booked himself on a morning flight to San Antonio.

He made the next call to the San Antonio Police Department, where a Sergeant Maydelle answered on the first ring.

McGuire introduced himself. "I have a Murder One investigation that concerns the son of one Ernest Edward Snyder of your city."

"Heard about that ol' dog this afternoon," Maydelle

drawled. "Y'all coming down here, shake some sand out of your boots?"

"I plan on arriving tomorrow to ask him a few questions, with the cooperation of your department."

"Glad to help," Maydelle said. "Give me your flight number. I'll have one of our young'uns meet you, give you a tour, maybe recommend a good place for a taco and beer."

McGuire recited his flight number.

"Look for a San Antonio officer holding a red file folder when you arrive at the airport," Maydelle instructed. "Bring your ID. We'll do the rest."

· ·

"I got ears. I heard," Ollie said when Joe returned to his room and began describing his conversation with Kavander. "He's going to shoot you down in flames, Joe."

"Not me, Ollie," McGuire answered, slipping into his top-coat. "I'm not going to ignore the only solid lead that's turned up on the case in six months and add another NETGO stamp to the file. I do that and I deserve to spend the rest of my life in the Bomb Shelter with all the files Fat Eddie has screwed up, just counting the days until I'm pensioned off."

"You never learned to play politics, Joe. That's your problem. Fat Eddie, he's not the greatest cop in the world but he knows the politics." Ollie shifted his head slowly, his eyes searching for the offshore light in the darkness, his hand still squeezing and releasing the tennis ball.

"And you did?"

"Damn right I did."

"How?" McGuire spread his hands. "I never saw any of it. Hell, you were twice as driven as I am. Ask anybody on Berkeley Street. Ask them if Ollie Schantz ever played politics. They'll all say 'Like hell he did.' When did you ever get down in the dirt with those political bastards? I sure as hell never saw it."

In a slow, almost creaking motion, Ollie's head swivelled

back to stare coldly at McGuire. "Maybe," he said, "I was so good at it that nobody ever noticed. Did you ever think of that?"

. .

McGuire slept fitfully, waking to imagined sounds in his apartment while his mind scrambled to regain vestiges of dreams. In the morning he dressed in a tweed jacket, flannel slacks, white button-down shirt and black knit tie. He threw socks, underwear, a clean shirt and toiletries in his suitcase, along with his Police Special revolver and cartridges wrapped in a heavy bath towel.

Climbing into a cab in the fading darkness on Commonwealth Avenue, he leaned back in the seat and allowed the winter chill to finish waking him up.

CHAPTER SIXTEEN

Leaving the aircraft at San Antonio airport, McGuire walked through endless shades of brown: chocolate-brown tiles on the floor, sand-brown stucco on the walls, coffee-brown complexions on the people he passed. Through the windows, the outside world shone dusty brown in the sun.

He collected his bag at the luggage carousel and quickly located a young police officer dressed in a starched sepia-brown uniform grinning in his direction and waving a red file folder like a semaphore.

"My name's McGuire," he said, approaching the officer and showing his badge. "Boston Police Department, Homicide Division. You looking for me?"

"Sure am!" the younger man chortled. "Knew it was you. Said to myself, now there's a police officer, soon's you come through the door."

The constable was pink-cheeked, crew-cut and so unfailingly cheerful that McGuire knew he wouldn't be able to tolerate the man's company for more than an hour.

"Constable First Class Melvin Pernfus," the officer said, seizing McGuire's hand and shaking it like an instrument in a rhythm band. "It's my pleasure to welcome you to Texas and to the great city of San Antonio!"

He led the way through the terminal and out into the heat of the day, where McGuire shrugged out of his tweed jacket and loosened his tie.

"Days like this, my daddy used to say the air was too thick for a dog to bark," Pernfus grinned as he wheeled the car out of the airport. "This your first visit to San Antonio?"

"First time in Texas," McGuire replied. A rivulet of sweat beneath his shirt was beginning to wend its way down his back.

Pernfus slapped his thigh, accelerating into the freeway traffic skirting the airport. "Hell, I can't imagine living anywhere else but Texas," he said. "My daddy, he said there's everything you need to see here. No matter where you go, people still chew their grits the same and instead of travelling for long days on a slow train, he'd rather stay in Texas and watch his dog grow old —"

"You know this man, Ernest Snyder?" McGuire interrupted. He was damp with perspiration.

"All's I know is what's in there," Pernfus said, removing the red file folder from the dashboard and handing it to McGuire. "Read a bit of it while waiting for you. Hope you don't mind. Mr Snyder, he sounds like he's got two kinds of diseases. They're called too many women and too much alcohol. We get epidemics of both in Texas."

McGuire opened the folder and studied the photocopies of official police reports.

Ernest Snyder had been born fifty-five years earlier in Brady, Texas. One of six children, he had drifted in and out of trouble as a juvenile, finally leaving school in grade eight. He spent two years in the U.S. Army and received a Conditional Discharge after serving time for two AWOL charges. While in the service a son, Andrew, had been born to Snyder and his wife, a fifteen-year-old runaway from Abilene who divorced him five years later and settled with the boy in California.

McGuire flipped the page to Snyder's arrest record.

He counted four convictions for D.W.I., including one laid as a result of the accident in which his second wife was killed, plus three charges of assault on women, five convictions for being drunk in a public place and two of common assault. In the most recent assault case, which occurred four years earlier, the attack was so vicious that his victim had been in a coma for two weeks. For this conviction, Snyder had been sentenced to two years in a state penitentiary. McGuire's pulse quickened as his eyes skipped ahead to read:

Subject was released on parole with conditions:

a) He is to refrain from alcohol for the duration of his sentence;

b) He is to enrol in an alcohol-abuse control group, preferably church-oriented;

c) He is to reside with his son, Andrew Ernest Snyder, who accepts responsibility for the care of his father. Subject is not to change his place of residence without prior approval of Texas Department of Corrections and notification to the San Antonio Police Department.

McGuire looked up from the file to see Pernfus swinging off the freeway at an exit. "Where's this old boy live?" Pernfus grinned at McGuire from under a haircut so close-cropped even a Marine boot camp sergeant would approve. "Westfield Road, is it?"

McGuire read the address aloud. He hitched up his flannel pants, scratchy in the heat, and pulled his tie further away from his collar.

"Got yourself all dressed up for winter there," Pernfus laughed. "If you're down here for longer than a day, better invest in some good old Texas chinos and a T-shirt. I tell you, you get yourself a cold Lone Star to sip and a cool place to relax along River Walk tonight, watch some of those nice ladies promenade along there, you might never go back north again. Lot of folks have done that. Wheel you by the Alamo later if you like."

The road from the freeway passed through a prosperous business district that quickly declined to a seedy commercial area. Soon they were passing blocks of empty stores and gasoline stations separated by small ranch homes, weedy lawns and abandoned cars.

"Not the best part of town," McGuire observed.

"Not the worst, either," Pernfus added, turning onto a narrow residential street.

They entered an area of cheap tract housing, each home identical in size and layout to its neighbour, differing only in the colour of its trim and the degree of pride its owners took in its appearance.

"Everybody in Texas drive a pickup truck?" McGuire asked after two blocks.

"Just about," Pernfus offered. "Most folks around here have a pickup in the driveway, a hound dog in the yard and a shotgun in the kitchen." He stopped the car, squinted through the windshield, then accelerated again and wheeled into a dirt driveway. "This would seem to be Mr Snyder's place of residence," he said with mock formality.

The house facing them was so neglected it appeared abandoned. Flakes of paint hung from the window shutters like dead leaves. Sheets of cardboard had been tacked over broken windows, a heavy blanket of moss grew along the edges of the roof, and the lawn was more brown than green, more weeds than grass.

At the end of the driveway a gap in the weathered picket fence indicated where a gate had once hung. Beyond the fence a hammock was strung between a dead tree trunk and a second tree, which clung to life and provided the only shade in the yard.

The hammock swayed gently. A country music song, thin and tuneless, floated in the still air.

"Looks like our boy is smart enough to take it easy on a hot day," Pernfus said, stepping out of the car. In spite of his non-stop grin, Pernfus dropped his hand to his holster. McGuire followed the officer through the gap in the fence and into the yard.

The man was sprawled on his side in the hammock, his back to the road and his eyes closed; one hand was behind his head, the other dangled and almost touched the ground. Three empty Lone Star bottles lay beneath him, along with a near-empty pack of cigarettes and a cheap transistor radio.

He appeared older than fifty-five, his face lined and leathery, hair thin and white like the stubble on his chin. He wore an oversized cotton shirt, greasy trousers cinched with a plastic belt, and heavy socks.

Pernfus settled on his haunches beside the hammock. Getting wind of the man's foul breath, he winced and grinned back at McGuire.

"Hey, old timer," the constable said, touching Snyder lightly on the shoulder. "Got a man here to see you. You Mr Snyder?"

The older man's eyes sprung open like traps; they flashed from the kneeling Pernfus to the standing McGuire and back again. He mumbled something.

"What's that?" grinned Pernfus. "Didn't quite catch your drift."

"I said haul your asses off my property!" Snyder spat at the men, looking at each in turn. "Go on! Git!"

Pernfus stood up and took a step backwards as the man swung his feet to the ground and rested his elbows on his knees. Snyder scratched himself with a curious concentration before looking up at the two men. "You still here?" he demanded. "Told you to git. Now git!"

His eyes remained in constant motion. Watery, red-rimmed and a surprisingly deep blue, they darted between the two standing men, the beer bottles on the ground, the cloudless sky, the police cruiser in the driveway, and back to the men again.

"You Ernest Snyder?" McGuire asked calmly.

Snyder's eyes rested on McGuire for a moment before resuming their motion. His mouth twitched and he rubbed his chin.

"This man's come all the way down from Boston just to talk to you," Pernfus said in his cheerful manner. "Probably just take a minute or two, then we'll let you get back to that siesta you were having. Looked like a pretty good one, too."

Snyder's eyes became less animated. "Got nothing to say to you sons of bitches," he muttered, holding each of the beer bottles up to the light in turn. He tilted the third to his mouth and swallowed its dregs.

"Relax," McGuire said, his back to the sun. "It's not you we want to talk to. It's your son."

"Who?" Snyder barked, shielding his eyes against the bright sky to look up at McGuire.

"Andrew Ernest Snyder," McGuire replied patiently. "Your son."

Pernfus, hands on his hips, looked from Snyder to McGuire and back again. He seemed quietly amused.

Snyder parted his lips, exposing a mouth full of yellow and broken teeth. "Son?" he said. He hiccupped with laughter. "My son? You see a son around here? Do you? Huh? I ain't got a son. What the hell you talking about, my son?"

McGuire waved the file folder. "Cut the bullshit, Snyder. We know you have a son. This is his house and you were sent here to live with him as part of your parole agreement."

"Bastard's dead." Snyder lay back in the hammock and closed his eyes.

"When?" McGuire demanded. He knelt on his haunches

and winced at the cracking sounds from his knees. "Where? How did he die? Give us some facts."

The older man ignored him.

"Sure would be nice to give the man here some information," Pernfus suggested. "Otherwise, might have to ask you to come downtown with us. No hammock or Lone Star down there, Mr Snyder. 'Course, you already know that." Pernfus stared off in the distance as he spoke. "Now, if I was you, I'd rather be having my siesta out here than down there. That's only my opinion, you understand."

Snyder remained silent for a moment before shifting his body sideways and raising a hand to cover his eyes. "I don't know where he's at."

"Well, which is it?" McGuire asked. "Is he dead? Or has he gone off somewhere?"

"Took off two years ago. Haven't seen him since."

"Where was he going?" McGuire demanded.

"West."

"That's all you know? West?"

"That's all I fucking know. Now both of you get the hell away from me." He rolled further onto his side, his back to McGuire.

"Well, we appreciate your time, Mr Snyder," Pernfus said. "We'll let you get back to your business now."

McGuire seized Pernfus by the shoulder as the constable walked past him towards the cruiser. "That's it?" McGuire snapped. "I come all the way down here for some drunk to tell me he doesn't know where his own son is?"

"Sorry, Lieutenant," Pernfus shrugged. "If we take him downtown, he might say even less. Probably get a legal aid lawyer." Pernfus glanced at McGuire's hand on his shoulder as though it were an insect he was about to brush away. His cheeriness had disappeared; in its place was a sense of quiet scorn. "Didn't bring a warrant with you, did you? One that's good in the state of Texas?"

McGuire saw the shrewdness and hint of contempt behind

the expression in the other man's eyes. "No," he said, dropping his hand. "No warrant. Just questioning."

Pernfus opened the car door. "Guess I could have done this myself. Saved you a trip." McGuire entered the car and fell back angrily in the passenger seat.

Pernfus started the engine and twisted his body to back out of the driveway. "Long as you're here, I could give you a tour of old San Anton'. Get you into the Alamo free. Watch while you sip a Lone Star or two." But the offer was empty and McGuire knew it. Pernfus slipped the car into drive and pulled away. "Lordy, I'd give a good huntin' dog to join you on a day like today, sitting in the shade just watching the ladies. Not in uniform, though. I mean, even in Texas, there comes a time you just have to pass up a cold beer."

McGuire stared at the man in the hammock who lay with his hands across his eyes. He could see those steel-blue eyes, wide open behind the splayed fingers, watching the police car pull away.

"How's that sound?"

"How's what sound?" McGuire asked as Snyder disappeared from view.

"Having a cold one at the Alamo?"

McGuire shook his head. "No sense wasting any more of your time or mine," he said. "Take me back to the airport. I'll catch a flight north."

Pernfus shrugged.

On the way, Pernfus told tales of his father's hunting dogs, his mother's garden, his sister's children and his wife's talent as a Tennessee clog dancer. "Won 'Best of County' three years running," he boasted as they arrived at the terminal building. "You get up in the Great Smokies, where Peggy's from, they're all clog dancing in their diapers practically. Well, here we are, Lieutenant."

McGuire grabbed his bag from the back seat and turned to shake the constable's hand.

"Bet you're not looking forward to going back, facing all that snow and cold in Boston," Pernfus said.

"You're right," McGuire replied. "I'm not looking forward to it at all."

He closed the door, nodded to Pernfus as the cruiser pulled away from the curb, and entered the terminal. Then he stopped, looked casually around and turned to the nearest car rental booth.

He was thinking about the weakness of the spoken word.

And the purity of physical violence.

CHAPTER SEVENTEEN

Barely slowing the car's speed, McGuire swung into the driveway, burst through the tired picket fence and rammed the dead tree supporting Snyder's hammock with the front bumper of his rented Ford.

He flew out of the car and grabbed the dazed man — who had been knocked sprawling to the ground — by the shirt collar, with one hand. With his other hand, he thrust the muzzle of his revolver at the older man's mouth.

"Open up, Ernie," McGuire hissed. He rammed the gun barrel between Snyder's thin lips and heard the blue steel clink against teeth.

Snyder's eyes, wide and frightened when the impact tossed him out of the hammock, focused on McGuire and began to narrow.

"Now tell me the truth about your son," McGuire whispered, trying to ignore the foul odour rising from Snyder, "or I'll blow your tonsils out your ass."

From behind the muzzle of the revolver, Snyder mumbled something.

"Let's hear it," McGuire said, withdrawing the gun from the man's mouth.

"Fuck you," Snyder said, his eyes mere slits in his weathered face. "Go ahead and shoot. You'll be doing me a favour."

Swinging the gun a few inches away from Snyder's face, McGuire tilted it at a shallow angle to the ground and calmly pulled the trigger.

Snyder winced at the blast. Ten feet behind him, a clod of dusty-dry soil exploded into the air. Dogs began barking in neighbouring yards and somewhere a screen door was hastily shut.

"Don't try to bluff me, Snyder," McGuire said. "You've been a two-bit drunk and a coward all your life. You know it and I know it." He ran the muzzle of the gun down the front of the man's shirt and thrust it behind the top button of his trousers.

"Maybe you think you're tough enough to suck this mother," McGuire said. "I doubt it, but maybe you are. So how about this?" He forced the gun in between the waistband of the man's pants and his stomach. "Every ten seconds or so I'll send a copper-jacketed slug in the general direction of your balls until I hit something. You ever seen a man take a bullet in the crotch, Snyder?"

"*What the hell do you want Andy for?*" Snyder screamed. His eyes had widened again and he struggled briefly in McGuire's grip.

"He left some dirty laundry in Boston."

Snyder frowned and almost relaxed. "Boston?" he said. "Andy's never been to Boston. Far as I know."

"All of a sudden you know a lot about him," McGuire said. The transistor radio was still playing, sounding louder in the strange near-silence of the neighbourhood that followed McGuire's gunshot. "Just tell me where he is. Or I'll leave you lying on the ground watching your pecker swing from a tree branch."

"Laredo," Snyder blurted. "He's in Laredo."

"For how long?"

"Two years. Maybe more."

"You're lying."

Snyder shook his head violently. His eyes were steady and focused.

"Where in Laredo?"

"Don't know. Works for a guy named Bledsoe."

McGuire stared in silence at Snyder, spread on the ground beneath him. The radio announced a classic country song by "the late great Marty Robbins."

"God's truth," Snyder said. His eyes were pleading.

McGuire slowly pulled the gun from inside the man's trousers. "I'm going to believe you're intelligent enough not to lie to me," he said, standing up.

Snyder ran the back of his hand across his mouth and tried to swallow, his eyes swooping away from McGuire's face and back again. "All. . . all the cops up in Boston like you?" he stuttered.

"No," McGuire replied evenly. "Some of us are real crazy bastards." He watched Snyder compose himself, keeping the revolver at his side. "What does your son do for this Bledsoe character?"

"Don't know." Snyder used the dead tree trunk as support and raised himself to a standing position. His hands were shaking violently. "Odd jobs." He nudged one of the empty Lone Star bottles with his toes as Marty Robbins, dead ten years, sang "Mansion On The Hill" through the tinny speaker of the transistor radio. "Wrecked my hammock," he said, nodding at the dead tree McGuire's rented car had wrenched from the ground, its roots exposed by the impact. "What the hell do I lay on now?"

McGuire ignored the question. "Where do I find this Bledsoe? What's he do?"

Snyder turned from the ruined hammock to look at McGuire with a changed expression, neither fear nor defiance in his eyes. "Make you a deal. I give you an address, you give me ten dollars for a couple cases of Lone Star. Whaddaya say?"

The man looked pathetic. Snyder, McGuire knew, was destined to do nothing more with the rest of his life than lie on his back, sip beer and listen to dead country singers. He peeled ten dollars from his wallet and handed it to the other man, who crumpled it quickly into his pocket.

"It's inside," Snyder said. "Wait here. I'll bring it out."

McGuire watched him shuffle across the baked earth to the rear of the house, where an aluminum door leaned on one hinge. Amazing what the eyes can tell, he reflected. Your whole body can believe you're telling the truth but your eyes can't lie for you. It's all in the way they widen, the way they shift, the way they move. Windows of the soul. Who said that? Who cares?

The rental company will probably care about the dent in the front bumper, he grinned, walking to his car. The driver's door hung open and the engine was still running. He collapsed behind the wheel, feeling the familiar lethargy he always felt when the first sudden rush of adrenalin had dissolved.

The sound of a cupboard door being slammed echoed from inside Snyder's house. McGuire tossed his revolver on the passenger's seat.

His energy level was low. He could feel it. In the middle of the confrontation with Snyder just minutes earlier, there hadn't been the same burst of strength he remembered from earlier years. He wondered if his body was producing less adrenalin as it grew older. Lately, it seemed to be producing smaller quantities of other vital fluids, he mused. . .

The screen door creaked open and clattered shut. Then he heard another metallic sound that was more precise, more emphatic. . . more familiar.

McGuire cursed and exploded into action, slamming the car door. He shoved the transmission lever into reverse and pushed the accelerator to the floor, spinning the wheels in the dirt driveway just as Ernest Snyder, his face twisted in rage, rounded the corner and raised the shotgun to his shoulder.

A shotgun in every kitchen, Pernfus had said.

The car's tires squealed in protest as they bumped over the sidewalk and began gripping the crude asphalt surface of the street. McGuire swung the car hard to the left. The motion threw him across the passenger seat as Snyder fired and a cloud of smoke appeared and dissipated above the hood of the car.

Dogs began barking furiously from unseen yards. McGuire sat upright again, jamming the car into drive while still moving backwards, and the vehicle shuddered forward as an ominous hammering noise clattered from inside the transmission.

Snyder stumbled down the driveway, the gun still at shoulder level. He stopped for another shot at the fleeing car. The blast sent curious neighbours back from their doors and into their houses, launched another symphony of hound cries and made a sound like scattered gravel against the rear of the Ford.

McGuire roared through blocks of tract housing, pounding the wheel in anger at his own stupidity. This wouldn't have happened in Boston, he told himself, wheeling onto the road leading back to the freeway. Yes it would, he reflected. And it'll happen again if you grow older and more reckless instead of older and smarter.

God-damn, he almost laughed. But the adrenalin got turned on after all, didn't it? he grinned. You old fool. You can still move your ass when somebody has it in their sights.

At the intersection with the freeway he frowned. Laredo? he asked himself when he had joined the flow of traffic on Highway 410 circling the city.

Where the hell is Laredo?

．．

"South of here, " said the waitress in the doughnut shop. She wiped the counter with a grey, greasy rag. "About a hundred and fifty miles. Just keep going south down Highway Eighty-one until there's no place else to go except Laredo. What the hell you want to go there for? Waste of good Texas gasoline, you ask me."

McGuire ordered a large black coffee and a sack of iced doughnuts.

"Not much down there?" he asked as he paid her.

"You got that right, mister."

· ·

Beyond San Antonio the highway ran through prosperous ranch land dotted with new housing developments. McGuire nibbled at the doughnuts and sipped the coffee, keeping the car's speed at the limit.

An hour out of the city the landscape began to change, growing rugged and craggy. Ranches and farms were smaller and less prosperous. In the empty pastures bordering the road, cactus competed with massive boulders for soil and space.

Even the vehicles on the road changed. He saw as many pickup trucks as ever, but they were older and moved more slowly, looking sad and tired with their dented fenders and cracked windshields. Most of the drivers were Mexican, their complexions as brown and their expressions as bleak as the landscape they drove through.

On the horizon, McGuire saw rusting water towers and lonely church steeples marking the locations of small towns abandoned by the interstate highway. Signs announced their passage: Pearsall, Dilley, Cotulia. He wondered what it was like to live in a sleepy Texas town called Dilley. Would it breed an Arthur Wilmer, so alienated and ignored by society that he would savagely murder a young woman just to prove he existed? Or a Marv Rosen, who once claimed he would have defended Adolf Hitler "if the retainer had been right"?

At Laredo the interstate sliced through an urban sprawl of

gas stations, chain motels, fast food restaurants and shopping malls. He ignored the exit signs until one announced "Last Exit Before Bridge To Mexico," where he turned and headed west through an almost deserted business section.

A narrow one-way street led him past empty stores whose whitewashed windows stared like blind eyes into the street; the abandoned parking lots grew neglected crops of weeds.

At the end of a street leading south he pulled over to the curb and left the car to walk to the river bank, where he stood and felt the afternoon sun on his face.

There was nothing grand about the Rio Grande. It was a muddy near-stagnant stream at the bottom of a weedy embankment. To McGuire's left, he could see the steel-and-concrete International Bridge clogged with traffic. Pedestrians moved across it faster than vehicles, which inched at a painfully slow pace, like the waters of the river far beneath them.

From Nuevo Laredo at the Mexican end of the bridge, mariachi music drifted back across the valley. Brightly lit bars lined the riverfront street and a sea of people swept up and down the main avenue leading south from the border. Nuevo Laredo seemed even poorer than Laredo, Texas, but much more alive.

McGuire nudged an empty beer can with his toe, watched it tumble down the eroded hillside and returned to the car.

. .

The pimply-faced attendant at the Exxon station on the interstate stared back at him blankly.

"Bledsoe?" he repeated. "Only Bledsoe I know is Mister Bledsoe, owns the big place over on San Bernardo."

"What big place?"

"The one that sells all the Mexican stuff. All them little statues and things."

McGuire asked how to find it.

"Two blocks over and turn right."

"What's the name? How will I know it belongs to Bledsoe?"

The attendant slapped his faded jeans. "Shee-it, mister," he sneered. "Can't hardly miss it. Takes up a whole city block."

. .

Bledsoe's Mexican Bazaar was indeed an entire block on what had once been the main north-south business avenue of Laredo, before the interstate highway carved a new path two blocks east. Now San Bernardo was a sad street, potholed and forlorn and lined with abandoned gas stations, dusty ice cream and doughnut shops and the uninviting rumps of motels flashing their glamorous fronts at the fast-moving interstate traffic.

McGuire parked across the street. "LAREDO'S BIGGEST IMPORTER OF MEXICAN ARTIFACTS" said a large hand-painted sign suspended on two massive steel towers, "WHOLESALE PRICES TO THE PUBLIC." A high chain-link fence enclosed the area. Two large gates opened onto San Bernardo; he watched as a truck entered a second gate from a side street. Nearby, in a small enclosed kennel area, a pair of Rottweiler guard dogs dozed in the shade.

Occupying the rear half of the property was a large hangar-like structure with offices and living quarters on the second storey. Wooden stairs led down past the dog kennel to the side gate.

Except for the area opening onto San Bernardo, every square foot of ground seemed cloaked in brightly painted ornaments whose designs stretched the boundaries of imagination and taste. From across the street McGuire could see birdbaths, elves, garden benches, ornamental outdoor tables, statues, fountains, oversized decorative planters and more, all manufactured from plaster, wrought iron, stone and wood.

At least a hundred plaster elves, identical in their tasselled caps, beards, pipes and waistcoats, stood near the entrance like a petrified army awaiting its marching orders. Beyond them, thousands of cheap ornaments were stacked higher than a man's head. Most were loose, perched precariously atop each other up to ten layers high; others sat on wooden shipping pallets, tightly enclosed in plastic shrink-wrap.

McGuire tucked his revolver in his jacket and walked casually across San Bernardo and down a corridor between pallets of plaster figurines. Plaster frogs crouched on plaster lily pads. Crudely made suits of armour stood at rusting attention. Filigreed iron furniture rose in tiers like building blocks. Half-sized marble statues of full-busted women gazed skyward, each with one hand modestly cupping a naked breast.

McGuire approached a middle-aged Mexican man in immaculate white T-shirt and khaki trousers who was crating plaster statues of fairies posing beneath plaster daisies.

"I'm looking for a man named Snyder," McGuire said quietly to the worker.

The Mexican glanced up, nodded his head towards the large open structure at the rear and resumed his work.

Entering the building, McGuire passed a chaotic world of smaller statues and papier-mâché decorations. Parrots, monkeys, reptiles and crude reproductions of cartoon characters were displayed on metal shelving under the harsh light of fluorescent lamps.

A man in his thirties with half-lidded eyes and a wispy beard watched McGuire enter. "What can I show you?" he called across the aisle.

McGuire studied him before replying. Like the Mexican, this man wore a T-shirt that shone brilliantly white. Unlike the Mexican, whose attitude was deferential, he carried himself with a swagger and a sense of authority, and he balanced himself on the balls of his feet as McGuire approached.

"Looking for Andrew Snyder," McGuire said softly.

The other man grinned, but his eyes narrowed.

"Andrew Snyder," McGuire said, taking another step closer. "He works here. Or he used to. Where is he?"

"I don't know who the hell you're talking about, mister." The grin grew wider as he shook his head and wiped the palms of his hands on his jeans. "Ain't nobody by that name working here."

"Bullshit." McGuire said it quietly.

The man sized him up carefully, measuring the age, height and weight of the older, shorter and lighter McGuire. He turned away for a moment, grinned even wider, and glanced back at McGuire again. He seemed to be stifling a laugh. "Oh, *that* Snyder," he said pleasantly. "Sure, he's right over here." He bounced away on the toes of his sneakers, gesturing to McGuire to follow.

Stopping at a scarred wooden door in the side of the building, he said, "Right in here, chief," and removed an open padlock that had been swinging on its hasp.

"Open it," McGuire said calmly.

His eyes still on McGuire, the younger man pushed the door inward. A dank, damp aroma wafted out of the windowless room.

"Now go in," McGuire told him.

"Sure thing, chief." The man walked past McGuire to enter the room before pivoting suddenly, his arm back and his fist clenched, legs spread to deliver the blow, just as McGuire's pistol crashed backhandedly against his cheek. He grunted a sudden curse of surprise and fell against the wall of the room, both hands at his face. Before he could scream, McGuire drove the fist of his other hand into the man's stomach, drew it back quickly and watched him fold at the waist to collapse, retching, on the dirt floor.

"Son, you're younger, bigger and heavier than I am," McGuire said to the prone figure. "But you're also twice as dumb and half as mean. I could see it coming with my eyes shut."

McGuire looked around. No one had seen or heard a

thing. He stepped out of the storage room and closed the door behind him, slipping the padlock through the hasp again, locking the beaten man inside.

He walked back to the Mexican labourer, his hand in his jacket pocket, the fingers gripping the pistol. "Show me Bledsoe," he said quietly. The Mexican looked up from his crouch and McGuire withdrew his pistol, letting his hand dangle at his side.

The Mexican blinked once before shrugging his shoulders and walking past McGuire to the main aisle leading to the street, with McGuire following a few cautious steps behind. On the way they passed two elderly women admiring a marble birdbath and a young couple arguing, with surprising passion, about whether to choose a green or a red papier-mâché parrot.

Ahead of them, a tall overweight man in an open-necked shirt stood with a clipboard in his hand. His complexion was red and raw and his eyes were large behind thick, rimless glasses. Nearby, two Mexicans in identical white T-shirts were stacking plaster flamingos while a younger man in sleeveless shirt and jogging shorts stood nearby, his well-muscled arms folded across his chest.

"*Señor* Bledsoe," the man with McGuire called out as they approached.

"What you got, Nando?" Bledsoe continued writing on the clipboard.

"I'm looking for Andrew Snyder," McGuire said before the Mexican could reply. He raised the gun to waist level. "And no jerking me around. Some other guy just tried it and now he's drizzling down his shirt in a storeroom around the corner."

Bledsoe looked up, adjusted his glasses, dropped his eyes to the gun in McGuire's hand and smiled. "Hey, hoss," he said, nodding at the revolver. 'What's this? Hell, you want a statue, you take a statue."

"I want Andrew Snyder," McGuire said evenly. "Just tell me where he is and I'm gone."

The two Mexicans looked briefly in McGuire's direction and, seeing the gun, quickly sat on their haunches, staring at the concrete floor. The young man in jogging shorts lowered his arms, watching McGuire.

Bledsoe stood, his mouth open in a broad smile, looking first at the muscular young man, then back at McGuire. He seemed to find the incident amusing. "What? You locked somebody in a storeroom? Who? What'd he look like? Must be Colin. Colin!" he called down the aisle of plaster figurines towards the street.

"The hell with him," McGuire said. "I want Snyder. That's all. Andrew Snyder. You Bledsoe?"

"Around here it's *Mister* Bledsoe," the younger man sneered.

"Where I come from, bullshit is bullshit," McGuire said. "Even if it stands six feet tall and wears glasses."

Bledsoe laughed aloud. "Ain't he somethin', Warren?" he said in admiration to his assistant. By his expression, it was clear Warren was unimpressed. "Hell, hoss, you can call me anything you want to." He leaned casually against a post. "Name's George Bledsoe, actually." He thrust a large pink hand towards McGuire. "What they call you at home?"

Stepping away from the hand, McGuire hooked the toe of his shoe around a plaster flamingo on the bottom layer of a pallet being loaded by the Mexicans. With a sudden kick, he dislodged the corner figure, sending several layers crashing to the floor.

Warren swore. The two Mexicans jumped up and stood to one side, their eyes still downcast.

McGuire leaned against another pallet of figures and smiled coldly at Bledsoe. "Amazing how clumsy I get with a gun in my hand," he said. "So before I start tripping over anything else, just tell me where I can find Andrew Snyder." George Bledsoe looked at the broken statues at his feet. The smile faded, then reappeared. "Hoss," he said, shaking his head. "I see that much shoot in a man's eyes, I figure it's time to start singing small." He handed his clipboard to Warren. "You know where the Old Mine Road is?"

"You going to tell me, or do I visit the tourist bureau?"

"You go back up the interstate about five miles. Look for an exit to the left. Big power plant there. Can't miss it. That's Old Mine Road. You go west about twenty miles till you see the sign. Bledsoe Mines. That's where old Andy works for me. Kind of a watchman. You go in there, you'll see Andy."

McGuire stared at Bledsoe for a moment. "If he's not there, I'm liable to come back mad and very clumsy," he said softly.

"Hell, hoss," Bledsoe grinned, "I'd have to be about as sharp as a bag of wet mice, bring a mean dozer like you here twice when I didn't want to see him once. You got business with Andy, that's Andy's lookout. Now, you mind if Warren and me get back to making a semi-honest dollar?"

McGuire angled his head towards the front of the building. "Go look after your customers," he said. "All of you. After I'm gone you might want to rescue the punk who tried to sucker me into a locked storeroom. But that's up to you."

Bledsoe ambled by, his heavy stomach spilling over his belt. "Right nice of you to take over like that," he drawled, avoiding McGuire's eyes as he passed. "Come on, Warren."

The other man followed, glaring at McGuire.

"You young ladies sure picked yourself a pretty birdbath there." Bledsoe's voice echoed through the building as he approached the elderly women. "God's truth, I was kind of saving that one for myself."

McGuire stepped quickly across the aisle and walked to the open gate facing the side street. He pocketed the revolver, circled the block and entered his car from the passenger side, keeping his eyes on the front gate.

Within the compound, Bledsoe watched him drive away.

Then, his faced clouded and severe, he spoke a few sharp words in Warren's ear and the younger man grinned before trotting to a telephone on the sales counter.

CHAPTER EIGHTEEN

The chimneys of the power plant stood like monuments on the horizon. When McGuire reached them, he turned west into the sun, a hazy orange balloon floating above a barren brown landscape.

Within a mile, the small houses, general stores, garden nurseries and gas stations lining the road gave way to pastures delineated by rusty barbed-wire fences.

McGuire checked his rear-view mirror repeatedly; no one appeared to be following him.

Soon the road surface began to deteriorate. The asphalt grew pock-marked; loose stones clattered against the car's fenders. There were no buildings to be seen and the patchy grazing land had been replaced with raw, red clay.

The sun sank lower, approaching the earth, and McGuire accelerated to race against the oncoming darkness. Half an hour after leaving Laredo, a tall metal structure loomed up from a field to his left. He slowed at a laneway where a faded sign announced "Bledsoe Mining. Unauthorized Persons KEEP OUT!"

McGuire withdrew the revolver from his jacket, placed it on the seat beside him and turned into the gravel lane.

Coming over a rise just beyond the entrance he passed a rusting dump truck, the hood and doors removed, the tires rotting on the wheels. At the top of the next rise he could see the full height of the ore-loading machinery, that had marked the mine's location from the road. Like the rest of the operation, it appeared to have been abandoned years ago; one end of a rubber conveyor belt dangled from the top of the structure like a dead serpent.

He drove cautiously through the mine site, feeling every nerve-end tingle as he passed a corrugated metal shed with "OFFICE" in faded white lettering over the open doorway and a long line of wooden buildings stretching down a weedy lane, their open windows staring blankly at the dying sun.

McGuire saw no sign of life: no vehicle tracks, no footprints.

He circled the grounds cautiously once, twice, one hand on the steering wheel, the other gripping his service revolver.

The gravel road continued beyond the office area and over another low rise. McGuire edged the car towards it, driving into the sun again, keeping his eyes moving and his senses alert.

Topping the rise was the mine head, marked by square timbers erected like some primitive wooden icon across an open pit. Rusting machine parts were scattered on the ground surrounding the pit, an open and bleeding wound in the red glow of the sunset. Gear-toothed wheels, levers, tools and other equipment lay where they had been discarded long ago.

McGuire stopped the car, switched off the engine and looked around. The silence covered him like a heavy blanket.

In the city, McGuire would frequently curse the unmuffled trucks, the piercing sirens, the incessant babble of humanity. Now, in a Texas desert glowing like molten metal in the light of a setting sun, he grew aware of the silent terror created by the total absence of sound — silence, without even a whisper of wind.

He scanned the horizon again. Deserted.

Except . . .

White, crisp and brilliant among the weathered wood and iron — a piece of paper, freshly nailed to the cross-beam timber over the mine shaft.

And a word printed on it in bold black letters.

McGuire stepped out of the car, his revolver in his hand. Moving in slow circles, he approached the mine head, seeing nothing but desolation, hearing nothing but his own heartbeat.

He reached the edge of the open pit and looked up to read the word on a large white envelope fastened to the cross-beam midway over the pit.

Snyder.

"Bullshit," McGuire muttered, then louder, shouting against the silence, "Bullshit!"

He wasn't going to crawl across a beam in the middle of the desert, hanging over an open hole in the ground. He looked around again, then walked towards the car.

He stopped. It could mean something. Anything.

He scanned the horizon again and circled cautiously back to the open pit marking the mine head.

The sandy walls at his feet sloped down to the dark, forbidding opening of the vertical mine shaft in the centre of the pit. Heavy machinery had once been installed in the pit to hoist ore from beneath the ground and convey miners up and down the shaft. Now only their concrete footings remained, set just beyond the rim of the crater; exposed iron reinforcing rods reached out of the concrete and into the air like spiny, rusting fingers.

McGuire studied the cross-beam above him again. The sturdy timber was more than a foot square. He pushed against the nearest upright supporting the cross-beam, testing its stability, confirming it was solidly fixed in the ground.

He shook his head.

Jesus.

Iron bolts on the upright beam would provide a grip for his feet. Crawling on his stomach along the cross-beam would bring him to the envelope. Which was probably empty. Which would make it all a trap.

You could drive away, McGuire told himself. See Bledsoe tomorrow. Except that he'll be ready for you. If it's a trap, he set it up. And he could have the same kind of trap waiting back in Laredo.

Or you could crawl up there, check the envelope and hope something inside leads you to Andrew Snyder. And the killer of Jennifer Cornell.

He scanned the horizon again. There was no sign of life. Darkness was creeping over the desert, the sky in the east already more ebony than blue.

He didn't really have a choice.

He said it aloud, wanting to hear the sound of his own voice again. "You don't really have a choice." Then he added: "You dumb son of a bitch."

Slipping the revolver into his jacket pocket, he began to shinny up the nearest vertical beam. This, he promised himself, was the last mine shaft he would ever crawl across in Texas.

At the top, he was bathed in the fading light of the sun, suspended just above the horizon. He lay lengthwise on the beam and began dragging himself on his stomach, closer to the envelope, telling himself not to look down, telling himself he would seize the envelope, return to the ground and be back inside his car in a minute. One minute. Sixty seconds.

The envelope was within reach when the wood beneath him exploded and the crack of a rifle shot echoed across the desert.

He remembered butterflies he had seen as a child. Where? A museum, probably. Collections of tropical butterflies displayed in deep cabinets. Each insect, its wings dutifully spread to display their vibrant colours and distinctive patterns, impaled on a shiny pin which pierced first their bodies, then the layer of cork beneath them.

He was the butterfly. He was pinned. He could not move.

From the direction of the setting sun, he heard the snick-snick of a lever-action rifle being reloaded. A hunting rifle, he told himself, standard Winchester probably. Equipped with a scope. For shooting deer, not butterflies.

The next shot struck just below his armpit, sending splinters flying into his face. His body jolted in response and he almost slipped from the beam as his reflexes screamed at him to put the beam between himself and his hunter.

The sniper was adjusting. First shot low and too far right. Next shot higher and to the left. Coming closer to the chest. Or the head.

He looked down. The vertical mine shaft gaped black, open and waiting, twenty feet below.

The snick-snick echoed again from somewhere near the sun.

Survive another shot, he told himself. Then survive the fall to the ground and survive the arrival of the sniper to finish you off.

One step at a time. That's all he could do. Survive one step at a time.

He shifted his body, trying to become a moving target while still hanging over the side of the beam. His arms were in near agony from the strain. His shoulders ached and his hands felt frozen. He had to hold on. If he dropped before another shot, the sniper would know he hadn't been hit. And he would lose the element of surprise.

He needed the element of surprise. It was all he had.

McGuire moved again, sliding his hands across the rough wood, hefting his hips upward to rest on the beam as the third shot echoed across the open sky and the air whispered just above his head.

Crying out, he dropped from the beam into the darkness below him, throwing himself away from the open shaft and sinking to his ankles in the sand. He fell forward and scrambled up the sides of the crevice, dog-paddling in the loose soil, hands and feet churning against gravity. His efforts loosened a large rock that crashed against his ankle and slid down the slope, plunging into the vertical mine shaft.

Only when McGuire had scurried around the side of the pit, clutched the corner of a concrete anchor and tried to calm his breathing did he hear the faraway sound of the boulder striking the bottom of the shaft.

Huddling against the concrete anchor, he tried to vanish within its shadow.

He has to make sure, he told himself, trying to keep his hand from trembling as he withdrew the revolver from his pocket. He has to come over here and see.

McGuire counted seconds, crouching ten feet below the western edge of the pit. Above him, the crimson light of the sun bled into the deeper blue of the sky.

If the sniper walked directly to the pit, McGuire could remain in the shadows until the last second. But if he circled to approach from the east, he would see McGuire easily. Then it would be a matter of firepower and accuracy. A Police Special revolver against a lever-action rifle at thirty feet.

McGuire grimaced. Even the butterflies had better odds.

Time expanded. It seemed like hours since McGuire had plunged from the beam before he heard the sound of footsteps taking long, slow strides on the loose soil.

The footsteps stopped.

He's looking around, McGuire told himself. Making sure I'm alone. Making sure there are no witnesses. Staying west of the mine head, keeping the sun behind him. If I hadn't climbed the beam he would have shot me before I got back to the car.

He set it up neatly. One good hit and I drop into the mine shaft. No blood on the ground. Neat.

The footsteps began again.

Don't circle, McGuire prayed.

He tensed at the first sight of the man's shadow cast into the pit by the setting sun. It crept over the rim above his head, grew down the walls of the pit to the open mouth of the shaft and began moving up the other side. A long, lean shadow elongated by the low angle of the light.

Son of a bitch is wearing a cowboy hat, McGuire frowned. John Wayne stalking Indians in the desert. God, he hated Texans.

A second shadow traversed the first and McGuire knew the man was carrying the rifle low across his body. He was relaxed, not expecting to fire again.

He heard the boulder fall, McGuire realized. He thinks I'm down there. Bledsoe called, told whoever is out there to bury me in the mine shaft. Probably suggested the envelope with Snyder's name on it as bait. Something to get me occupied, keep me from blowing the bastard's head off. McGuire extended his arms slowly, the revolver steady in his right hand, his left gripping his right wrist, and waited for the man to arrive at the brink of the pit. To hell, he said silently, with the Marquis of Queensberry.

Suddenly the other man was there above him, his eyes on the opening of the mine shaft beyond the place where McGuire lay. McGuire sighted on the arm holding the rifle, squeezed the trigger gently and felt the gun jump in his hand.

Like catching a sidearm fastball, he thought: the recoil of the gun slapping his hand, stiffening his wrist, driving his arm up and his shoulder back. Like catching a hard-thrown baseball.

The rifleman screamed in pain and surprise as he flung the rifle in front of him, the bones of his forearm shattered by the bullet from McGuire's gun. He stumbled forward, off balance and intent on his agony, as the rifle sailed into the pit. McGuire slid quickly aside to avoid the man, who was falling towards him and screaming a second scream which masked the echo of the first.

With his back to the plunging man, McGuire heard the

sickening liquid impact and a third scream, a long, shrill cry of agony and terror, and knew the man could fall no further than the top of the concrete anchor.

He gripped the side of the pit and pulled himself to the top. You have to look, he told himself. You have to look at him. He glanced quickly down at the man, groaned and turned away, then looked back again.

A butterfly.

Dressed in a tan shirt, matching chinos and lizard-skin boots, the man atop the concrete anchor had lost his hat in the plunge, spilling thick blond hair that hung back from a long angular face. He had twisted onto his back while falling, landing on the rusting iron rods which jutted from the concrete anchors up to the blood-red sky. Now he lay pinned there, his body jerking in spasms, his eyes wide and fearful.

McGuire returned his gun to his pocket and dropped down to the injured man. He counted six rods piercing the body, heard the man's laboured breathing and some strange liquid sounds he didn't want to think about.

"I'll get help," McGuire said, touching the man gently.

The man's eyes, swerving wildly in their sockets, found McGuire, rolled upwards, found him again.

"Snyder," he whispered. "Is that you? Are you Andy Snyder?"

The eyelids lowered. One leg moved in spasms.

In the rear pocket of the man's chinos, fastened to a belt loop by a long and elegant silver chain, was a worn leather wallet. McGuire removed it carefully, took out the driver's licence and read the name.

William Raymond Edwards.

McGuire seized the man by the shirt and began to lift him away from the rods, anger exploding within him. "God-damn it, you know! Tell me where Snyder is!"

His eyes snapping open again, the other man made an animal noise, long and loud and filled with agony and terror. Stunned by the sound, McGuire sat back on his haunches for a moment before swallowing once, hard, and bringing his mouth close to the dying man's ear. "Tell me where Snyder is," he said quietly. "Or I'll do it again."

"Cat . . ." the man began. Then: "Cat . . . alina . . ."

Blood began to spout like a geyser from around a rod which had penetrated the man's neck. It pulsed at a heart-beat rhythm, and as McGuire stepped aside, the man's spine curved upwards like an archer's taut bow and a final scream rent the air, echoing again and again from dark distant hills.

McGuire lay back against the side of the pit and watched the body relax, bathed in red beneath an angry crimson sky, before stumbling to his car and speeding away from the mine, seeing demons in every shadow cast by his headlights.

CHAPTER NINETEEN

"**Y**ou're the guy was looking for Mister Bledsoe, right?"

The pimply-faced youth studied McGuire curiously from the door of the service station office before draining his can of cola and crumpling it in his hand. "You find him?"

"I'm not looking for him any more." McGuire stepped out of the car, feeling the cool night air wash his skin. "I'm looking for a place called Catalina. Ever heard of it?"

The boy stared off across the interstate. "Not 'round here. 'Less'n you mean Catarina. Sure it's not Catarina? That's up near Crystal City."

"It could be. How far is that from here?"

"'Bout seventy-five miles. Just go north and take Highway Eighty-three. Can't miss it."

McGuire thanked the attendant and climbed into his car.

"'Less you mean the Catalina Bar," the youth offered.

"Where's that?" McGuire settled back in the seat.

"Just across the bridge. In Mexico."

"I don't think I'm looking for a bar."

"Thought you might be looking for that one."

McGuire shifted into drive. "Why?"

The youth flipped the crushed soda can in the air, pivoted on one foot, and caught it behind his back. "'Cause it's owned by Mister Bledsoe. Hell, everybody 'round here knows that."

. .

The International Bridge stretched from the dark emptiness of downtown Laredo, Texas, to the shining energy of Nuevo Laredo, Mexico.

Its pedestrian walkways were crowded with two-way traffic. American tourists, returning north with cheap souvenirs and duty-free liquor, wove past Mexicans walking in sullen silence, toting groceries in white plastic bags.

Vehicles on the bridge moved at two speeds. The faster line flowed into Mexico; painfully slow traffic crawled northward, where U.S. Customs inspectors harangued anyone with a brown face and a diffident manner.

Driving into Mexico, McGuire watched the crowds overflowing the streets ahead of him. At the Mexican end of the bridge, an official in a peaked cap gave the briefest of glances at McGuire and the car's Texas licence plates before waving him past.

The farther McGuire travelled along the southbound main street of Nuevo Laredo, the blacker the night became. Within three blocks, he was beyond the last of the garish neon-lit bars and shops catering to tourists. He swerved into a side street, parked and locked the car, and began walking back to the main avenue.

"*Por favor, Señor?*"

McGuire almost stumbled over a tiny Mexican girl, perhaps four or five years old, whose face shone in the weak glow of a streetlamp. One small hand, palm up, stretched towards him. She had thick, matted black hair and wore a shapeless and filthy cotton dress. Her feet were bare and dirty.

Fishing a dollar from his pocket, he placed it in her hand.

She looked at it solemnly, nodded "*Gracias*," and ran away into the darkness.

He walked through another block crowded with children and old women who beseeched him with empty hands and pleading gestures. You can't save the world, he told himself as he made his way between them, avoiding their eyes and keeping his hands in his pockets.

On the main avenue he shouldered past American tourists in polyester slacks and open-necked blouses and shirts, laughing their way back to the bridge that led home, ignoring bare-footed children with sad eyes who offered packages of gum, shrivelled bouquets of flowers, and strings of dried chilies and garlic buds for sale.

"*Buenas naches, Señor.*"

McGuire turned to see a cocky Mexican boy in T-shirt and jeans sitting on the fender of a car parked at the curb.

"What can I show you, *Señor?*" the boy asked, grinning lewdly. "You want donkey show? Young gorls? Young boys? I take you there. Tell me what you want, I take you."

"Where's the Catalina Bar?" McGuire asked.

The boy's smile grew wider and he looked away in mock disgust. "What you want to go there for?" he sneered. "Plenty more bars in town. With young gorls dancing. Nothing on. Nothing on top, nothing on bottom. Good margaritas, good mariachi."

McGuire thrust a five-dollar bill at him. "Just take me to the Catalina Bar," he said. "That's all."

Shrugging, the Mexican youth crumpled the bill into his pocket and slid from the car. "It's not far," he said, walking back in the direction McGuire had come from.

A block beyond McGuire's car, the boy waved him forward, crossed the avenue and stood at the corner, smirking back at him.

At the end of a short dead-end street, a large adobe building faced the avenue, crowned with blazing red and yellow neon signs. "Catalina Bar," the sign spelled, "A Favorite

Gringo Watering Hole Since 1925." Two overweight couples were stumbling through the wooden doors, arguing loudly among themselves in Texas drawls. The women wore their hair in beehives; the men growled at each other from beneath sweat-stained Stetsons.

The Mexican youth was already making his way back to the bridge, his hands in the pockets of his jeans.

McGuire waited for the tourists to pass, then stepped up to the entrance of the bar and opened the carved wooden door.

He walked into a cavernous room filled with smoke and hard-edged laughter, where groups of tourists sat nibbling food, sipping beer from long-necked bottles, and laughing and poking their companions. Sombre-faced Mexican waiters in white shirts and black trousers with stained aprons tied at their waists sped between the tables and the long bar against the wall to McGuire's right. Sawdust lay scattered on the floor, faded photographs hung in antique frames on the wall, and an unseen piano player hammered out ragtime music from somewhere at the rear of the room.

It was a contrived reproduction of a western saloon, untidy enough to appear authentic and efficient enough to quiet the qualms of middle-class Americans.

McGuire approached the bar where a platoon of waiters wore blank and weary expressions as they opened beer bottles, mixed oversized margaritas, and dispensed elaborate drinks topped with tiny plastic cactus plants. He leaned against the bar, ordered a Corona, and turned to watch the tourists nibbling on tortilla chips and melted cheese. Their conversation reached him in a muted roar, as thick and mingled as the tobacco smoke hanging in the air above them.

The Corona arrived cold and sweating in a clear glass bottle. McGuire tossed two dollars on the bar and drank the beer quickly, trying to wash away the dust and the visions that clung to him from the mine site. When he finished he motioned to the waiter, who leaned across the bar to retrieve the empty bottle.

"Another Corona?"

"No," McGuire said softly. "Just tell me where I can find a man named Andrew Snyder."

The waiter nodded solemnly. "Around the corner, to your right," he said, wiping the countertop. "Second door down."

McGuire scanned the room again before walking to where two arrows marked "Senors" and "Senoritas" pointed down a hallway at the end of the bar. With a last glance behind him, McGuire slipped a hand in his jacket pocket to grip his revolver and entered the corridor.

On the frosted glass panel of the second door, McGuire read "PRIVATE" in faded gilt lettering. He withdrew his gun and, with his free hand, turned the knob quietly.

Behind a desk in the middle of the small room sat a man with his back to the door, hunched over a book on a low table.

McGuire quickly closed the door behind him. "Don't even twitch," he ordered, the gun extended, "or I'll blow your head off."

The man, who had begun to straighten at McGuire's entrance, nodded his head slowly, still facing the wall.

"You Andrew Snyder?" McGuire barked.

The head nodded again.

"Raise your hands where I can see them."

The head nodded a third time. Then, with deliberate slowness, the arms began to rise from the desk top.

McGuire swallowed, turned away and lowered the gun, shaking his head in disbelief. Instead of hands, two shiny steel hooks extended above the other man's head. "May I turn around now?" he asked, still facing the wall.

"Sure," McGuire replied. "Turn around. Stand up and dance. Do a cartwheel out the door. Who cares?"

Andrew Snyder swivelled in the chair to face McGuire. He

had a boyish face, the nose slightly upturned, the eyes clear and large, the hairline just beginning to recede.

"You're kind of old to be doing this, aren't you?" Snyder asked. He rested his forearms on the desk, crossing the two hooks in front of him.

"Some days I'm too old to get out of bed." McGuire dropped his revolver back into his jacket pocket, then frowned and asked, "Too old to be doing what?"

"Working for Mister Bledsoe."

"Bledsoe?" McGuire snorted. "What makes you think I work for Bledsoe?"

"Because he sends people here," Snyder said. "New people. To see me." He raised the steel hooks. "As a warning." Sensing McGuire's confusion, he dropped the hooks heavily on the desk again. "In case they get any ideas about stealing from him. He tells them to meet me and ask what happened. And I tell them."

"You tell them what?"

He said it calmly and without emotion, as though he were describing a shopping trip or visit to the dentist. "I tell them Mister Bledsoe cut off my hands with a hatchet for stealing half a kilo of cocaine."

. .

"What's your interest in Bledsoe?"

Andrew Snyder gripped a small glass of tequila and ice between the tongs of one hook, watching McGuire warily. They were seated in a rear corner of the barroom, opposite the old upright piano painted a garish pink and purple. Taking a break, the piano player slouched on the stool, looking as tired and tuneless as the piano itself.

McGuire had ordered another Corona. "I don't give a damn about his narcotics business if that's what you think," McGuire answered. "I've had enough experience in drugs to know that you can't get as big as Bledsoe without a lot of important local people helping out, and a lot of other people just not giving a damn. They want to put up with that crap in their own backyard, it's fine with me, so long as they keep it there and leave me out of it. So whatever you say on that score isn't going any further than me." He offered his hand.

Snyder cocked his head and smiled indulgently at the natural gesture, raising his right hook and arching his eyebrows.

McGuire withdrew his hand. "Joe McGuire," he said. "Boston Homicide."

Snyder shrugged. "You're right." His voice was soft and he punctuated his words with slight grins that vanished almost as soon as they appeared. "People around here know the score. They've either been bought off or choose to mind their own business. Everything from here to Brownsville comes through Laredo. What he can't sell in San Antonio he ships further north. Austin, Dallas, sometimes as far as Tulsa."

"Cocaine?"

"Yeah, up from Colombia in trucks, vans, whatever's moving. Then over the border every way you can think of. Some you can't."

"How did you connect with a guy like him?"

Snyder sipped his tequila and smacked his lips. "The word gets around. You prove yourself on a few small deals and you get an offer for something bigger, a chance to make more money with less risk at the wholesale end. I'd been doing a little dealing up in San Antonio. Made enough to buy a house. I was like everybody else back then. Thought I would just make enough to get settled and go straight. Find a wife. Have a family. Then my father moved in with me."

"I met your father," McGuire interrupted.

"How is he?" Snyder seemed genuinely interested.

"Taking it easy."

Snyder's face darkened. "Did he say anything about me?"

"Hardly anything at all. Just told me you were working for Bledsoe. Didn't even hint it might be illegal."

Snyder searched for the truth in McGuire's eyes. "He

knows and he doesn't know. About me, I mean. Doesn't want to know too much." He glanced away, then back at McGuire. "Why were you looking for me in the first place?"

"Do you have a sister?"

Snyder grinned. "Hell, no."

"Ever been to Boston?"

"Never. So what's this all about?"

McGuire leaned back in his chair, trying to decide whether he could believe this man, watching him in silence. "Tell me why Bledsoe did it," he said finally, indicating Snyder's hooks.

"I told you. I slipped a half-kilo bag into my pocket one night. I was working at a place out on the Old Mine Road —"

"I've been there," McGuire broke in.

Snyder looked at him with renewed interest.

"I'll tell you about it later," McGuire said before Snyder could speak.

Beginning hesitantly and growing slowly in confidence, Snyder described what happened.

"One of the other guys saw me take the coke. That night, after we finished, Mister Bledsoe and two of the others said they were coming over the border to do some business and have a party. Said there were some new whores in from Mexico City. Told me Bledsoe booked them for us for the night. He owns a brothel west of here."

Snyder looked around the room, gathering strength to continue.

"I don't talk about it much," he said apologetically. "The details, I mean." A waiter approached with another tequila and ice for Snyder and a Corona for McGuire. When he left, Snyder continued.

"They invited me along. Practically ordered me. I didn't want to look suspicious so I had to go. I left the drugs in my car. I planned to leave the next day, sell the coke in San Antonio and go back to California. Maybe see my mother. Anyway, they took me to this place south of town." Snyder clicked one hook around his glass and stared into it. "How much do you want to hear?"

"As much as you want to tell me."

"As soon as we got in the room, the two guys with Bledsoe grabbed me. They forced my arms down on this old table and Mister Bledsoe came in with a thick leather belt and a hammer. He nailed the belt across my arms. Then they did it."

McGuire said nothing. He picked up his beer to take a sip but changed his mind.

"They used an axe," Snyder said in a voice dry of emotion. "First he told me why he was doing it. Then he showed me the towels they had brought. So I wouldn't bleed to death. He said he didn't want to kill me and he would even give me a job when I recovered. But I had to learn a lesson."

"How could you handle that?" McGuire whispered. "Sitting there, knowing what was going to happen?"

Snyder shook his head. "I wasn't there. Sometimes . . ." He looked away, then back down at his drink. "I met a girl once who had been raped in San Francisco. Over and over again, for hours, by a motorcycle gang. I asked her the same question. She told me 'I wasn't there. My body was there but me, my mind and me, we went somewhere else.' And that's all I can say about it."

Snyder told of being driven to the hospital in Nuevo Laredo, the towels wrapped around the stumps of his arms to staunch the bleeding. He described staggering into the hospital unable to speak, welcoming the fog of the anaesthetic, and waking with the hope that it had all been a nightmare until he saw the drab grey walls, smelled the aroma of the sick and dying, and felt the pain like glowing coals filling the space where his hands had been.

In the afternoon, a Mexican police officer arrived to cluck over Snyder's misfortune and suggest that people be more careful when working with hay balers.

"So Bledsoe bought off the police?" McGuire asked.

Snyder fixed him with a cold smile. "They've been bought off for years. You go over there now, to the police station, and ask to see my accident report. If you can read Spanish, it will tell you I lost my hands in a hay baler on a farm south of town." He snorted, a short sarcastic laugh. "Which shows how arrogant they are."

"Why?"

"Nobody bales hay around here. There's not a hay baler between here and San Antonio."

McGuire nodded. "Why are you still here? How can you associate with a man who would do this to you?"

Snyder bit his bottom lip. "It's the best deal I can get. I run the place. Make a good profit too. Bledsoe pays me well and I only see him four, five times a year. He acts like nothing happened. Puts his arm around my shoulder, asks how my girlfriend is, how her family's keeping. She's Mexican. She's very pretty, very sweet. I love her and support her family. Without me, they would be begging in the streets. And . . ." He studied the sawdust on the floor. "I don't want to go home like this." He gestured with his hooks. "I couldn't if I wanted to."

"Why can't you?"

"Because Bledsoe would have me killed. He promised if I ever cross the border, he'll kill me. I believe him."

"So tell the Border Patrol," McGuire began, before seeing the expression in Snyder's eyes.

"Come on, McGuire," Snyder said with contempt. "How do you think a man like Bledsoe moves a hundred kilos of coke across the border every month? You think he's just lucky?"

"He can't buy off the entire Border Patrol."

"He doesn't have to!" Snyder snapped. "All he needs is . . ." He glanced around and lowered his voice. "Look, I could tell you . . ." he began and faltered again. "There's a car that belongs to one of the guys at the bridge. The way he parks it in the morning, nose in or nose out, tells Bledsoe something. A blind lowered in an office window tells him something else. There's never any contact. Never any direct payoff. Just some deposits made in bank accounts in Juarez. Ten seconds after I blew the whistle on Bledsoe, he would know about it. He would get rid of the evidence. Then he would get rid of me. In jail, in a safe house, wherever." He shrugged. "I'm better off here. I'm safe. I'm as happy as a man without hands can be."

"You said he owns a lot of property over here. What does he do with it? Use it to launder money?"

Snyder nodded. "But it's not as easy as it used to be. Time was, he could come over here and buy up a block of property with cash. But soon every property owner here knew what he was doing. They inflated their prices and offered him peanuts when he was ready to sell. I heard the last deal cost him sixty cents on the dollar. And now there's a glut on the market. Everybody's in the business. The price on the street is maybe a third of what it used to be," Snyder explained. "He's cancelled shipments for a few months until the price goes up. Meanwhile, he just sits on his cash."

"How much?"

"I heard ten million. I believe it."

"Where?"

"In that dumpy office apartment over the warehouse on San Bernardo. Probably under the floorboards." Snyder grinned and shook his head. "He can't spend it over here because the locals will rip him off. He can't take it to the bank because they have to report deposits that big to the Feds. He even lives alone up there, over that junkyard he calls a business, because he can't trust having anybody in the same room with him and his money. So there he is, stuffing it between the rafters like insulation."

"Nice to know money still can't buy happiness," McGuire smiled.

"Did you see the dogs?" Snyder asked suddenly.

"The Rottweilers? Good guard dogs."

"They're killers. Sometimes he sends Warren and Colin out at night to pick up stray cats, bring them back to San Bernardo. The three of them sit on the porch and drop the cats into the kennel with the Rottweilers and watch the dogs tear them apart." He sipped nervously at his drink. "Warren told me Bledsoe once had a guy killed by those dogs. Out near the mine site. I believe him."

"Maybe you're better off over here after all."

Snyder leaned back in his chair and shrugged. "I have a good life here. I take care of Bledsoe's investment. I run the bar well. There's no way I could get another job as good as this with these things," he gestured with the steel hooks.

"And Bledsoe uses you to keep his people in line."

"Something like that."

"When did this happen? With your hands?"

Snyder closed his eyes. "One year and two months ago. And ten days," he added. "Think I can forget something like that?"

The two men sat and contemplated a shared horror, one attempting to wrap his imagination around it, the other striving to extinguish the memory. During the silence between them, the piano player slid back on his bench and began a Scott Joplin rag in a jagged rhythm. No one in the room seemed to notice; not a head turned, not a conversation paused.

In an almost conciliatory tone, McGuire asked: "Did you know Jennifer Cornell?"

Snyder raised a hook and scratched his right ear. "I know the name."

"She was the daughter of your father's second wife Suzanne."

"Jennifer. Yeah, I remember her now. I only met her once. No, twice. Second time at her mother's funeral."

"What do you recall about her?"

"Not a lot. Let's see, the first time would have been just

after Suzanne and Pop were married. Jennifer was talking about going to college or something. I remember she kept pumping me about California. She was thinking of going to school there. Lots of glamour, she thought. What's she up to now?"

"She's dead." McGuire watched for a telltale response. "She was murdered last summer. In Boston."

Snyder shook his head. "She was a bright girl. A little stuck on herself but kind of attractive." He looked at McGuire with a crooked smile. "You think I had something to do with it?"

McGuire ignored the question. "Last summer, just before she died, someone was living with her and posing as you. She was showing him off. She introduced him as Andrew Cornell and said he had been living in California."

"Hey, McGuire," Snyder interrupted. "I spent a couple of hours with the woman once. We drank some beers and I listened to her talk about herself. She was one of those women, she'd talk about anything as long as it had something to do with Jennifer Cornell. I never saw her again until she came down for her mother's funeral."

"Did you spend time with her then?"

"Not a lot. To tell you the truth, she was pretty angry at me because my father was driving the car when Suzanne was killed. Naturally, she grouped both of us together. I remember she made a point of not even helping me into the limo on the way to the cemetery."

"Why would you need help?"

"Because I was on crutches. I was in the car when Pop rolled it. Broke my right ankle. Suzanne was thrown halfway out the window and the car rolled over on her."

"Tell me how it happened."

"We were all drunk. I was passing through town doing some . . . What the hell, I was dealing coke. Made a score in Philly. So I stopped off on my way back to California to see the old man, take him out to dinner. We all drank too much and I fell asleep in the back seat on the way home. Next thing I know, I'm lying on the grass and Pop, he's bent over Suzanne, trying to wake her up. Anybody could see she was dead. Pop, he came out of it without a scratch."

McGuire drained the last of his beer. "Whoever was posing as you in Boston last summer," he said, studying the empty bottle, "was the last to see her alive. And he disappeared the night she was murdered."

"I've never been in Boston in my life," Snyder said in an even voice, his eyes never wavering from McGuire's. "And even if I had been there last summer, I would have been wearing these," he added, displaying the hooks. "How was she killed?"

"Struck from behind with a club and left to drown."

"You think I could swing a club with these?"

McGuire shook his head solemnly and stood up to leave.

Walking across the room with McGuire, Snyder stopped to give instructions to a waiter, told a barman to bring up a fresh block of ice, and congratulated another waiter on the birth of his son.

"You run a tight ship," McGuire said at the doorway.

They stepped outside. The night air smelled fresh and they both breathed deeply to clear their lungs of smoke and the aroma of stale beer.

"It's not a bad place," Snyder said, looking up at the darkened sky. He grinned slyly at McGuire. "Be a hell of a lot nicer if we didn't have to put up with so many loud Yankee tourists."

"Are you afraid of Bledsoe?" McGuire asked.

"No," Snyder replied without hesitation. "He needs me. I'm valuable to him. George Bledsoe takes care of his valuables. As long as I keep doing well here and never cross the bridge, he'll take care of me. I like what I'm doing. I love my girlfriend. I even feel more Mexican than American sometimes." He shrugged. "But I still want to kill him."

McGuire turned to walk away. He had taken three paces

when Snyder called his name suddenly and McGuire stopped to look back.

"You said you were at the mine today, right?" Snyder asked.

"For a few minutes," McGuire said cautiously.

Snyder closed the space between them and lowered his voice. "Did you see anybody there? Guy with long blond hair and a hump on his nose? Stands six-two, six-three?"

"What about him?"

"Did you see him or not?"

"I saw somebody who looked like that."

Snyder cursed. "Edwards," he said, staring at the ground. "Billy Ray Edwards."

McGuire said nothing.

"Remember I told you they used the axe on me?" Snyder said, avoiding McGuire's eyes. "Well, it wasn't Bledsoe. He got Billy Ray to do it. Didn't have to ask Billy Ray twice, either. He's an animal. He's so crazy, Bledsoe tries to keep Billy Ray at the mine. Afraid to have him in town too much. So he pays him to be a watchman and do the work Bledsoe and the others can't stomach." Snyder shook his head violently. "Crazy. He's a crazy man."

"Don't worry about Edwards any more," McGuire said softly.

"Why?"

"Just don't worry about him, that's all."

"Is he dead?"

McGuire smiled silently and turned to walk away again.

"He's dead, isn't he?" Snyder said to McGuire's back.

"What difference does it make?" McGuire called over his shoulder.

"Because I wanted to ask him."

McGuire stopped again and looked back at the man with

hooks for hands standing silhouetted in the red and yellow lights of the bar sign. "Ask him what?"

"What he did with them. My hands. What did he do with my hands?"

CHAPTER TWENTY

By ten o'clock the town had been returned, as it was every evening, to its inhabitants. The souvenir shops, abandoned by the tourists, had closed their doors and darkened their lights; metal screening had been drawn across the liquor stores and the street vendors had trundled their carts off the avenue.

McGuire walked slowly back to the car, his shoulders slumped. He felt old; he felt weary. Most of all, he felt defeated.

As he walked, he passed men slouched on benches in a dusty space which had once been an elegant town square. A woman carrying a small baby papoose-style was bent almost double into a trash container, the upper half of her body hidden inside the barrel as she searched for food. On her back the baby wailed sadly, its tiny face creased with pain and hunger and anger. Adolescent boys, their faces so hardened that their eyes seemed to withdraw deeper into their sockets, offered McGuire drugs and women.

McGuire sat behind the wheel of his car collecting his thoughts. He wouldn't bother to confirm Snyder's story. Snyder didn't match the description of Andrew Cornell.

McGuire was convinced he had never been in Boston. And he hadn't killed his stepsister. They were further from solving the murder of Jennifer Cornell than ever.

And nobody cares but me, McGuire reflected.

Anger and frustration began to boil in him.

In what he had always considered an unfair world, McGuire devoted his life to redressing the balance, tipping the scales in defiance of perpetual injustice. Suddenly, the unfairness seemed overwhelming to him.

He had gambled on discovering a new clue to the murder of Jennifer Cornell — not for an abstraction like justice, or even for practical gains like deterring crime. Or to satisfy a need for success and achievement.

He did it because it was his job. More important, it was his identity.

Now he had lost the gamble. The Cornell file would remain ignored and forgotten. No one would care except McGuire. And few people would even understand *why* McGuire cared. The little girl with the solemn face who had accepted his hand-out an hour earlier was doomed to the same unmourned, forgotten fate as Jennifer Cornell.

He started the car. You don't need to care, he told himself. Nobody ever told you to care, so nobody will give a damn if you stop caring.

. .

From the moment he cleared U.S. Customs and began driving north into Laredo, he knew he was being followed.

McGuire turned casually down one street, then another, watching the dark pickup truck trailing several car lengths behind him, two men inside.

On San Bernardo Avenue, he wheeled into the parking lot of a fast-food restaurant and watched as the truck drove slowly past. McGuire recognized the driver and passenger as Bledsoe's men: Colin, wearing a fresh bandage across his cheek, and Warren, the muscular dark-haired man.

McGuire entered the restaurant, ordered a take-out coffee and emerged to see the truck parked at an abandoned service station across the street.

Leaning against the car, he sipped the coffee in full view of the men and considered what they might do. They could follow him north to San Antonio and simply ensure that he left town. Or watch him check into a motel and perhaps fire-bomb his room. Or sideswipe him on the interstate. Or fire a shotgun through his window as they passed him on the darkened highway . . .

Or McGuire could choose to do something — something for Andrew Snyder's hands and for the little girl across the bridge who begged for money while Bledsoe crammed his floorboards with it. It would be a way of pointing the finger, of redressing the balance.

So let's do it, McGuire told himself. You want to give me a reason to care? he mused. Maybe you have. "Let's do it," he said aloud, and tossed the empty cup into a waste container.

Back in the car, he drove north on San Bernardo, turning east and passing under the interstate a few blocks before Bledsoe's Mexican Bazaar, watching the pickup truck match his speed a hundred feet behind him. He passed shopping malls, trailer parks and baseball diamonds before the land opened up and a highway sign told him he was fifty-eight miles from Freer, Texas. The road was two lanes wide and empty of traffic — a thin ribbon through empty range.

"Let's do it," McGuire repeated angrily, and he pushed the accelerator to the floor.

The engine came to life with a roar and the Ford lurched ahead into the darkness. He switched his headlights to high-beam, slipped the revolver from his pocket and watched the speedometer climb past sixty, seventy, eighty. In the rear-view mirror, the pickup lagged behind momentarily before matching McGuire's pace.

His headlight beams revealed a rise in the road perhaps half a mile ahead. He measured the distance in his mind, fixed his eyes on the crest of the hill and quickly turned off his headlights, becoming all but invisible to the truck pursuing him.

His eyes grew accustomed to the darkness, and McGuire could make out deep ditches lining the road. The lights of the pickup bounced in his rear-view mirror as he felt the car heave over the low hill. Beyond the crest, the truck's lights vanished in the mirror; McGuire steered the car across the dark road into the other lane, slowed his speed, then jammed down on the brake pedal while twisting the steering wheel sharply to the right.

The Ford's tires howled in protest as the rear of the car swung around in a smoothly executed hundred-and-eighty-degree manoeuvre and the vehicle slammed to a stop in its own lane again, facing back to Laredo and the oncoming truck, whose headlights were glowing like a corona just beyond the crest of the hill.

McGuire had the door open before the car ceased shuddering. He tugged at the headlight switch as he rolled out of the car onto the grassy shoulder and dropped into the dry ditch beside the highway.

At eighty miles an hour, the pickup crested the rise in the road to encounter McGuire's car in its own lane, the high-beam headlights shining brightly into the driver's eyes.

Momentarily blinded, the driver tried to brake his vehicle and swing into the other lane to avoid McGuire's car. But McGuire's manoeuvre had been practised, controlled and anticipated; the driver of the pickup relied on instinct and surrendered to panic.

From the ditch, McGuire watched as the truck swerved away from him into the darkness, suddenly lurching to the left before rising in the air and crashing into the open ditch on the other side of the highway in an explosion of twisted metal and shattered glass.

In the eerie silence that followed, the truck's horn blasted from the wreckage, steady and undying.

McGuire pocketed his revolver and began crawling from the dry run-off ditch just as a voice cut through the night air, crying in anger and pain.

"Where are you, you bastard?" the man screamed. "I want you, whoever you are!"

McGuire ducked below the edge of the ditch again as footsteps came running raggedly up the road to his car, its headlights still piercing the night.

A rifle fired, the bullet striking McGuire's car with a metallic whine.

"You sumbitch, I'll feed your liver to the dogs, I swear!" the voice screamed hysterically.

The man reached the door of McGuire's car and wrenched it open with one hand. In the crook of his other arm he carried an automatic rifle. The interior light of McGuire's car illuminated his face as he thrust his head into the empty car. McGuire could see a piece of the man's scalp was torn and crumpled like an orange peel; blood flowed freely down his face and into his thin beard.

"Colin," McGuire called out from the shadows of the ditch.

A shot rang from the rifle, scattering dirt wildly behind McGuire, who ducked below the rim of the ditch and ran crab-wise several steps to his right.

"First you kill Billy Ray and now Warren's dead!" Colin screamed. Two more shots blasted in McGuire's direction.

McGuire moved further along the ditch as Colin stumbled away from the car, shouting curses. He fired another shot at the ditch where McGuire had been waiting, the muzzle blast flashing red in the blackness.

"Leave it be, Colin," McGuire called, before ducking away as another shot from the rifle struck the wall of the ditch behind him.

To the other man, McGuire was a voice in the dark. But to McGuire, the muzzle flashes pinpointed Colin's location as though he were standing in the noonday sun.

Surrendering to instinct, McGuire raised his gun in a two-handed target stance, aimed at the location of the last muzzle flash and squeezed off three shots in rapid succession.

He heard the rifle clatter to the roadway. Something soft and yielding followed it to the pavement.

McGuire pocketed his gun and climbed out of the ditch, walking to where Colin lay face down on the shoulder of the road near McGuire's car. He nudged the man with his toe, then rolled him onto his back. In the spill from his car's headlights he could see three entry wounds in the man's chest. They bubbled with the last intake of breath before Colin shivered and relaxed a final time.

The motion dislodged something inside Colin's denim jacket and McGuire reached down to withdraw a plastic bag of white powder.

Headlights flashed in the distance, somewhere to the east. McGuire moved quickly to his car, slipped it into gear and swung the vehicle to the other side of the road, heading west, back towards Laredo.

The sound of the pickup's horn faded with the distance, an endless moan grieving for the two dead men he left behind.

· ·

"I seen more of you than I seen of the sun today." The teen-age gas station attendant slammed the trunk shut. "Looks of things, I won't be seeing you again for a spell. You heading somewhere into open country?"

"Kind of," McGuire replied, handing him money. "Know where I can get some hamburgers this time of night?"

"How you want 'em?"

"Thick and juicy."

"Fat Frank's. 'Bout a mile up on your right."

McGuire slipped behind the wheel. "You're a tribute to the Texas tourist board," he smiled as he drove away.

· ·

Precisely at midnight, McGuire stood in a telephone booth directly across the street from Bledsoe's Mexican Bazaar. He dropped a coin in the slot and dialled a number.

In the lighted living quarters above the rear of the warehouse, a shadow moved behind a drawn blind.

"Bledsoe," a man's voice growled in McGuire's ear.

"I just killed your dogs," McGuire said.

"Who the hell is this?"

"Your dogs, Bledsoe. They're dead. At the front of your yard. Right at the fence. Haul ass out here and see for yourself."

He hung up, dropped another coin in the slot and dialled 911.

"There's a fire at Bledsoe's warehouse on San Bernardo," McGuire said to the woman who answered. He measured his words carefully, knowing they were being recorded — "Now," he added, and hung up again.

Leaving the telephone booth, he walked casually across San Bernardo to stand in the darkness near his car, arriving just as Bledsoe emerged from his apartment carrying a rifle. His eyes sweeping the yard, Bledsoe reached out a hand and pulled a large electrical switch near the doorway.

Suddenly quartz lights flooded the open area in a harsh green glare. Gnomes, cartoon characters, flamingos, rusting armour, Venus de Milos — thousands of plaster creatures stood and pranced in the brilliance of the floodlights like denizens of a grotesque miniature world.

Near the locked gates at the San Bernardo entrance lay the two dogs, the remains of several hamburgers in their stomachs, each heavily laced with the cocaine McGuire had taken from Colin's jacket.

At the sight of the dogs, Bledsoe looked furiously around him, stopping only once to smell the air and frown at the smell of gasoline drifting over the complex.

"Where you at, hoss?" Bledsoe shouted. "I find you,

you're lizard shit, hear me?" He looked around again and clambered down the stairs, running to his dogs.

McGuire stepped from the shadows and crossed to the side gate. He stopped at the wet trail leading under Bledsoe's stairs through the hole in the wire fence he had forced with a tire iron as the Rottweilers lay dying.

Casually withdrawing a match, he lit it, watched it flare, and dropped it into the dampness at his feet.

The gasoline ignited into a path of fire which raced through the fence to the five-gallon can directly under Bledsoe's wooden stairway. With an explosion of flame that momentarily rivalled the glare from the floodlights, the fuel erupted into the air and began consuming the structure.

McGuire turned his back to the inferno. He could feel the heat through his jacket. He could hear Bledsoe running and screaming in panic through the yard, colliding with plaster gnomes and stumbling over ceramic birdbaths in his race to reach the stairs.

The Ford started easily. McGuire drove slowly, methodically away, without looking back.

. .

He woke the next morning in a motel room on the edge of town. The air conditioner clattered at the window, its decorative grille cracked and dusty. He showered, dressed and stepped into the heat of the late morning.

In a coffee shop across the street he ate breakfast and eavesdropped on the conversation of men sitting astride chrome stools at the counter, men who pushed their greasy caps up from their foreheads before speaking and stirred sugar into their coffee with exaggerated arm motions. They all spoke in lazy drawls separated by long periods of silence, as though they were assembling their sentences in precise order before voicing them.

"You hear how much money they found up there?" The

speaker was thin and wiry, dressed in a faded rodeo shirt with fancy stitching and silver trim on the collar and cuffs.

"Millions," replied another. He was fat and balding with a black beard, thick and wild on his chin. "And that's what weren't all burnt to hell. Most of it's ashes now."

"Fellow I know on the fire department, he says the floorboards were all stuffed with money like an old maid's mattress." The speaker was out of McGuire's line of vision. "Thing I'd like to know is, where in hell did Mister Bledsoe get himself so much money anyhow?"

The fat bearded man laughed over his coffee. "Shee-it, Henley. What'd you do, get yourself raised by armadillos? Hell's bells, everybody knows where he got that money. Just never knew he'd be such a damn fool to keep it all together up there."

"I had that much money, I'd be gone," said the man in the rodeo shirt sadly. "I'd just be gone to some place where I could sit by the ocean, watch people fish, and have young women bring me drinks all day. Wouldn't stay in this dust bowl."

"Hear he's hurt bad," someone offered.

"He'll live," another suggested.

"Guy on the fire department, he says it took three of 'em to keep Mister Bledsoe from going back in there. Said his shirt was near burnt off him and he was still trying to get up-stairs."

"It's all tied in with those two dudes they found out on Highway Fifty-nine," the bearded man added. "Colin what's-his-name and that Warren guy. You know, Booker's cousin."

"Couple of white trash," someone said bitterly. "No loss."

"Deputy Morrison, he's telling everybody it was a settling of accounts," the bearded man continued. "Drug stuff. Prob-ably Mexicans or them crazy Colombians. Says Bledsoe probably didn't pay for a shipment or something. Says it looks like that to him, and he don't plan to break any speed records hunting down that scum. Probably halfway back to South America by now anyway."

"Let 'em all kill each other off," somebody observed. "Damn well shouldn't waste taxpayers' money chasing them," he added amid a chorus of murmured agreement.

McGuire finished his coffee and left.

. .

He took a side road north of Laredo, cruising slowly through dusty towns with names like Asherton, Carrizo Springs and Crystal City. In Uvalde he turned east to drive through Sabinal and Hondo and Castroville, where the highway became a four-lane expressway. McGuire almost regretted the disappearance of the brown desert wasteland replaced by strips of gas stations and billboards.

At the San Antonio airport, the rental car attendant questioned a bullet hole in the Ford's rear fender.

"Drive through a lot of open country?" he asked, and when McGuire replied he had, the attendant nodded. "Probably deer hunters. Can't find a buck to shoot at, they'll bury a slug in a car fender for kicks. Looks like somebody dinged your front bumper too. Good thing you took the collision coverage."

"Good thing," McGuire agreed.

McGuire waited for his flight to Boston in the bar drinking beer and thinking of nothing, remembering everything.

Two hours later he watched the dry Texas landscape grow smaller beneath him as he flew home, north towards a cold sun.

CHAPTER TWENTY-ONE

The sun followed McGuire home. He awoke the next morning to discover it shining through his bedroom window, melting the last of the snow that had fallen three days earlier.

An hour later he was greeted at the door of the house in Revere Beach by Ronnie Schantz, who thrust a mug of coffee in his hand and kissed him on the cheek. "Missed you," she said. "And guess who else has?"

. .

"How many laws do you think I broke?"

Ollie Schantz had listened in silence, arching his eyebrows at McGuire's description of the incident at the mine and the deaths of Warren and Colin. His right hand continued to squeeze the tennis ball, whose surface had split from the constant flexing. The muscles and sinews on the back of his hand, once withered and weak, now stood out in relief. A new speaker-phone sat on the bed near his right hip.

"In Texas, probably none," Ollie replied. "Except maybe drinking Mexican beer instead of Lone Star. So what are you going to do now?"

"Give the Cornell file back to Kavander. Maybe with my badge on it. And then get away from this cold weather. San Antonio's a long way from heaven, but at least you can live through November down there. There has to be some place just as warm but nicer." He stood up. "I'll drop back later, let you know what happened with Kavander."

"Wait a minute."

McGuire turned at the open door. Ollie was frowning at him, his hand squeezing and releasing, squeezing and releasing the tennis ball. "Snyder, he was in the car when her mother died?"

McGuire nodded.

"Broke his ankle?"

"That's what he told me. The old man wasn't hurt at all."

"And he's hobbling on it when the Cornell woman comes down for the funeral?"

"What's the point?"

Ollie rolled his head to the side. "Who said there was one?"

McGuire shrugged and left the room.

. .

"I'm back."

Jack Kavander lowered the memo he had been reading and glared over the sheet of paper at McGuire. "What's this, you doing an impression of MacArthur returning to the Philippines?" he growled. "Where the hell have you been?"

"Away." McGuire sat in the chair opposite Kavander's desk. "I needed to get away. To think."

"Other guys go fishing or sit in a bar to work things out. McGuire, he has to go away to think. What the hell do you think they invented bathrooms for?"

McGuire tossed a thick brown manila envelope on the desk.

Withdrawing the toothpick from his mouth, Kavander used it as a pointer. "What's this? Your lunch?"

"The files, Jack. The grey files from the Cornell murder. You can have them back. I'll attach a NETGO form on them. I'm stumped."

Kavander's eyes narrowed. "Never thought I would hear you say that. You were always like a bull terrier when you got your teeth into a case."

"Well, I was younger." McGuire leaned back in the chair, his hands behind his head. "Even bull terriers lose their teeth when they get old. And this one's going to spend a week on a warm beach somewhere. Maybe the Bahamas. Bernie Lipson once told me about some little towns in the out islands where you can sleep in the shade all day and eat conch fritters and drink beer in a quiet little pub all night, just watching the sun go down."

"Yeah, another day shot in the only life you'll ever live." He waved his hand across the desk, wiping away the thought. "What the hell, McGuire. Do it. It will give both of us less to worry about."

"Rosen's having me followed," McGuire said softly.

Kavander stared at him. "You sure?"

"He told me himself. He has me pegged for breaking up Janet's marriage."

"Rosen threaten you?"

McGuire nodded. "With two witnesses who will swear he didn't. He wants me to walk, Jack. If I do, he drops all the charges. And if I walk, so will Wilmer at his retrial."

Kavander turned and studied his wall. "Leave it with me," he said after a moment.

"You going to back me against him, Jack?"

Kavander reached for another toothpick.

"Are you going to back me, Jack?" McGuire repeated.

"I'll have to discuss it."

"With whom?"

Kavander shook his head in silence.

"You bastard," McGuire spat at him. "Somebody upstairs wants to throw me to the wolves, don't they? Who? Who is so pissed at me that they'll use me to get out from under a lawsuit and let the crazy kid back on the streets —"

"Joe —"

"— *the kid who gutted that poor girl like an animal?*"

"Nobody is throwing you anywhere, McGuire. Your problem is that you always work on the surface of things. You never see what's going on underneath."

"Yeah, I'm a lousy politician," McGuire responded bitterly. He stood up and waved his arms as he spoke, feeling himself becoming more agitated and refusing to fight it this time. "Hey, I'm proud of that. Damn proud. You know why? Because the world needs politicians like it needs a second rectum. You, the commissioner, Don Higgins, the rest of them, you're all politicians. You're all smart enough to win the game and dumb enough to think it's important."

Kavander smiled indulgently, like a parent waiting for a small child to finish his tantrum. "Maybe you shouldn't waste any time picking up your ticket to the Bahamas," he said.

McGuire thrust his hands in his pockets and stalked from the room.

. .

"Ralph says you left Max." McGuire entered Janet's office, closing the door behind him. "Is it true?"

Janet Parsons swivelled in her chair, the telephone receiver at her ear. "What?" she mouthed to him silently. "Yes, I'm listening," she said aloud into the receiver.

"Did you leave him? Is it over?"

She rolled her eyes to the ceiling and began scribbling on a yellow legal-sized pad, thrusting it at him when she finished.

McGuire leaned across her desk. "What's it to you?" he read from the paper.

"Yes, I'm just getting that down now," she was saying into the telephone. She pulled the pad back. Beneath her message to McGuire she wrote an address and telephone number.

"You don't happen to know what kind of car it was, do you?"

McGuire seized her hand and yanked her towards him, staring into her eyes.

"Excuse me just a moment, will you please?" she said in an apologetic tone. Carefully setting the receiver on her desk, she pressed the "hold" button before raising her hand and slapping McGuire's face. "What the hell do you think you're doing?" she demanded through clenched teeth. "Maybe you and Ollie Schantz can lie around playing private-eye games but I've got a lead on a Murder One suspect here and I'll be damned if —"

McGuire grabbed her free wrist in his other hand, pulled her towards him and pressed his lips against hers. "You twitched," he said when they separated, smiling back at her green eyes flashing with anger. "You were trying hard, but I definitely felt you twitch."

"Let me go, damn it, or I'll have you charged with assault," she said softly.

"No, you won't."

"Where were you?"

He relaxed his grip on her wrists. "In Texas. On my own. I was following a lead."

"I mean for me. Couldn't you see what I've been going through for the past week? Couldn't you tell I needed you to help me through this damned mess you were part of?"

He stood up and looked away. "Some things you have to work out for yourself —" he began.

"That's your opinion. Not mine. Not something like this."

"I'm going to the Bahamas." He looked down at her. "As soon as I can get a booking. Tomorrow, the next day, whenever. I'll make reservations for both of us in some quiet place on the out islands. Thanksgiving weekend is coming up. You could squeeze a couple of days out of here and tack it on. We'd have almost a whole week together, but we have to do it now. Tonight."

"I'm busy tonight." She picked up the receiver.

"With what?"

"Having dinner."

"Anybody I know?"

She smiled like an errant child, teasing him. "Ralph Innes."

"Ralph?" McGuire looked around her office as if he had just awakened from a lengthy sleep. "A date with Ralph? Where, in the back seat of his car? Ralph Innes? Jesus, Janet."

She pressed the "hold" button and swivelled in her chair. "Sorry to keep you waiting," she said into the receiver. McGuire was left staring at her back. "There are just a few more questions I need to ask."

. .

Two hours later, McGuire had opened his second beer, loaded a Paul Desmond CD into his player, and sat down to a chopped sirloin dinner heated in his microwave.

A knock on his door disturbed the mood.

"I brought lunch." Janet Parsons stood holding a paper sack smelling of hot cheeseburgers.

"I'm just having mine," he growled at her. "Besides, I wouldn't want to ruin your dinner tonight."

She brushed past him, tossing the bag of burgers on a chair. "I do detect a hint of jealousy in your voice." Sliding out of her coat, she tilted her head towards the stereo system. "The late Paul Desmond. Wonderful music to make love to. I understand he sounds especially good on warm nights in the Bahamas."

"What the hell are you up to?" McGuire muttered from the open doorway.

She began unbuttoning her blouse. "You," she smiled.

. .

She lay against his shoulder, one leg out from under the

covers, the knee resting on his hip. The music had ended long ago.

"What happened to your Murder One lead?" he asked.

"Came up empty. Mistaken identity. I'm back where I started."

"And your husband?"

"It's over. I guess. One day it's over, the next day he wants to try again. For now, it's over." She looked up at him with her green cat's eyes. "Are you really going to the Bahamas?"

"Do you really have a date with Ralph Innes?"

She rolled on her side and rested her arm on his chest. "He's amusing, in a coarse way. Kind of like a naughty little boy. Underneath, I really think there's a decent guy."

"Janet, there's nothing under Ralph's skin except a goat in heat." He rolled to face her. "Come with me. Get out of the cold for a few days. You need time off and Kavander will give it to you. We can fly down tomorrow night and have six, seven days together."

"Damn it, I was angry with you." Her voice conveyed both anger and sorrow. "I needed you. But you, you're so damned independent, you think everyone else should be the same way."

"You had to work it out —"

"*And I needed you to help me!*"

He lay back again and covered his eyes with his forearm. "I'm sorry," he said.

When he raised his arm and opened his eyes after a long moment's silence, she was watching him with a wry smile. "I never thought I would hear you say that," she said. "I didn't think you knew the word." Leaning over to kiss the tip of his nose, she whispered, "I have to get back."

"Have a nice time tonight," he said as she was dressing.

"I plan to."

"Take some aspirin with you."

"Aspirin? What for?"

"To hold between your knees!"

. .

He slept the rest of the afternoon, waking once from a dream in which he saw men pinned to the ground on iron stakes like butterflies.

When he awoke for good, the sun was going down somewhere beyond Cambridge. He showered, swallowed a cup of instant coffee, called a travel agency and drove north to Revere Beach.

. .

"I booked a trip to the Bahamas." McGuire reached for the last of the cookies Ronnie Schantz had brought him when he arrived. "Place called Green Turtle Cay. Off Abaco. Rented a cottage on the beach near the only town on the island. I'll just lie in the shade for a week, drink beer, eat shrimp and think about nothing."

Ollie Schantz was staring at the ceiling. "And the Cornell case?"

"The hell with it. I gave the grey file back to Kavander."

Ollie grunted. "Don't need it anyway."

"I'm not walking away from Berkeley Street, Ollie. Not yet. I'll just slip into a lower gear until I retire." He stood up and stretched. "Tell you the truth, if I like the weather down there, maybe I'll look around for something to do. Even a place like Green Turtle Cay might need a cop. Somebody to go around, check for unlocked doors. No politics. No ambitious guys nipping at your heels."

McGuire looked down to see Ollie watching him. "Sit down and go through all the Cornell suspects again," the other man ordered.

"Ollie, I'm through with the case —"

"Well, I'm not!" Ollie snapped. "Run through it again from memory before you leave to go build sand castles on some desert island, God-damn it!"

McGuire sat. "There's Reich, the super," he began.

"Except he's dead and his wife says he was in bed when the victim was killed. Then there's the insurance man, Milburn, who was at the Fens when she died. He says he was drunk and asleep on a bench. I guess Andrew Snyder is a possibility, but hell, Ollie . . ."

"Keep going."

McGuire sighed. "Okay, there's Fleckstone, who had a violent fight with her. She might have bugged him enough for him to kill her, I guess. There's Irene Hoffman, who I never did meet. Jennifer Cornell ruined her business, which is motive enough. Then I guess you could include Marlene from Pour Richards, but where's the motive?" He stared back at Ollie and shrugged his shoulders.

"Let's assume," Ollie Schantz said, "that the brother's dead. Or at least he disappeared as soon as the Cornell woman was murdered. Good assumption?"

"Good assumption."

"I'm going to ask you something. And don't answer until you've let the idea ricochet around inside that melon you carry on your shoulders. Think about it: Who was the only person who ever claimed to see both the victim and her brother together?"

McGuire looked away.

He frowned. His face became clouded, then suddenly animated and he leaped to his feet and said a name slowly, his words tinged with disbelief.

"Nice going, killer," Ollie smiled. "And I'll bet you've figured out what happened to Andrew Cornell."

"How long have you known, damn it?" McGuire demanded.

"I suspected it the day you left for Texas. When you came back and told me about Andrew Snyder, it all fell into place. The accident cleared up a couple of nagging little details. It's all been in your notes, Joseph. The ones you made when you were looking at the murder-scene pictures. Her hair, Joe. Look at her hair. And the callous. That's what clued me in."

"I'll need something. Maybe the old glass sandwich number."

"That'll work. Match them up with Norm Cooper's files." Ollie's right arm swung in jerky motions to his night table. His hand released the tennis ball and one finger hooked the drawer handle.

"You've got a fair bit of movement there now," McGuire observed.

The drawer slid open, revealing a scattered collection of dated snapshots and news clippings, a gold badge, plastic sealed ID card and .38 revolver.

McGuire chose what he needed. "How long has your gun been here?" he asked, frowning down at the weapon.

"Since I asked Ronnie to bring all my junk down from upstairs. Close the drawer."

· ·

McGuire slept fitfully that night, waking often to assure himself it was true, that Ollie's theory was the only plausible solution and that they had all been blind not to see it.

CHAPTER TWENTY-TWO

The morning air traffic was heavy into Logan Airport. McGuire stepped out of his car, the weak sun at his back, as a 747 passed low overhead, its wheels dangling from beneath the craft's underbelly.

At the sound of the doorbell, the dog gave a warning bark.

"Good morning," McGuire said to the face that appeared at the partially opened door. "Sorry to arrive unannounced."

Frances O'Neil's sister, Mona, stared back at him, holding the black Labrador by its collar.

"I'm Lieutenant McGuire, Boston Police Department," he said, smiling. "I was here about a week ago to talk to your sister Frances. Remember?"

The woman nodded, her face devoid of expression.

"I have to talk with her again," he said when she made no gesture to invite him in. "Actually, I just want to show her a photograph. If she can identify the individual in it, she could help us in our investigation. It won't take a minute."

She opened the door and stepped aside without a word. McGuire entered the house and glanced into the living-room where Frances O'Neil stood near the fire, a moss-green cardigan over her shoulders, her arms folded in front of her.

"Hello, Miss O'Neil," McGuire said, smiling warmly. "Sorry to drop in like this. Wonder if you can help us with something."

Frances O'Neil walked to the centre of the room, her cautious smile growing wider as she approached McGuire.

"You promised to call me Frances," she said. "But I forgive you. Come sit by the fire and we'll talk."

"I can't stay long." McGuire allowed himself to be led away from the sister, who stood at the door watching them before dragging the protesting dog into the kitchen.

"Not even long enough for tea?" she asked. She tilted her head, her eyes crinkling as she smiled.

McGuire withdrew a small brown envelope from his topcoat. "Miss O'Neil," he began.

"You promised Frances," she repeated coyly.

"Okay, Frances." He removed a photograph from the envelope. The picture had been bound between two small squares of glass that McGuire had purchased from a hardware store that morning, the edges sealed with paper tape. "Tell me if you recognize the person in this photograph."

"It's not you, is it?" she smiled. She took the photograph from him, tilting it in the light from the window to see the image through the glare from the glass.

."It's a little fuzzy," she said frowning. "Hard to see the face."

"Does he look familiar at all?"

"No. I can honestly say I have never met this man."

Mona walked briskly into the room from the kitchen where the dog cried and danced excitedly behind the door. "Who is it supposed to be?" she demanded, peering over her sister's shoulder.

Ignoring her, McGuire asked Frances to turn the photo over and read the writing on the back.

Frances brought the glass-encased picture closer to her eyes and squinted. "It looks like 'Provincetown, 1956,' " she said.

"Does that mean anything to you?"

She shook her head. "Sorry."

"How about the writing? Does it look familiar?"

"Let me see," Mona insisted, reaching for the picture.

"Please." McGuire held a hand up to dissuade her. "Please let your sister study the writing. This is very important."

Mona glared at him before retreating to the fireplace.

"I have no idea whose writing this is," Frances said. She looked up at McGuire and giggled. "I didn't do very well, did I?"

McGuire retrieved the photograph from her. "It's not your fault," he said, handling it carefully by the edges. "If you don't recognize him, it was a false lead. Happens all the time."

"Who is he?" Mona snapped, trying once again for a glimpse at the picture.

"Someone who might have helped us find the murderer of Jennifer Cornell." McGuire slid the picture back into the envelope. "Right now, it looks like I've hit a dead end. Sorry to trouble you." He turned and headed for the door.

"Will you be back?" Frances touched his elbow, walking quickly to match his pace.

"Only if I have more questions." McGuire seemed distant, deep in thought.

"Can't we talk again like we did the other day? I enjoyed that. You're a wonderful listener, you know. That's a very special gift. Some people think listening is easy, but they're wrong. It's a gift; it takes real talent."

He paused at the door to turn and take her hands in his. "Tell you what. I promise we'll have another chat soon. And when we do, I'll listen to everything you have to say." He looked over her shoulder at Mona, who had taken her sister's position near the fireplace, where she stood watching them with hooded eyes. "Thank you," he called across the room.

Frances followed him to the top step, wrapping her arms

around her to ward off the chill. "Don't mind Mona," she said softly. "She's been, well, tense lately. She's very protective of me. You can understand."

"Go inside," McGuire said.

"Not until you tell me when we can talk again."

"Soon."

"Promise?"

"Promise."

. .

"Coop!"

McGuire had nodded at the security desk officer, skimmed past the officers and stenographers crowded near the vestibule elevators, bounded down a side corridor of Berkeley Street Police Headquarters and burst through the door marked "Bureau of Identification" at the rear of the building. Now he stood behind a counter separating him from the best police ID expert in Massachusetts.

Norm Cooper looked up from a microscope. He adjusted his horn-rimmed glasses and grinned at McGuire across the battered oak desk. "Ah, the countenance of a strange and haunted man," Cooper said with an exaggerated English accent. His face was so round it might have been drawn with a compass, his button nose serving as the centre point; it was crowned by dark hair which refused to be tamed by comb, brush, gel or bricklayer's mortar. "Are you here in the process of exercising deductive abilities? Or have you come to bid farewell to this decrepit vale of tears?"

"I need a favour, Norm." McGuire circled the counter and walked across the room, past several assistants examining hair and skin samples, fabric fibres, and other detritus of crime investigation. "Won't take you more than a couple of minutes and I even have a file number to cover the paperwork. Can you handle it?"

Cooper studied him cautiously. "Is it apt to put Kavander's nose in a meat grinder?"

"It could."

"Then no problem. What's up?"

McGuire explained what he needed, handing Cooper the brown envelope.

"Have it for you in an hour," the ID expert nodded. "Soon as I finish a blood match. You need it written?"

"Just your well-qualified opinion over the telephone," McGuire said, already heading for the door. "I'll call later."

The high-ceilinged lobby of the old Police Headquarters building had grown crowded by the time McGuire reentered it. Detectives, police officers, secretaries, lawyers, forensic staff and others crisscrossed the marble floor between the exits and the elevators, or stood chatting in small groups.

McGuire elbowed his way through the throng, receiving pats on the back from some of his colleagues while others avoided his eyes. He planned to spend the next hour devouring eggs, coffee and the morning paper at a nearby diner, but a grey-haired police officer called out to him as he passed the security desk.

"Captain Kavander told me to send you up," he said, with as much authority as he could muster.

McGuire strolled over to the desk. "How did he know I was here?"

"I told him. Saw you enter. I was ordered to let him know if you were still in the building."

"I'll drop in some other time."

"He said right away."

McGuire looked at the old cop at the security desk, his face lined from years of walking a beat in every kind of weather, his hair thinning and his eyes watery behind thick glasses. Making one last stop before retirement after forty years on the job, McGuire speculated, and probably hating every minute of it. McGuire smiled back at him. "You got it," he said, and turned to the elevators just as the doors of the nearest one opened and two familiar faces stood staring back at him. One of them, Bernie Lipson's, broke into a wide grin at the sight of McGuire.

"Now there's a man who can solve it, I'll bet," Lipson said as he left the elevator.

McGuire glanced at Ralph Innes who had shared the elevator with Lipson. "What," he asked, "happened to you?"

Innes licked his swollen upper lip. The flesh around one eye was the colour of kosher wine. "Accident," Innes replied, brushing past him.

"Damned if we can figure it," Lipson said as he and McGuire watched Innes stride to the front door. The doors closed and the elevator began descending to the basement. McGuire punched the 'up' button again. "He goes out of here last night higher than a kite. Won't tell us what's up. Says he'll give us all the hairy details this morning. So we figure he's up to something. Probably something carnal. Then he comes in this morning looking like that. Won't talk about it. Can't kid him either. One of the guys upstairs tried to make a joke about it and I thought Ralph was going to throw him through a window, and what the hell are you smiling at, McGuire?"

"I think I know what happened." McGuire laughed aloud. "See you, Bernie," he added, stepping towards the elevator now coming up from the basement. Its elaborate brass doors opened to reveal a morose Tim Fox glaring angrily at the floor. "Hey, Timmy," McGuire said as he stepped aboard and the doors closed behind him. "What's the matter?"

Fox looked up briefly at McGuire, his hands thrust in his pockets. He shook his head slowly. "The bastard, Joe," the detective said in a low voice. "You wouldn't believe it. The little bastard."

"Who? What the hell happened?"

"We were on Huntingdon half an hour ago," Fox explained. "Me and Sadowsky, on our way to check a weapons ownership. And this woman comes running out into the street, right in front of us. She's screaming, she's hysterical, wearing a bathrobe. Sadowsky, he's driving, he almost runs over her. She tells us some guy broke into her apartment while she and her roommate were getting ready for work. Guy tied them up in separate rooms. She got free and he's still in there with the roommate. So Sadowsky and me, we go up, and he's still in there with a knife, cutting up this woman on the living-room rug. God-*damn*!"

McGuire grunted. "So you brought him in?"

The elevator doors opened to the third floor as Fox grunted, still looking at his shoes. "He's down in the interrogation room. Looking like he just came off work in a slaughterhouse. Worse than that." Fox looked up at McGuire. "He's your man, Joe. Arthur Trevor Wilmer, out on bail for doing the same thing to that co-ed from Boston College six months ago."

. .

McGuire bolted from the elevator and charged down the fire stairs to the basement, where he entered an unmarked door off a side corridor.

In the dim light of the observation room, a swarthy face turned to meet McGuire's from behind the glow of a cigarette. The sound of slow, steady breathing hissed through a speaker on the wall.

"Joe," the man said softly. "I hear you know this piece of rat-shit."

"Yeah, Lou," McGuire replied, waiting for his pulse to calm. "I know him."

Two police officers standing near the far wall stepped aside and nodded as McGuire approached the large glass area in front of him. Through the one-way mirror looking into an adjacent small room, McGuire could see two men sitting across from each other at a low wooden table, a small desk microphone between them. A large electric clock hung on the wall opposite the observation room, positioned to face a video camera and taping equipment. The microphone fed sound from the interrogation room to both the taping equipment and the speaker in the observation room near McGuire's ear.

McGuire knew the men at the table. The burly crew-cut detective who sat with his massive forearms on the table and his small, piercing eyes on the young man seated across from him, was Don Sadowsky, Sergeant of Detectives.

The other man, smiling nervously and drawing invisible patterns on the table top with his finger, was Arthur Trevor Wilmer.

"When are they going to clean him up?" McGuire asked softly.

"What's the rush?" Lou Cummings, the detective who had greeted McGuire, stood at his elbow.

Wilmer's heavy cotton shirt was soaked with blood. Smears of it ran across his face like streaks of paint on a textured wall.

"What else, Arthur?" Sadowsky's voice growled through the speaker.

"He tell us anything worthwhile?" McGuire whispered, his eyes still on Wilmer.

"Everything." Cummings turned away, drew a last puff on his cigarette and crushed it in an ashtray. "Didn't leave a thing out. Started babbling before Sadowsky could read him his rights."

Wilmer's voice came through the scratchy speaker. "Nothing." He shrugged his shoulders. "Can I get a shower and maybe something to eat now?"

One of the cops near the door swore. "He's hungry," the officer said, shaking his head. "Do you believe it? The little prick's *hungry*."

"Christ, how can Sadowsky stand being in there with that?" the other cop said in a stage whisper.

Wilmer's voice, electronic and disembodied, came through the speaker again. "Is Mr Rosen here yet?"

"I don't know," Sadowsky replied.

"You called him, didn't you?" Wilmer whined. "You said you would call him. That's what you told me. You promised."

The door behind McGuire swung open and all four men in the room turned to face the newcomer.

"My God," Jack Kavander muttered, walking to the window in two long strides. The uniformed officers stood a little straighter but remained silent. "What the hell did he *do*?"

"You'll have to read the transcript," Cummings replied. "Otherwise you'll never believe it, Jack."

"Rosen's outside." Kavander stood with his eyes still on the blood-soaked figure of Wilmer, who had begun cleaning his fingernails. "Send the son of a bitch in."

"In here?" Cummings asked.

"No, damn it! In *there*! Show the slime-bucket what his client has done while it's still fresh and smelling up the room!" When Cummings left, Kavander turned to McGuire. "I didn't come down here to see this," he said in a low voice. "I came down here to see you."

"Figured that." McGuire folded his arms. Neither man looked at the other.

"Detective Parsons asked for a few days off starting tomorrow," Kavander said. "Now what do you make of that?"

"You take an infinite number of monkeys and give them an infinite choice of holidays over an infinite amount of time . . ."

Kavander turned to McGuire, his mouth agape. "What in *hell* are you babbling about?"

"The world is full of coincidences, Jack."

"World's full of bedbugs like Wilmer, too. I still don't know what you're getting at."

The door of the interrogation room opened and Marv Rosen entered, a camel-hair coat tossed over his shoulders like a cape. At the sight of Arthur Wilmer, he froze on the spot and brought a hand to his face.

"Frankenstein meets Jack the Ripper," McGuire muttered.

Rosen's voice trembled through the speaker. "I want, want my client examined by . . . by a court-appointed psychiatrist." Rosen's face grew pale.

"Looks like he got a whiff of his client," Kavander said.

Rosen turned quickly away from Wilmer, who had stood up at the sight of his attorney. McGuire could see the lower portion of his shirt glistening with blood. "Hi, Mr Rosen," Wilmer said, a broad smile spreading across his face. He stepped towards the lawyer, extending a hand. "Thanks for coming. Soon as I got here I said 'Call Mr Rosen,' like you told me to if I ever . . ."

"*Stay there!*" Rosen shouted, backing away.

Sadowsky angled his head and smiled coldly.

"Sadowsky's stomach is built like a septic tank," Kavander remarked.

"I do believe Rosen is about to see his breakfast again," McGuire added.

Rosen had stumbled to a corner of the interrogation room. McGuire grunted as he watched the lawyer's shoulders heave and heard him retching through the sound system while Wilmer watched, mystified. Sadowsky glanced at the lawyer before turning to face the one-way glass, spreading his arms in a gesture of helplessness.

Leaving the observation room a moment later, McGuire stepped around Rosen, who stood in the corridor wiping his face with a handkerchief, his brow glistening with perspiration.

"Spilled something on your coat," McGuire said without expression as he passed the lawyer before walking up the stairs and through the exit, anticipating the clean aroma of fresh air.

CHAPTER TWENTY-THREE

At his apartment McGuire changed into cotton slacks, sweater and light-weight jacket before tossing T-shirts, swimming trunks, faded jeans, shorts and sneakers into a battered suitcase.

Five minutes later he stood on Commonwealth Avenue, flagging a cab and trying to keep his teeth from chattering in the frigid air.

After a stop at a travel agency on Boylston, he directed the cab to Revere Beach. Passing Suffolk Downs, the driver glanced in his rear-view mirror and grunted; he pulled to the curb as two police cruisers flew by, their sirens wailing and lights flashing, reminding McGuire of a pair of hysterical animals fleeing an unseen pursuer.

He watched them disappear in the traffic without interest. Risk your necks, cowboys, he thought. Keep the siren howling and the pedal to the floor. It will give you something to talk about tonight over your beer.

Seconds later an ambulance roared past, chasing the cruisers.

From North Shore Road, McGuire saw the lights of the cruisers and ambulance reflected from the sides of the small wooden houses along Ocean Boulevard. Domestic trouble, probably. Maybe a wife beating. Just after lunch, middle of the week, not a lot of things can happen —

He sat upright and cursed.

The three vehicles were angled in front of a familiar white frame house. Knots of curious neighbours gathered on the sidewalk while two figures in blue flanked the open front door.

"Move it!" McGuire shouted to the cab driver. "That's where we're going! Where the ambulance is!"

The two cops at the door, young and clean-shaven, barred the entrance to Ollie's house as McGuire leaped from the cab and bounded up the walk.

"Stay back," one of them ordered. "Police investigation."

McGuire flashed his badge at the rookie, who nodded and stepped aside.

In the hallway, McGuire elbowed between two ambulance attendants, who paused in their conversation to watch him rush by and stop abruptly at the open doorway to Ollie's room.

He recognized the two uniformed officers, both almost Ollie's age. One sat next to Ollie's bed, the chair reversed and his arms folded across its back. The other leaned against the wall looking down at Boston's most decorated homicide detective. Near Ollie's right hand, which made feeble gestures as he spoke, lay his Police Special revolver.

"So Jack takes another swig of the rye and throws up again," Ollie Schantz was saying as McGuire entered. "And he does it a couple more times. Finally Hayhurst, he opens one eye lying there on the floor and he says 'Hey, Jack,' he says, 'if you're only practising, would you mind using the cheap stuff?'"

Laughter erupted from the police officers, ending at the sound of McGuire's angry voice.

"What the hell is this?" McGuire demanded. "A meeting of the God-damned benevolent society?"

The three men looked at him, their smiles fading. "False alarm, Joe," said the cop seated in the chair. "Almost broke our necks getting here and . . ." He shrugged and stood up. "Take it easy, big guy. You need anything, give us a holler."

"Won't use the nine-eleven though," Ollie said.

"Yeah, maybe not," agreed the second cop. "Barker here almost took out a fire hydrant turning off Shore Road."

Barker's smile flashed briefly. "Just warming up for the time trials at Indy," he said, rising and touching the peak of his cap at Ollie. "Hell, Ollie. All I've had lately's been cats in trees and lonely women in hair curlers."

The two officers nodded at McGuire as they left the room.

"You were going to kiss the old .38 crucifix, weren't you?" McGuire spat the words out angrily. "You made a nine-eleven. You hit the buttons on your speaker-phone and told them to get the hell out here. What'd you say it was? Suicide? Accident? Murder? Or just an old cop, gets hungry, decides to chew on the end of a Smith and Wesson?"

"Fuck you," Ollie said softly, looking out his window at the sea.

"Those guys, they know what it's like, don't they?" McGuire jerked his thumb over his shoulder at the departing police officers. "That's why they're so forgiving when they get here. They probably thought about gnawing on a muzzle a couple of times themselves. I'll bet you were going to spare Ronnie, right? What'd you do, send her out to buy some more tennis balls? She gets home and the ambulance attendants are washing your brains off the wall while the cops hold her back and ask who they can call for her. That the way you planned it?"

Ollie's head swivelled slowly until it faced McGuire. "You're one bright bastard, aren't you?" he sneered. "Keep it up, you might make top cop some day."

"No, I won't," McGuire sighed. He sat heavily on the chair next to the bed. "No, I won't," he repeated.

"Kavander's right. The best brains in the department sleep in this room. Me, I'm just a pair of legs for you."

The two men stared at each other in silence. Slowly, painfully, Ollie's right hand twitched its way across the bedsheets where McGuire grasped it in his own.

"I've been working up to it all week," Ollie said, his eyes shining. "Ronnie's out at a bake sale somewhere. Took me ten minutes to get the drawer open and the gun out. Told nine-eleven to haul their asses out here, there'd been a shooting." He squeezed McGuire's hand. "Feel that?"

"Like a vice," McGuire nodded. "How many tennis balls you go through?"

"Four. Five. I don't know. Only half the muscles are working but they're strong enough. Would have been easier on an automatic though. Damn Smith and Wesson takes a ten-pound trigger pull."

"So what happened?"

The other man's eyes closed. "It seemed like such an easy way out. Remember what I said about leaving ugly? Maybe that's how I should go. Bitching and scratching and being as big an asshole as ever to the world. Instead of making it fast and clean. I'm lying here, Joe, just ticking over and going nowhere. I'm like a clock in an empty house. What the hell is there to do?"

"*Do?* Look what we've done together in the last two weeks. More than that herd of hyenas over on Berkeley have accomplished since you . . . since you left. You know why? Because nobody's setting the pace. Nobody's up front giving a damn anymore. Two kinds of guys over there, Ollie. Just two kinds. One kind is holding on to their pension like a life raft, not giving a damn where they're drifting to. The other is too busy shafting their buddies just to get a shot at making lieutenant or captain or, Christ knows why, maybe even commissioner. And nobody's doing the day-to-day slogging work, a cop's work. Nobody's got an Ollie Schantz to look at and say 'That's the way it's gotta be done. That's the way you do it, like Ollie does it.' Not anymore. These days, they all act like two-bit politicians trying to board the last bus to the White House."

Ollie had listened with his eyes closed. Now he opened them and stared out the window as he spoke. "You blaming Kavander for all the mess?"

"Why not?"

"Whatever you think of Kavander, he cares. Trouble with Jack is, he's too busy keeping the dogs off his own ass to kick anyone else's. What Kavander needs . . ."

"What Kavander needs is an Ollie Schantz to get the Goddamn job done like it should be."

"Maybe that's you."

"No," McGuire said, almost wistfully. "Two, maybe three years ago, it might have been. But not now. He needs somebody more dedicated than me. Somebody who could just take the load off the backs of Fat Eddie and Bernie and Sadowsky, all those guys. Maybe then they'd be able to get into the bones of some of these . . ." McGuire stopped, frowned, looked at the floor.

"What's the matter?" Ollie Schantz asked. His head turned from the window in a series of short twitching motions.

"Nothing," McGuire replied. "Just an idea . . ."

"On what? Our case? What'd Norm Cooper say? Did we get a match?"

McGuire snapped his fingers and reached for the telephone, switching it from speaker to receiver operation. He dialled Berkeley Street, asked for Norm Cooper's office, and uttered a few monosyllables. "Thanks, Norm. And I'll ask him," he added before hanging up.

He turned back to Ollie. "They're hers. And Norm likes the picture but he wants to know what happened to all your hair."

"Pulled it out waiting for that horseball to match prints," Ollie grinned.

"One more call," McGuire said. He was still speaking to Janet Parsons when the front door opened and Ronnie's footsteps clattered frantically down the hall. "Everything's all right," McGuire was saying as the door opened. "See you in half an hour."

He replaced the receiver and turned to see Ronnie Schantz standing in the doorway, her eyes brimming with tears.

McGuire stood and hugged her. "It's okay," he said. "Nothing happened."

She brushed past him to throw herself on the bed next to her husband.

This time Ollie Schantz didn't turn from her to stare out the window at the distant light. This time he smiled up at her tear-streaked face.

"Hiya, sport," he said.

. .

The thought nagged at him as the taxi headed south from Revere Beach. The more he considered the idea the stronger it grew, flourishing with new offshoots, new benefits, new rewards.

In Winthrop, he instructed the cabbie to park near a telephone booth where he deposited a coin and dialled Berkeley Street Police Headquarters.

Jack the Bear answered his direct line in a tired, resigned voice, like a man who had just lost an argument with his wife.

"It's me, Joe," McGuire announced, and waited for at least a short eruption of obscenities.

Instead, Kavander asked: "What's up? Lipson and Fox left here saying they're meeting you somewhere . . ."

"Wrapping up one of your grey file cases. Which is why I'm calling. I've got an idea that can help two tough old cops, you and Ollie Schantz."

"I'm listening."

"Remember you talked about being overloaded? How Fat

Eddie and the rest can get the details down but don't have time to do the feet-up thinking?" Without waiting for a reply, he continued: "Who's the best feet-up thinker you and I ever worked with? And don't take too long to guess."

"Gotta be Ollie Schantz. Only cop you ever showed any respect for," Kavander said.

"Jack, he needs something to keep a muzzle out of his mouth. You hear about a call to Revere Beach today on a nine-eleven?"

"What about it?"

"That was Ollie, Jack . . ."

"Jesus, he didn't . . ."

"No, but it was close." McGuire lowered his voice and tried to speak slowly, keeping his excitement under control. "Jack, just think about this. Promise you'll think about this, okay? You take some of your grey files, the stuff with good background material, and you send them over to Ollie. Ronnie, his wife, can pick them up, handle the organizing, take the notes. Ollie reviews them, looks for the stuff Fat Eddie and Ralph and the rest are all spinning their wheels over. Says 'Talk to this guy again,' 'Get a make on that guy,' 'Match the bank records to the travel schedule,' all those things Ollie used to think of with his feet up, not even moving out of his chair."

"And how are my guys going to feel, having their work second-guessed all the time?"

"Same way I felt working with Ollie for ten years. Like I'm getting something done. Like I'm learning from the best in the business. Like I'm a rookie on the Celtics and Larry Bird is showing me his layup shot over and over, telling me I can do it too." McGuire took a deep breath, forcing himself to relax. "Just call him, Jack," he said, calmer now. "Call him, then come out and see him. Tell him it's your idea. Bitch about how slack the guys have become on Berkeley Street. Bitch about *me* if you want, I don't care."

"McGuire," Kavander said slowly, "if I *didn't* bitch about

you, Ollie would ask what I've been smoking." A pause.
Then: "I'll call him now."

McGuire slapped the side of the booth with glee. "Jack,"
he laughed, "I take back at least half of those lousy names I
called you over the years." Still laughing, he hung up in the
middle of an insult which had something to do with gorilla
shit.

. .

The taxi rolled through Cottage Hill in the late afternoon
sun, pausing only long enough for McGuire to ring the doorbell of the chocolate-brown house on the narrow winding
street several times before driving slowly around the curve of
the shore to a low stone wall, where a solitary woman sat
with her eyes on the city skyline and tears coursing down her
cheeks.

She looked around as McGuire stepped from the cab and
spoke some instructions to the driver. Then she looked
quickly away.

McGuire watched the cab disappear around the next
curve. He walked to the low wall and sat beside the woman,
who was staring at the city skyline.

"Hello, Frances."

"Finally," she replied, looking down at her hands folded
on her lap. "You finally start calling me Frances."

"Do you know why I'm here?"

She avoided his eyes. "Yes, I know. God, I'm so dumb.
Mona knew. She realized you didn't want me to identify that
man in the picture. You just wanted my fingerprints, didn't
you?" She began blinking back tears and withdrew a damp
handkerchief from her pocket. "Who was he? The man in
the picture? Not that it matters. I'm just curious."

"My partner, Ollie Schantz," McGuire said. "It was taken
on his honeymoon. He's the one who figured out what happened."

She looked directly at him for the first time since he had sat down. "Everything?"

"Enough. We know you killed Jennifer. Out of anger or frustration."

"Try humiliation."

"Whatever. I'm no lawyer, but I would say the charge is more likely to be manslaughter than murder."

She shook her head sadly. "Do you know, I actually persuaded myself that I had gotten away with it? Me, this little mouse." She laughed dryly. "There were times I wanted to tell the world about it. Look at me, Frances O'Neil. Ex-school teacher, ex-librarian, ex-waitress. I killed a woman in the Fens and fooled the entire Boston Police Force."

"Did Mona know?"

"Of course she knew." The smile faded and Frances turned back to the harbour view. "Mona knew," she nodded. "She's at her lawyer's now. Or maybe they've already left his office for the police station, I don't know."

"To turn you in?"

"No, to turn herself in. To explain what . . . why she killed . . . why she pushed Henry Reich down the stairs."

McGuire sat back abruptly. "Your sister killed Reich?"

She turned to him, her expression almost coy. "So you didn't know everything after all."

"I suspected it wasn't an accident."

"It practically was. He was so drunk."

"He knew about it, didn't he?"

She nodded.

"And he was blackmailing you. To have sex with him."

Turning her back to him, she answered "yes" in a choked voice. An aircraft passed low overhead, the noise of its engines drowning the sound of her voice. In the silence it left behind she faced him again, with tears flowing freely down her cheeks, and sobbed, "You don't know what he made me do. He was . . . he was *horrible* . . . an old man like that. Old enough to be my father. Making me do things down in that cellar and out on the fire escape. Warning me that if I didn't he would tell the police and I would go to jail."

"And when Mona found out, she killed him."

Frances nodded. "I was to meet him in the Fens one evening. That day I broke down completely and told Mona what happened. I was ready to go to the police but Mona said no. She said she could get him to stop, so she went instead. When he pulled up in a cab and got out carrying a case of whisky, she followed him into the apartment building, just to talk to him, to insist that he leave me alone. She was behind him in the corridor, and when he almost stumbled at the top of the stairs, she pushed him."

"He saw you leaving Jennifer's apartment the night she died."

Frances nodded, and McGuire continued.

"You were going down the back stairs carrying Andrew Cornell's belongings when Henry Reich came out to see what was going on. He thought it was prowlers or addicts shooting up on the fire escape. And somehow he recognized you."

"He'd been in Pour Richards a few times. I think he fancied Jennifer. He would try to talk to her there. That's how he remembered me."

"What were you doing with Andrew Cornell's belongings?"

She shrugged. "Getting rid of them. Everything. I wanted it all to disappear — his clothes, shoes, jewellery. I didn't want anyone to know what really happened. Who he really had been. I put everything in plastic garbage bags and was carrying them down the back stairs when Henry Reich came out. He grabbed the bags from me and demanded to know what was in them. I panicked. I dropped them and ran."

"So he hid them," McGuire said. "He found the watch later and sold it. Probably burned the rest in the incinerator. And all you left in the apartment were your fingerprints." McGuire rested his hand on her shoulder. "She was one hell of an actress, wasn't she?"

Frances studied his hand before placing hers on it lightly. "Do you know what she did?" she asked, leaning to rest her cheek on her shoulder, cushioned by their hands. "She wore elevator shoes to look taller and taped a stone inside one to make her limp. I saw it when I gathered everything together. She had sewn padding inside the sports jacket to conceal her bust. That's what made Andrew look so muscular. She would stuff cotton in her cheeks and put something on her hands to make the skin feel rougher. She cut her hair short and wore a man's hairpiece and tinted contact lenses. It must have taken her an hour to make herself up."

"There were clues all over the place," McGuire said. Frances watched sadly as he removed his hand from under hers. "Running from the fight with Milburn. Telling Fleckstone she'd prove to him she was a good actress."

"He was the cause of it." Frances was staring out at the harbour again. "Fleckstone told her she could never be a convincing actress. She became obsessed with proving him wrong. So she was going to arrive at his office as her brother. I really believe, when she was dressed and made-up as Andrew, I really think she became him. She modelled herself after him so completely. If you had seen her, you would understand. It wasn't just a woman in men's clothing, talking like a man, gesturing like a man. She carried herself differently. She *became* him. And she loved it. She loved fooling the world, even those who knew her. She revelled in it."

"Tell me what happened the night she died."

Frances breathed deeply and stared at the base of the stone wall. She swung her feet back and forth, striking the wall with the heels of her shoes: the nervous mannerism of a frightened little girl.

"I was enjoying the walk so much. I even suggested we sit together near the Fens and look at the stars. It was a beautiful night and Andrew . . . Jennifer as Andrew . . . You know, I still think of him, that person I walked with, I still think of him as someone else, another person, somebody who wasn't

Jennifer but was everything she might have been. And she said, in Andrew's voice, 'Wait here and I'll come down with a surprise.' I was a little frightened, waiting all alone there. There was some traffic on the street but you know the Fens isn't safe at night. It can be dangerous for a woman alone. So I waited, for almost an hour, watching the lights in the apartment. And finally it was Jennifer who came out. She took my arm. She seemed edgy, nervous. I was confused. Where was Andrew? But she said she had something to say to me and there was someone around, near her apartment, she didn't want to meet."

"Milburn," McGuire offered.

"Is that who? Anyway, we went down into the ravine by the water and under the bridge. I was afraid. I thought she was going to tell me to stay away from Andrew. I kept asking where he was. 'Where's Andrew?' I kept pleading. And then she said, in Andrew's voice, 'Right here.' "

McGuire watched her silently, waiting for her to continue. She wiped her eyes with her hands and leaned forward, resting her elbows on her knees.

"I thought she was just imitating him," she began. "I laughed. I said she was being silly. Maybe she was drunk. I could smell alcohol on her breath. I think she had a drink in the apartment while I waited. And I asked where Andrew was again. And then she began limping towards me and I saw that sweet smile on her face like Andy used to have. And, oh my God, I got hysterical. Because I knew what she had done."

"Did she apologize?"

Frances shook her head angrily. "No, no, no, no. She was *proud* of it. She taunted me. She laughed and laughed and said, 'You were ready to kiss me on the way here, weren't you?' And she laughed again and said how much she had fooled everyone at the bar and how she was going to prove something to Fleckstone. Then she would go back to Pour Richards and tell everyone. Tell them everything, including how she had deceived me. And I was crying and angry because all of my life people have been making a fool of me and using me. I wanted to hurt her. Not kill her. Not really. Just hurt her because she had hurt me. So I picked up a piece of wood. She had her back to me, looking into the water and telling me about her audition with Fleckstone. And while she was talking, I swung it at her head."

Another aircraft passed overhead, flaps and landing-gear lowered, engines screaming.

"Did you know you had killed her?" McGuire asked.

"I did later. When I struck her, I dropped the wood and ran away, under the bridge. I stood there and cried until there were no tears left. Then I returned and saw she'd fallen in the water and hadn't moved."

For the first time, she looked at McGuire with fear in her eyes.

"Honestly, I didn't mean to kill her. But when I saw she was dead, I picked up the keys from the ground . . ." She froze, looking over McGuire's shoulder.

He turned to follow her eyes. An unmarked detective car, police cruiser and taxi were rolling slowly around the curve towards them from the direction of the chocolate-brown house.

"Are they for me?" she asked.

McGuire nodded and took her hand in his. "I don't know how this will turn out," he said gently. "But it will probably be a relief just to get it all over with."

Her face, inches from his, began to crumble. Behind him, car doors opened and slammed shut and footsteps walked briskly in their direction. McGuire turned again to see Tim Fox and Bernie Lipson leading two police officers, one male and one female.

McGuire stood and nodded to Fox and Lipson. "See you in a week," he said as he walked past.

At the detective car he opened the rear door and extended his hand.

Janet Parsons stepped out, a small carry-on bag over her shoulder. Together, she and McGuire walked to the cab while behind them, still seated on the low stone wall, Frances O'Neil watched them silently as Tim Fox read her legal rights and Bernie Lipson fastened her hands behind her back in cuffs.

The last of Fox's words were lost in the roar of a descending aircraft gliding low overhead, returning to`earth reluctantly on extended wings.

John Lawrence Reynolds

THE MAN WHO MURDERED GOD

A mild morning in Boston, filled with fresh sea air and the promise of spring…until the calm is broken by the violent, shocking murder of a gentle, harmless priest in the sanctum of his own church. The savage killings continue and Lieutenant Joe McGuire — one-half of the best homicide team in Boston's history — starts searching for the killer whose violence has touched so many. And behind it all, slouched in a damp corner of an ancient building, is the source of the tragedy — *the man who murdered god.*

"Lieut. Joe McGuire has a big future. I'm sure of that."

The Vancouver Sun

"…a distinguished piece of writing that, while diverting and entertaining, keeps a firm hold on the realities of human character."

The Ottawa Citizen

Peter Robinson

GALLOW'S VIEW

Short-listed for the John Creasy Award

Chief Inspector Alan Banks of the Criminal Investigation Department has been recently transferred from London to Eastvale, a town in the Yorkshire Dales. His desire to escape the stress of city life appears to be satisfied by Eastvale's cobbled market square, its tree-shaded river and its picturesque castle ruins. But the village begins to show a more dangerous side . . .

As a Peeping Tom disturbs the peace of Eastvale women, police are accused of underestimating the seriousness of the crime. At the same time, Banks is also investigating the case of two local teenagers whose crimes are escalating from theft to violence. The two cases weave together as this tough, gritty novel of power and suspense reaches a terrifying and surprising climax.

"This is a first novel that will knock you over with its maturity."

Howard Engel

"Offers all the suspense and local colour that anyone could expect, plus a few surprises."

Toronto Star

"A Fast-moving, gripping mystery story."
Winnipeg Free Press

Peter Robinson

A DEDICATED MAN

Nominated for the Arthur Ellis Award

It was a perfect summer. The weather was unusually warm for the Dales, and Harry Steadman, who was preparing a book on the area, and his wife, Emma, enjoyed their holiday at the Ramsden Bed and Breakfast.

But ten years later the memories of that peaceful summer are shattered by Harry Steadman's brutal murder. Inspector Banks is back, and investigating a case just as confounding as his first. Who would kill the kindly scholar? Penny Cartwright, a beautiful woman with a disturbing past? Harry's editor or the shady land developer? And is it possible that young Sally Lumb, locked in her lover's arms the night of the murder, could unknowingly hold the key to the case?

"A perfect little portrait of a village in the Yorkshire dales. . . . First-rate stuff for the detective story buff."
Province (Vancouver)

"A cast of interesting, human characters—especially his wry and introspective hero."
Star Phoenix (Saskatoon)

"A first-class story. . . . One of the most completely realized detectives in Canadian crime fiction."
The Toronto Star

Ellen Godfrey

MURDER BEHIND LOCKED DOORS

By the author of the Edgar Award-winning
By Reason of Doubt

When the vice-president of a large software company is found dead in the computer room, Jane Tregar plunges into the corporate world and executive boardrooms to discover the killer. But in the business world, competition can be so tough that people will do anything — including murder — to come out on top.

"The charcterization of this novel is admirable; we watch the small circle of suspects evolve from mere names into real and complex human creatures."
The Sunday Star

"A fast-paced, high-tech mystery."
Quill & Quire

"Deft characterization draws the reader into a cut-throat world of computers, technology, mergers and takeovers in this well-written mystery."
Publishers Weekly

Medora Sale

MURDER IN FOCUS

When Toronto homicide detective John Sanders is chosen to go to Ottawa for a week-long seminar in anti-terrorist techniques, he expects to suffer five days of mind-numbing boredom. Instead, he finds himself plunged into internal chaos among the RCMP, CSIS and the local police force. And his professional interest is sharpened when a construction worker is found brutally murdered in a high-risk security zone.

Sanders' life is further complicated when he bumps into an attractive and independent photographer, Harriet Jeffries. It is Harriet's photograph of two men who don't want their picture taken, especially together, that initiates a ruthless and dangerous chase to destroy vital evidence of murder and conspiracy.

". . . refreshingly filled with clever dialogue and suspense."

The Leader Post (Regina)

"Medora Sale has given a new spin to the theme of the less than perfect detective . . . the whole investigative procedure has been corrupted."

The Toronto Star

". . . well-structured and original."

The Windsor Star

". . . a solid series debut."

The Vancouver Sun

"The story is well crafted, the parallel development of love and suspense skilfully handled."

The London Free Press

Howard Engel

A VICTIM MUST BE FOUND

In his sixth important case, Grantham's own Benny Cooperman finds himself mixed up in the art world. More out of water a fish can't get. After all, Benny only heard of Picasso last year and now he's hot on the trail of some missing paintings by Wallace Lamb — a trail that leads him to the people who buy, trade and sometimes steal pictures in the bosom of Grantham's elite. The sleuth soon learns that art can lead to murder — Benny's own client is found dead and the shoes peeking under the curtains at the scene of the crime belong to Benny!

"Benny is as scruffily charming as ever. . . . A delightful, original creation."

The Gazette (Montreal)

"Another winner. . . ."

Publishers Weekly

"The Engel/Cooperman wit remains in top form, the characters continue to be interestingly odd and well drawn and the convoluted plot is worth puzzling out."

Sun (Vancouver)

"First-class entertainment, stylishly written, the work of an original, distinctive, and distinctively Canadian talent."

Julian Symons

"One of the best of the series."

The Globe and Mail

Laurence Gough

HOT SHOTS

A Willows and Parker Mystery

Hot Shots are smacks of undiluted heroin that kill with the ultimate high. When Alan Paterson, a man with a failing computer business, stumbles across millions of dollars worth of heroin, he thinks his money problems are over. But Paterson is only to become a wild card in a game of ruthless professionals.

Psychotic millionaire drug dealer Gark Silk surrounds himself with a killer elite whose only threat to him is their taste for the high life … and revenge. As cross and double-cross weave their tightening net over the city, innocent and guilty are trapped together in the intricate tangle of *Hot Shots*.

"In lean, hard prose … Gough tells a story as shocking for its sudden explosions of violence as it is engaging for its unfolding relationship between Willows and Parker."

The London Free Press

"It doesn't come any more chilling than this."

The Windsor Star

Laurence Gough

DEATH ON A No. 8 HOOK

Mannie Katz is a sleazy two-bit low-life who fancies himself as a killer. So when Felix gives him his first contract, on three teenage hookers, he sets up a nice artistic job with plenty of false clues. Mannie likes meaningless props.

Detectives Jack Willows and Claire Parker don't. So it's really very bad luck on Mannie that each of them stumbles on a body. . .

"Jack Willows and Claire Parker . . . look to have the stamina for many future yarns."

The Times

"Terse characterization and screwed-up tension take this new author into the McBain class at one stride."

Observer